D0063793

Moonshot

Copyright © 2016 by Alessandra Torre
All rights reserved.

No part of this book may be reproduced or transmitted in any form or by any means, electronic or mechanical, including photocopying, recording, or by information storage and retrieval system, without written permission of the Publisher, except where permitted by law.

This book is a work of fiction. Names, places, characters, and incidents are the product of the author's imagination or are used fictitiously.

ISBN-13: 978-1-940941-78-3
Digital ISBN: 978-1-940941-77-6

Editor: Madison Seidler
Proofreaders: Angie Owens, Perla Calas
Front Cover Design: Perfect Pear Creative Covers
Image: Perrywinkle Photography
Cover Model: McKinli Hatch
Formatting: Erik Gevers

Anderson Public Library
Lawrenceburg, KY 40342

Moonshot

by

ALESSANDRA TORRE

for girls with dirty hands and pure hearts

PROLOGUE

Pittsburgh

When my foot first stepped up, high and hesitantly, onto a team bus, I was seven. I liked My Little Ponies and Hanson. A brand-new coloring book was tucked under my skinny arm, a Lisa Frank backpack high on my back, full of my Most Important Items.

He stood at the top of the steps, one hand on the rail, the other on his hip. His jeans were stiff and dark, the bright yellow T-shirt tucked into the top of them. I raised my eyes from the neck of the shirt, past his scruffy jaw, his mouth, and landed on eyes that I had rarely seen.

"Hi Tyler." His mouth lifted in a smile, and I tried to match the gesture.

"Hi Daddy."

His smile broke a little, his mouth tightening, and he took the steps between us quickly, awkwardly sticking out a hand. "Let me take your backpack," he said, his voice gruff.

I moved obedient arms through the straps, and carefully lifted one pink plastic shoe up another dirty step, then a second, depending heavily on his hand, my small palm gripping it tightly, our progression up the short flight an awkward dance of strangers.

When I got to the top, I stopped, a long aisle stretching before me, a chorus of male faces, *strangers'* faces, staring at me, an uncomfortable hush settling over the big bus.

"Go ahead, Tyler. Find us a seat." My father pushed gently on my back, and I took my first step down that aisle.

It was April of 2001, and six days after Mom died.

TEN YEARS LATER
2011 Season

APRIL

"At the start of that season, the curse of Chase Stern was nothing—none of it had even begun. And back then, there wasn't a person on that team who knew what they were getting into. Back then, there was nobody *dying*. It was just another season starting, another year of baseball."

Dan Velacruz, *New York Times*

 **1**

New York

I hung on the edge of the fence, my cleats digging into the wood, my eyes glued to the field, on Danny Kiloti's face, an ump who should, given that last call, hang up his whistle.

"Come on, Ump!" I yelled. "Quit squeezing the plate!"

He ignored me, his hand on Hank's shoulder, their own discussion of sorts unfolding on home plate. I glanced at my dad, who leaned right and spat, his shoe stubbing at the pitcher's mound.

We were down by three, top of the ninth. Fucked, in nice lady terms. Especially with the bats we were swinging tonight. I rested my chin on the ledge, closing my eyes briefly, sucking in the sounds, the atmosphere ... even on a losing night, it was magic. Especially here, in Yankee Stadium. The greatest place in the world. It wasn't the old stadium, didn't have the history of the greats, but it was still incredible. Even more so, in ways. Our life, inside the dugout, had certainly improved in the new digs.

But on this April night, ten games into the season, a cool breeze blowing, the scent of grass and dirt competing with peanuts and beer, music thumping in tune with the stomp of fans, and the entire stadium on its feet, defending our play ... there was nothing like it. Especially not from this spot—eye-level with the field, the shift of the world's finest players behind me, the greatest stage in the nation before me. I opened my eyes and found Dad's on me. He winked, and I smiled. Rubbed underneath my nose, and he did the same. Our sign, solemnly decided upon one night, a decade ago. To a seven-year-old girl, it had meant everything. To me, now, it was just another piece of our connection, one strand of a thousand.

"Hey Ty!"

I didn't turn my head, Franklin's voice coming from the bench. "What?"

"Grab my inhaler?"

"On it." I pushed away from the rail, my eyes on the mound, the game back in play, my dad winding up. I turned, knowing before I even heard the smack, that it was a strike. Two-seam fastball, and there wasn't a better executioner in the game.

I left the stage and pushed through the swinging door, my sneakers slapping against the floor, my fingers trailing along the wall until I picked up enough speed and jogged, my fists swinging at my side, my chin nodding to a manager who passed, the entrance to the locker room ahead. I pushed through the door without hesitation, bee-lining for Franklin's locker, my hands quick as I reached into his bin and found his inhaler.

Franklin's inhaler.
Mount's dip.
Henderson's knee brace.

Someone always needed something. In the game that must go on, the players' minor needs are often crucial to our success. I heard the cheer of the crowd and quickened my return, my push on the dugout door in tandem with my toss of the inhaler, caught easily by the man.

"Struck out. Ramirez is up," Franklin updated without my asking, my glance at the scoreboard confirming. The opponent's first base coach looked my way and smirked, his eyes skating down my front. I smiled, giving him a front-row view of my middle finger, the crack of a bat distracting us both, and I watched the ball soar high and left—a foul.

I stared at Dad and willed another out to happen. One out, then we just needed the big man upstairs to hand out a four-run miracle.

 2

Baltimore

"We need help." Pre-calculus got covered up by a meaty hand with a long career of cleat scars. I looked up into Shawn Tripp's face and pulled the pencil from my mouth.

"Fernandez is having a breakdown over his wife. We tried." He shrugged, and I was pretty sure that had been the full extent of any trying done.

"I've got..." I pushed his meat cleaver to the side. "Three more problems."

"Come on, Ty."

I glanced across the room at Fernandez, who tipped back a beer. "What idiot gave him alcohol?"

"It's Fernandez."

I snorted. "Fair enough." I stretched, pushing back the textbook, and stood. Fernandez's wife was on her third or fourth affair, but the first he had found out about. It hadn't been pretty. We'd all dealt with the aftermath, through Boston, then Toronto, and now here.

I pulled at the chair next to Fernandez and sat. Reached over and stole a scallop off his plate. He raised his eyebrows but said nothing.

"Want to talk?"

He shrugged. "Nope."

I hitched my chair closer to the table. "You finished eating?"

He lifted his chin in a nod, and I grabbed a fork. Went to work on the remainder of his plate and met his eyes. He watched me warily, a good five minutes of silence between us before he let out a loud sigh. "You think I should leave her?"

I chewed his final scallop, musing over the question; my advice on affairs limited to midnight reruns of *Dr. Phil.* "Are you going to change?"

"Me?" He lifted his eyebrows.

"Yeah. Bring her on the road with you. If I was stuck at home for nine months a year, I'd cheat too."

"No, you wouldn't." His thick accent was so adamant, I laughed.

"I might." I reached for his beer, and he held it out of reach. "You don't know me, Fernandez."

He snorted. "Please, pepito. You wouldn't."

I leaned forward. "You would. You *do.*"

He avoided my stare. "I'm…"

"A guy? A future Hall-of-Famer?" I scoffed. "Don't give me that shit. It's the same. You don't get a free pass because you have a bat of gold."

"So what?" He looked me in the eye. "Two cheaters. What does that mean? We're meant for each other?"

I stand up, my wisdom fountain almost dry. "Think about whether you're ready to stop. If *you're* ready to behave. That's what you need to think about."

He said nothing, just slouched in his seat and worked at the label of his beer. I leaned over and kissed his cheek. "Love you, F."

"You too, Ty."

I did. I loved them all. I would do anything for those forty guys. And they would fight to their end for me. This team was my family, my soul. And I think that was what made everything that happened so damn complicated.

 **3**

Chase Stern leaned forward, sliding the mane of red hair over the shoulder of the woman, tapping a line of white powder down her spine, a dot between each vertebra. She giggled, squirming beneath him, and he put a hand on her ass, squeezing hard, holding her still. "Don't move."

"Hurry." She bounced back on his cock, the wet slide reawakening him, and he chuckled, leaning forward and taking the line, momentary spots of black in his vision before everything became blindingly, perfectly, clear. The squeeze of her around his shaft. The bounce of her breasts as he rolled her onto her back. The slow blink of eyelashes as she groaned, taking him fully in, the push of his thrust deep. The dig of her heels into his lower back, the gasp of her mouth, the taste of her skin as he lowered his mouth to her.

"Oh my God, Chase." Nails scraping across his back. A sharp tug of his hair. Slick skin rubbing, his stomach against hers, her breasts hard against his chest. Her teeth dug into his shoulder. She contracted around him and screamed his name, shrill and sharp, over and over, a record on terrible repeat.

He was close, his balls tightening, his grip on her harder, his thrusts quicker, when the hotel door slammed open, bright light in the dark space. He lifted his head, a curse on his lips, his body unprepared when hit with two hundred pounds of muscle.

Everything so clear. The fall of his body, away and out of her, his dick still hard, still ready, still close. The huff of male breath, the smell of onion. Pain in his shoulder, a hand on his chest, a fist coming down. He ducked his head easily, pushing off, a bare hand against a T-shirt, the face hitting the light of the hall, a burst of recognition blaring. *Davis*. Of course. He laughed at the sheer ridiculousness of it all and pushed harder. Another punch. Another easy miss. Everything so slow in this world of mortals. He snapped up his elbow and watched the connection. The widening of eyes, the crack of teeth, the connect of elbow and jaw, Davis's head going back, hands limp, the edge of the dresser right *there* and finishing the job. Davis out. He wiped the back of his hand over his mouth and stood, noticing the figure in the door—a woman from the hotel. A manager. Cheap shoes. Mouth half open. Face pale. Eyes darting, a ping-pong game of nervousness. To his dick. To his chest. Back down again. He twitched his cock and chuckled at her flinch, her eyes returning to his face.

He grinned, eye contact made, and winked. "Come on in, honey."

The woman on the bed picked that moment to scream, a shock of red hair scrambling across the bed and to her husband's side, a stream of Puerto Rican curses pouring out and directed at Chase. He smirked and glanced back to the door, his grin dropping when he saw the new face in the opening.

John Stockard. His and Davis's manager. The head of the Dodgers' MLB coaching staff. And he looked *pissed*.

 **4**

I propped a foot on the desk and blew on my toes. Second coat: perfect. I shook the bottle of clear and leaned back in the chair.

On the TV, SportsCenter ran. I rested my head against the chair and watched, an occasional push of my foot keeping my chair in movement. Nothing exciting. The NBA lawsuit, an NHL coach who needed to be fired, a steroids idiot who got caught at USC. I was starting to doze when Chris Berman straightened in his seat, something catching his attention.

I listened to his first few words, my own back coming off the chair, my hand reaching forward and grabbing the remote, turning up the volume. "Dad!" I called, my eyes on Berman's face, the screen changing to a highlight reel of sorts, showing clips I'd seen a hundred times, the man in them the current dominator of our world.

Chase Stern. The best bat to hit our game since Barry Bonds. A shortstop who made Ripken look like a rookie. A body built for baseball, a face that made *GQ* editors swoon, and enough swagger to fill Dodger stands with females. Chase Stern had played for Stanford for two years before blowing through the Minors and landing on the big stage. That was four years ago. Around the time I traded in my training bra for a real one. I wasn't immune to a little hero worship. The boys in the dugout had given me more than a little hell for my blush when he walked out on our field. I once caught a ball he tossed on his way to the dugout, and he'd *winked* at me. I'd been fourteen, and did everything but trip over myself in response.

But it wasn't his looks that had sucked me in. It was his play. His effortless grip of a game that we all struggled with. His swing, his throw, the dip of his body when he scooped up a ball, the stretch of his six-foot body when he leapt in the air … it was my porn. I would die a happy woman for one slow-mo clip of his swing, the bite of his bottom lip, the squint of his eyes, his fingers sliding over his bat's handle, the slow release, the easy swing of his body he jogged around the bases, oblivious to the crowd, to the cheers, to the madness.

He was beautiful.
He was perfection.
And he had, according to the news report title, been a *very* bad boy.

CHASE STERN: AFFAIR WITH TEAMMATE'S WIFE, THEN FIGHT.

"Dad!" I yelled loudly and reached forward, banging my fist against his hotel room wall.

MAY

"When Stern did that, it broke the cardinal rule of sports. You don't mess with your teammate's wife. And you certainly don't *punch* the guy after messing with his wife. That put Stern on *everyone's* radar. No one expected him to go to New York. But we expected someone to snatch him up. Nobody who bats four hundred is going to go unclaimed. And that summer, he was the hottest name in the game."

Dan Velacruz, *New York Times*

 **5**

"You're fidgeting, Ty."

"And you're drinking too much."

"It's coffee."

"It's not good for you. I've got juice in the fridge that I pressed this morning."

"I'd rather have coffee."

"Is it the kale you don't like? I can do it with just spinach and carrots."

"Stop changing the subject from your fidgeting."

"I'm not. I could try adding kiwi. That's what I do for Duncan."

"He's not coming here, Ty."

"Who?"

"Don't play stupid. It's not attractive."

"He *might* come here. The Dodgers can't keep him after this. And you know we should have gotten him straight out of the—"

"He's not coming. You know the reputation we keep. His bullshit isn't going to fly here."

"Maybe he'll change. Maybe it was a one-time thing. It might not even be *true*; you know how the media spins things."

"Good. Then they'll have no reason to trade him."

"How can you *not* want him on our team? He's Chase Stern."

"I have a teenage daughter. That's the only reason I need."

"I'm, like, five years younger than him."

"You're not that dumb, Ty."

"You *know* he'd be good for the team. Admit that."

"He's not coming here, so it's a moot point."

"We *need* him. Especially with Douglas's sprain. And Corten is a few years from retiring. And—"

"Ty. *Stop.* Finish that damn essay you've been staring at for two hours."

"Pour out that coffee, and I'll do my essay."

"Do your essay, or I'll tan your hide."

"I don't think you're allowed to tan my hide anymore. I think that stops at, like, age eight."

"I'm pouring it out, okay? Now shut up."

"Thank you, but I finished the essay. Sent it in fifteen minutes ago."

"Damn you."

"I love you too."

 **6**

"This is bullshit." Chase leaned back in his seat and tossed a plastic pen, watching it flip through the air before catching it.

"Can you get your shoe off my desk?" Floyd Hardin, his agent, moved around his heavy desk and swatted at Chase's tennis shoe. "I need you to focus."

"I'm focused. Dodgers don't want me anymore. So what? I'm sick of you Californians and your damn sunshine. You told me this was temporary, anyway. You know what I really want." He sat up, rolling the pen through his fingers before sticking it in the edge of his mouth.

"Yeah, the Yankees. And you haven't let me forget it. But they didn't need you then, and *now*..." Floyd raised his hands, the action showcasing the three World Series rings he'd probably picked up at Sotheby's. "You're not giving me a lot to work with, Chase."

"I've got the best stats in the league. What the hell else do you need?"

"You know their club as well as anyone, Chase. They like players who are *clean*. No drugs, no skeletons, no drama." He leaned over and tapped the front page of the paper, Chase's photo front and center. "Not this."

"They need me," he said stubbornly. "And I'm not signing with anyone else."

"It's not your decision. You're getting traded. It's up to the Dodgers where you go next. I've tried to talk to the Yankees, but they aren't biting. According to their camp, you're out."

"They said that?" Chase scowled, stopping his chew on the end of the pen and pulling it from his mouth.

"Yes. But my guy at CAA says Milwaukee might be making a big play. Have a blockbuster deal they're fronting."

"I won't do it. Milwaukee? *Fuck* that."

"Once again…" the man said slowly. "You. Don't. Have. A. Choice."

"I'll refuse to play. Error my ass off."

"And you'll get black-balled and never play for a major league team again. Including the Yankees." He crossed his arms over his chest and watched Chase.

Chase tilted his head back and groaned, his eyes searching the ceiling. "All this over a shitty lay," he said quietly.

"Learned your lesson?"

"With women?" he laughed, a hard and bitter sound. "Sure."

"You had a million Los Angeles women to choose from. I don't expect you to be celibate. Just *think* next time you feel like unzipping your pants."

He stood, lifting a baseball cap and pulling it on. "You think, too, Floyd. Get me in pinstripes, or I'll find an agent who can."

7

Packed over a six-month season, there were 162 baseball games every year. That was 162 times players warmed up, 162 times they walked onto a field and risked their career with swings, steals, and plays. Eighty-one times we stepped off a bus and onto an opponent's dirt. Eighty-odd times we dealt with opponents' fans, their jeers, their shitty locker rooms, the cloud of contempt that surrounded a visiting team. Especially when that visiting team was the greatest ball club in the world, the team every player wanted to be on, every fan wanted to secretly root for. It could be hell being a Yankee. But then we had home games. Times in the magic, an entire city's energy swirled in the air—the love strong, powerful, and coursing through our boys' lungs, fifty thousand souls storming to their feet for no purpose other than to celebrate our awesomeness.

It was one hell of a schedule. Exhausting by the time it ended. And that tally didn't include the playoffs—an extra twenty games to cap off the season. The most emotional games all year, each win celebrated in full fashion, assuming we got there. Assuming we pulled a constant stream of Wins.

But then again ... we were the Yankees. Did I need to dignify any other possibility?

I sat in a corner of the equipment manager's office and stared at a page in my biology textbook, the chapter on Population Ecology. Boring stuff. I doodled a flower in the right margin of the page, then stopped. Refocused and read the paragraph again. This office was the worst place to study: absolutely empty and quiet, especially this time of day. An hour before the team arrived, my freak of a father the only player in these halls. Everything was already set for the game, the balls mudded this morning, uniforms delivered from the cleaners and hanging in lockers, our food deliveries still three hours out. It was a tomb, which was why Dad loved to stick me in there. Good for biology, bad for my entertainment. I wrote down a few notes, reading over the sentences a few times to make them stick, then turned back to the book.

I wasn't a brilliant girl. Ask me a question about baseball and I'd ace your test. Put a math equation before me and my eyes glazed over. I used to have a tutor. Dad was focused on A's, thought that was crucial to my success. Three tutors quit before he gave up. Now, I taught myself, scanning in assignments to a home-school company in Jersey. They graded my work and required me to be present for exams four times a year. They also decided, at the end of the year, if I'd learned enough to graduate. It was May. One more month, four finals, and I'd be done with high school forever. I'd ditch my bookbag at home, say sayonara to books, and fully commit my time to the pinstripes.

I already had a contract penned for after graduation. Equipment Staff Assistant Manager. Not the most glamorous title in the world, but it'd keep me on the team bus. I wasn't really sure what the next step would be. Denise in Marketing had been trying to get me to intern up top with promises of a more permanent job. But I couldn't imagine breathing in the air of an office and not the field. I couldn't imagine looking out a window and down onto the action.

My graduation both loomed and beckoned. I was probably the only teenager in the city who didn't want to grow up.

Anderson Public Library
Lawrenceburg, KY 40342

 **8**

If fans leaving a game looked closely on the subway, they might see Frank Cinns. Our back-up third baseman pulled on a maintenance shirt and cap and turned invisible. He lived in Manhattan, as did Madden and Tripp, but their deep wallets used drivers to get home. Brooklyn held another five or six, a few preferred the Hamptons, but Dad and I lived in Alpine. Dad liked to drive, and used the twenty-mile trek to clear his mind after a game. I typically fell asleep. Something about the hours of intensity followed by the quiet hum of road … it was my lullaby. That and the nineties country music Dad lived by. A lethal combination to wakefulness, especially at one in the morning. Tonight was even later, an extra-long press junket holding up everything, a litany of questions drilled at every member of the Yankee organization, all regarding the same topic: Chase Stern.

They asked Tripp how he'd react if Chase slept with his wife. Tripp laughed. Fernandez, when asked the same question, broke his pencil in half. Dad didn't get that question. Even reporters occasionally have tact.

They did ask Dad if he thought Chase would be a good fit for the team. I had straightened in my seat, my eyes on my father, but true to form, he gave little more than a grunt.

Half awake, I stood in bare feet before my bathroom sink, and washed my face. Leaning forward, I examined a zit that hadn't quite decided to live or die. Once moisturized, I clicked off the light. When we traveled, I typically fell asleep to the TV, lulled to bed by an ESPN reporter. At home, it was nice to have the quiet. I stood on my bed and reached high, turning the window crank, the cool breeze immediate, the sound of the waves soothing. Our home perched on the short edge of a cliff, the crash of water against the rocks constant. Squatting on the bed, I pulled back the top blanket and crawled in, reaching out and flipping the switch beside my headboard, my room going dark.

Twenty-two miles away, in an executive conference room of Yankee Stadium, a printer hummed, spitting out the pages of Chase Stern's new contract.

 9

It wasn't lost on me that I was sitting in the wrong place. On the other side of the pool, a cluster of teenagers, their music floating over. I had caught bits of their conversations as I'd passed them— once by the food, once in the house. Bits of a foreign language that discussed Adele and parties, Spring Break, and Twitter. I knew most of them, we'd been clubhouse brats together, back when we were eleven or twelve. Then they'd moved on to private schools and new friends, weekends spent somewhere other than the club, my spotting of them less and less, their game seats up in boxes and not in the dugout. It had been a clear parting of ways and now, I was a million miles away. Sitting next to their fathers, chiming in on conversations that would cause them to roll their eyes and itch for an escape.

They were all glued to their phones, clustered together in the cabana. I watched them, half of their heads down, their conversations seamless, despite the constant movement of their thumbs. Maybe having friends was the secret ingredient needed for a phone addiction. I watched Katie Ellis giggle and tried to recall where I'd left mine. Probably the truck. My last sighting of it had been days earlier, no real need for it when I was with Dad.

In the past, he'd tried to push me to join them, had seemed to think that social interaction with them was crucial to my happiness. But over the last few years, he'd thankfully given up. I didn't want their friendship, certainly didn't need it. Not when we had absolutely nothing in common.

"Need a drink?" Thomas Grant stopped by my chair, putting a gentle hand on my shoulder.

I looked up with a smile. "Sunkist, please." I liked the man, the patriarch of the Grant dynasty, which had owned the Yankees for the better part of the century. A man who had taken me under his wing at a young age, a beam crossing his face whenever we met, my future in the Yankee organization all but guaranteed with his fondness for me. And the occasional hints that I should marry his son and live happily ever after as a member of the Grant family? I could handle those.

"You got it." He squeezed my shoulder and stepped toward the house.

The conversation around me was about a Cleveland Indians trade, and I pushed out my feet, settling deeper into the chair, the warmth of the fire heating my shins, the weather still cool on the Hampton coast. We were at the Grants' massive Hamptons estate, an impromptu barbeque grown bigger by the inclusion of wives and kids, the four teenagers on the other side of the pool just a small part of the party. Tobey Grant, a sophomore at Harvard and the future king of the Yankee empire, caught my eye, his cup lifting to his face, his gaze holding mine as he took a long sip, then lowered the drink. I looked away, back to the fire. We'd had a thing, once. Two years ago, during spring training. A few stolen kisses in a Hilton hallway, his hand sneaking up my shirt. He'd been my first kiss. It'd been okay, the second time better. I thought it had made us *something*; he hadn't. It was really just that simple.

I watched red-hot embers flake off wood and float into the sky. There were times when I loved the idea of dating Tobey, when I warmed to the Grants' not-so-subtle push of us together. There were times he loved the idea of dating me. Those times just never managed to line up, our occasional make-out sessions never enough to convince each other that a dedicated relationship was worth pursuing.

One wife trickled over to our group, her curvy body draping over Cook's lap. She was a new one; his last had had an issue with prostitutes, and his use of them. This one had been around for two years. I had a side bet with Dad that she wouldn't make it to five.

"Love has its own timeline, Tyler. Remember that."

He told me that in the moment before he took the field, the crowd roaring to their feet, swallowing my response. I was upset over Tobey, my frustration hidden behind fifteen-year-old attitude, my sunglasses masking any flash of irritation his occasional presence sparked. He'd walked into the stands, moving sideways down the row in Section 17 with a girl. Some tart in cut-off shorts and a tight tank top, her hair straightened, enough makeup on that I could see her eyelashes from my spot by the first baseline. Dad must have caught my look, my quick glance away. He stayed silent for two damn hours before slapping my back on his way out to the mound, his advice tossed out gruff and concise, no opportunity for discussion, the game needing to be played, strikes needing to be thrown, teenage feelings muffled.

It hadn't been the greatest advice in the world. And for me, a confused teenager who wasn't even sure I liked Tobey, it was useless. I asked Dad about it later that night, in a booth at Whataburger, the restaurant empty, one employee mopping the floor.

"You said that love had its own timeline. Was that the problem with you and Mom?"

He wiped his mouth, setting down his burger, his brow furrowed in his glance at me. "Problem? Why would you ask that?"

"You just weren't around a lot."

"You know this life, Ty. It's not one for a baby."

"So ... before me, she came on the road with you?"

He nodded, lifting his coffee cup to his lips. "She did."

"I'm sorry." I busied myself with the edge of my burger's wrapper. "For messing that up."

"Don't be. She came with me because we couldn't really afford anything else. Once I moved to the Majors, she would have stayed home anyway. Even without you."

"And missed all this?"

He chuckled. "Yeah, Ty. And missed all this."

He thought I was joking, our 2 AM fast-food dinner not exactly high-living, despite what we had in the bank. But I wasn't. For me, everything about our life, from the long hours, to the hell of a schedule, to the sweat and smells of the locker room … it was all magic. I couldn't imagine ever walking away from it.

I felt a nudge against my foot and looked up from the fire, Dad's eyes on mine. He tilted his head to the house. "They're putting dessert out."

I stretched, pushing to my feet and grabbed my empty Sunkist bottle. "Want anything?"

"Nah."

I headed to the house, my flip-flops loud against the deck, and I tossed my bottle toward the trashcan, movement in the side-yard catching my eye.

 **10**

At the private airport, the setting sun glinted off the tail of the Citation jet. Chase Stern stood by the back of the car, waiting as men loaded his bags into the plane, his phone out, fingers busy.

"Ready, boss?" the pilot stopped before him, and he glanced up.

"Yeah." He looked back at the car. "Got everything?"

"Yes, sir."

"Then let's roll." He stepped toward the plane, his long legs eating up the space, and he was up the steps and into a seat too quickly, his head still playing catch-up with the fact that this was *it*; he was leaving Los Angeles and headed to New York, to the place he'd dreamed about since he was a kid, to wear a jersey that had, for so long, seemed unattainable. This would be his future, where he would stay, his jersey hung next to the greats, his number retired, records forever broken and kept in his name. He glanced out the window, the driver already back in the car, no crowds recording this moment, not a single soul showing up for his exit. Not that he'd broadcasted the news, but it was in that moment, the airport rolling by, that he realized how few connections he had made in Los Angeles. Maybe it had been intentional—the push away from others, a part of him knowing it wasn't a permanent situation, stopping the dig of emotional roots.

Still, as the plane gained speed, the engines roaring beside him, it would have been nice to have *someone* there to see him off. He had a brief thought of Emily, and his heart tightened. Not that she'd have been holding a sign. No, she'd have been in the seat next to him, catching his eye with a smile and toasting his future before they even lifted off.

 **11**

He tasted like peppermints. I opened my mouth wider, and his tongue moved faster, an excited dart of flesh pushing against my gums, the clash of teeth brief, then he pulled back a little. We were on the side of his house, a palm tree beside us, my back against the brick. In the dark, only the moon lit his face, pale highlights on his lashes, the tip of his nose, and bruised lines of his lips.

"I've got to go back," I said, breaking away, Tobey's hands sluggish in their drop from my waist. "My dad—he'll be looking for me."

"Okay." He smiled shyly, and it was Tampa all over again. The meek boy with the pushy tongue. The one who slipped notes under my hotel room door and then dirty-danced with girls down by the pool. I didn't know why I'd followed him over here. I'd seen him standing in the shadows, his phone out, a beer hidden down by his leg, and had veered off course. And then … somehow … my hello had turned into this.

There was a shout from the house, one picked up and carried by the wind, almost lost. But a few people heard it and turned. I tucked a loose strand of hair behind my ear and took a step away from Tobey, to the edge of the deck, where I could hear better. And there, in the float of conversation carried, I heard *his* name.

I didn't glance back at Tobey, my feet launched me down the steps and toward the house. I ran, the wind whipping my hair, and couldn't help but smile.

I knew it would happen. He was born to wear our pinstripes.

 **12**

"Dad!" I ran after him, my hand catching his elbow, his turn sudden, and I came to a stop, my breath hard. "We got Chase?"

"Yeah."

"Who'd we lose?" The only negative of new blood, the sacrifice of our weakest lambs.

"Just Collende, and a Minor guy. Probably some draft picks and cash."

"Damn. Anyone talk to him?" I wanted to be sad. But we'd all known Collende would leave at some point. I'd spent the last two days analyzing our roster and had already prepared for the emotional break. Not that the loss was anything to cry over. Collende was a prick. A prick with one hell of a bat, but a prick regardless.

"No. You gonna be able to handle this, Ty?"

"What?" I looked up into his face and tried to understand the question. "Collende leaving?"

"No. *Stern.*" He lowered his voice and put a hand on my shoulder. "I don't want your hero worship of him to affect..."

I didn't help the man out. I let him dangle in the Atlantic wind, one struggling father on a limb that was shaky at best.

He swallowed before continuing, "...to affect your judgment. He's gonna go straight for you, Ty. I know he is."

I didn't know what to say, my father's opinion biased, the likelihood of Chase Stern even noticing my existence was slim. And that was fine. He was a baseball god. My excitement was at having him on our field, his glove and bat our new asset. "Dad. It's Chase Stern." He could change everything for us. He could take us back to the World Series, put us on the record books. One day his name would be mentioned in the same circles as Ruth and Gehrig, and *we would have shared a field with him.* "He's not gonna mess with me," I protested. "Don't worry about that."

He pulled me to him, a rare hug between us. "Oh, Ty. So smart and still so dumb."

I leaned into his arms and said nothing. He was wrong, a rarity for my father. But still, my blood hummed with excitement.

 **13**

Two Days Later
Bronx

Our original stadium was built in the twenties. Two years ago, due to an aging infrastructure, excess cash, and the need to one-up everyone else, our new home was built. We now had fifty thousand seats. Fifty-two skyboxes. A press box that caused erections. And a locker room that trumped every MLB club out there. A locker room that, fingers crossed, held Dad's wallet.

"It's not gonna be there. You check, you always check."

"It might be in the drawer. Sometimes you stick it there." I grabbed a pair of sunglasses from the glove box and pushed them on. I pulled at the seat belt to try to get some breathing room. "Just let me run in and check. Otherwise we're dealing with…" I rummaged through the center console, snagging a wad of spare bills and counting them out. "Nineteen dollars."

It was an old conversation, one we'd had a dozen times. After games, both of us tired, things got left behind. My backpack. His medicine. His keys, though we never got too far without those. His wallet was a constant source of stress, never where it should be; typically in Alpine when we needed it in the Bronx. Once he left it in a Cleveland hotel room, the team jet at thirty-five thousand feet before Dad reached for his back pocket, a curse leaving his lips.

He looked at the dash and cursed. "And … I'm low on gas."

"It'll be there," I repeated, passing him the gate card, the players' lot empty, today an off day. Everyone was at home, neglected families getting attention, jealous spouses getting updates, muscles worked by masseuses. Sometime today, Chase Stern would take off from LA, his stuff packed up by movers, everything in motion so that he could play tomorrow.

"Be quick." Dad came to a stop by the gate, and I grabbed the door handle, my feet already out, the truck door slammed shut as I jogged down the walkway and to the door, my fingers quick on the keypad, his personal code entered, and then I was inside.

 **14**

Chase Stern sat naked on wood planks, his back against warm stone, his arms loose at his side, eyes closed. There was a knot in his right shoulder blade that needed to be worked out. He rolled his neck to the side and inhaled deeply, the steam thick and hot, his skin pinpricking with the heat.

Yankee Stadium. It felt unreal. His tour had been short, the rep from the owner's office concise, nothing much to show. Every club was the same: offices, facilities, locker rooms, and fields. Here, everything was just better; the owner's money was spent well, the locker room one that put the Dodgers' to shame.

When he'd seen his locker, his name already in brass up top, his uniform pressed and ready, size 13 cleats in place ... that was when it'd really hit home. That was when he'd dismissed the short man with the wingtips and had a moment of reverence, of realization that this was *it*, he was *here*. In the big house, with pinstripes that bore his name.

He coughed, clearing his throat, and waved at the air, suddenly claustrophobic in the sauna, the steam so thick he couldn't see his hand in front of his face, sweat pooling behind his knees. He stood and wiped at his eyes, reaching for the handle.

 **15**

"Hey Ty."

"Hey Mark." I smiled at the maintenance worker, jogging down the hall, the path one I'd taken a thousand times. Easier on days like this, when the place was deserted, no conversations to halt forward progress, no packs of bodies to squeeze around, no executives to avoid. Not that I ever had to hide. But the less I was seen, the better. Yankee management has been extremely understanding about my travel with the team, my role as ball girl, and my constant presence over the last seven years. Prior to the Yankees, we'd been with Pittsburgh, a ball club who hadn't been nearly as understanding. Maybe the Yankees allowed me around because I was Mr. Grant's favorite. Or maybe it was because Dad was the best closer in the business, and they liked to collect rings. Whatever the reason, I was grateful.

I rounded the corner and hit the player lobby, the front desk empty, Dad's code getting me through the double doors and into the locker room. I slowed to a walk, moved past the club chairs and ping pong tables, grabbed an apple from the food bar and leaned on the door to the inner sanctum, a place I rarely went during peak times, the possibilities of a penis sighting too high; *that* was something I had no interest in seeing.

I took a bite of the apple and pushed off the door, letting it swing shut behind me. Then I stumbled to a halt, my world stopping dead at the man who stood naked before me.

16

I'd seen naked men before. The locker room was a freaking sideshow of male genitalia, and my presence there was sometimes unavoidable. I'd learned to keep my head down and walk quickly, a trip in and out typically knocked out within thirty seconds.

Not this trip. My head had been up, my teeth deep in the apple, my eyes widening as they encountered the utter beauty that was a naked Chase Stern.

Torso facing me, he had a white towel lifted to his neck, the action tensing every perfect ab, his shoulders wide and strong. His head was down, his mess of dirty blond hair showing as he rubbed his neck, the other hand loose on his hip—*God, the cut of that hip*, a hard line of definition that pulled my eyes down to the *thing* that hung between his legs, big and proud. His penis. I was *staring* at Chase Stern's *penis*. I couldn't breathe, couldn't move; I just stared. It was darker than his legs, thicker than I had imagined that organ would be, and it swung slightly when he chuckled.

Chuckled. My brain registered the sound right before he spoke.

"Like what you see?"

 **17**

She was a fawn, caught in headlights. Long, bare legs leading to a baggy tee, a bright green apple lifted to her mouth, her eyes huge, focused on him. It was about time she reached his face; she'd certainly spent enough time examining the rest of his anatomy.

She moved the apple away, her mouth full, and chewed, her eyes darting away, her face deepening in color, bright red by the time she swallowed, her feet suddenly in motion. She crouched before a locker, her hands quick, rummaging through its contents. He stepped closer, his eyes narrowing. "Hey, what are you doing?"

She ignored him, jerking open the drawer at the base of the locker, her hand shoved inside, and then she was full height, just a few inches shorter than him, something gripped tightly in her hand.

"You didn't see me. I didn't see…" She flushed. "You. In case someone asks."

"You can't steal that." He reached out, grabbing her arm, his fingers closing easily around her tiny forearm. She jumped, yanking away, her eyes snapping to his.

"I'm not stealing." She held the item against her chest. "It's my dad's." She spun, and in a burst of legs and blonde hair, she was gone.

 **18**

I ran as quickly as I could. The stupid apple was still in hand. Dad's wallet in the other. This was *bad*. Dad would *freak*. All of his worries, everything I had dismissed, and *this* had happened.

Like what you see?

Oh my God. He had caught me *staring*. How long had I stood there, just *examining* him like some sort of pervert? And then he'd thought I was stealing? He probably didn't believe me, was probably pulling on clothes and heading to the security office right now, would describe me, and they'd pull video, and of course Marty and Shaun would recognize me, and of course they would tell Dad, and *ohmygodIthinkImgonnavomit*. I stopped in the middle of the hall, breathing hard, my stomach heaving, the damn apple still in my hand, no trash can nearby. I leaned against the wall and closed my eyes, tried to calm my breathing, tried to sort through this in my head.

Dad would know something was wrong. My poker face was terrible. Once, when I was eleven, I cheated on a math test, a calculator stowed under my notebook. Dad had known something was up the minute I passed the Scantron over. But this wasn't an elementary school test. This was a hundred times worse. I tried to think of something, a distraction for my father, a lie prepared in case he asked what was wrong.

I came up with nothing, God punishing me for my actions, my deceit given absolutely no backup. I pushed off the wall and took the final steps to the end of the hall, the sun shining brightly through the door's windows, the world outside oblivious to my demise.

I pushed on the exit bar and stepped into the sunshine, chucking the apple in the trash. At the curb, Dad's truck idled.

"Got it." I held up the wallet and slid into the passenger seat, slamming the door shut and busying myself with the seat belt.

"Where was it?"

"The drawer." I pulled up my foot, resting my tennis shoe on the seat and busied myself with the laces, tightening them and retying the knot.

"You okay?" He was staring at me; I could feel his eyes, the truck not put in gear, his head turned to me.

"Yeah. Just pissed that I didn't check—" My sentence was cut off by the ring of his phone, coming loud through the speakers, and I let out a sigh of relief, followed by a moment of panic. Maybe it was the security office.

"Hello?"

The voice that responded was brash and feminine, and I relaxed against the seat, letting our housekeeper's voice carry my father into distraction, my chance at getting caught dissipating with each of her raised vowels.

Chase Stern. Naked. Staring at me. The deep laugh in his voice when he'd asked if I'd liked what I'd seen.

I dropped my head against the seat, replaying the interaction. Our misunderstanding over Dad's wallet. My sprint out the doors. I hadn't even introduced myself. Though … what would I have done? Shook his hand? I couldn't have, not with all his nakedness right *there*. No, it was probably for the best, me leaving when I did. Before someone else came in. Before he said something else. I groaned as quietly as I could and turned away, resting my forehead on the glass window.

Talk about ruining me for life.

19

Chase stood, for a long moment, his towel still in hand, and stared at the swinging door, almost expecting her to reappear. *It's my dad's.* He glanced back at the locker, ROLLINS printed on a brass nameplate across its top. *Frank Rollins.* A name that needed no introduction, the closer's place in the Hall of Fame already guaranteed, his rookie card one that Chase had behind glass somewhere. He'd heard that Rollins had a daughter—the sort of lewd comments always tossed around a locker room. He hadn't paid much attention. Now, he wished he'd listened harder, his mind blank on anything but her father's accomplishments.

He gave her one last chance at a return, then wiped at his face and headed for the shower.

Jesus Christ. Talk about the last thing he needed.

 **20**

Moonshot. They say the term comes from Wally Moon, a player from the fifties, who hit bombers that the local press dubbed 'moonshots.' Dad had taught me the term when I was twelve, and desperate to hit my first home run. An impossible feat for a scrawny blonde in a Major League stadium, but Dad hadn't told me that. He'd just kept me swinging, his pitches easy, my breath huffing smoke in the cold night air, my hits short after short after short.

He stood behind me, his hands over mine, and we swung. A practice stroke, over and over, my sore muscles learning the motion. "Look to the moon when you swing," he instructed. "That's what you want. A ball that disappears into it. One that goes to the moon and past. A moonshot."

"Sounds stupid," I grumbled, my eyes on the dirt, my swing down.

"Everything's stupid if you look at it a certain way. Some people think it's stupid for a girl to be named Ty."

I looked up with a smile. "That was stupid. Ty Cobb? You couldn't have picked a Yankee?"

"Would Thurmon have been better? Or Red? Or Whitey? Yogi? Lou? Mickey?"

"Mickey isn't bad. Or Babe." I grinned at him, tapping the end of the bat against my cleats.

He scowled. "Let's focus on the moon. I'll worry about stripper nicknames later."

A moonshot had been impossible for me. I woke up the next day with a task almost as improbable: avoid Chase at all costs. Eye contact would be dangerous, any conversation disastrous.

**21**

I knotted my hair into a low bun. Skipped makeup. Pulled on a baseball cap, low over my eyes. Wore jeans instead of shorts, and a long-sleeved T-shirt, the biggest one I owned.

I stared at myself in the full-length mirror and hoped that I looked different. Maybe he wouldn't recognize me from the girl who had stood, limp-jawed, in the middle of the locker room.

"He's my dad."

God, why had I said that? Talk about sticking a giant kiddie nametag to my chest.

I heard the rattle of metal on metal, our garage door opening, and turned at the sound. Striding down the hall, I grabbed my bag off the hook and headed for the door.

Our night games had a schedule, like clockwork, and hadn't changed in the last decade. Got to the park around two. The team ate together around five. Hit the field around six. National Anthem at seven. Showtime.

Everything was the same, yet everything was different, the change palpable in the air. Chase Stern's arrival at the Yankees hit like an atomic bomb—so loud it was silent, the cloud of effect rippling out from his person in a giant wave that touched all of us. Muttered conversations, bits of gossip jumping amid the staff, a subtle shift of change in the air, everything moving aside for greatness, then settling back into place around him.

Despite myself, despite the dread I had at seeing him, the energy was addictive. My own personal drama aside, we needed his glove, his bat, his fans. With him here, we could do anything.

Avoid Chase at all costs. Dad must have heard my inner mantra. He dragged me with him to the bullpen, way out at the end of the field, strict instructions barked at me to finish my history project. A project that could wait for the weekend, but I didn't argue. Arguing would have raised red flags, and he was more on edge than I'd ever seen him. So I pulled out my laptop and sat on the ground, leaned against the wall, and worked.

It took two hours to knock out my report—an analysis on Civil War motivations and the consequences of the war. My back tight, I stretched, closed the laptop, and pushed it into my bag. Dad sat at the end of the bullpen with two relievers, his hat off, elbows resting on his knees, his chin lifted at me in acknowledgement. As the closer, he was the best arm on the team, and brought in only when we were trying to preserve a close lead. The majority of the game, he was out in the bullpen, far enough to be out of my hair, close enough to be part of the game. I smiled at him. For an old guy, he was handsome, in a wiry kind of way, even with his hair sweaty and rough, his skin lined by too many years of squinting into the sun. In another life, he might have remarried, but I'd never even seen him consider dating. Maybe that was my fault. I'd never asked for another mom, wasn't really interested in anything to interrupt our bond. I looked away and stepped to the fence, peering through and across the field. The dugout was empty, no players in sight. I glanced at the stands, a few fans already moving down stadium steps, drinks in hand, smiles in place. The gates must be open, go time near. It was time for the boys to get their asses on the field, time for me to get down front. Close to the action, close to Chase. My palms sweated.

My father's voice stopped my reach for my backpack.

"You should go to the hotel."

"What?" I let go of the strap, and it fell, loud and heavy, on the metal bench.

"I spoke to Frank. The ball boys can cover for you."

"No." I could count on one hand the number of times I'd refused him. I could also count on one hand the number of times he'd been this stubborn.

His eyes hardened. "You've got school work to do, and I don't want you working the game. Now go. Take the truck. I'll get a ride."

I glanced toward the other pitchers and stepped closer to him, lowering my voice. "This is bullshit. I've never missed a game." And I hadn't. Not in ten years. Not when I'd been sick, not when I was seven and had tears running down my face over Mom. We were Rollins. We didn't miss games. And we didn't fight with each other; we griped, we gritted through with sarcasm and wit. Not like this. Not with a hole in my chest, my breath suddenly short, the possibility of not working the game, not even *going* to the game—that was something that had never crossed my mind.

"I'm sorry, Ty. It's just a big day. Lots of energy in the air with a new player. You know that."

"All the more reason to have me out there. Someone you don't have to worry about messing up." Snagging a fair ball as foul. Too much Mississippi mud on the balls. Grabbing the wrong bat. Not having dip, braces, lotion, headphones … all of the idiosyncrasies that set up each player for success. Yes, I was a ball girl—the job typically done by prepubescent boys. But I was the best one in the league. And it was ridiculous for him to pull me from this game, to punish me for … what? Chase Stern's presence? "I'm going to the game." I crossed my arms tightly in front of my chest, swearing on Babe Ruth's grave that I was *not* about to cry, not right here, on sacred soil, with the eyes of the others on us, my father's face as old as I'd ever seen it.

"Don't fight me on this." He hung a hand on the fence beside us. Long fingers, cracked at the seams. Talented appendages linked with a structure designed to keep worlds apart. There was an analogy there; I just didn't see it. "You're seventeen, Ty. You're beautiful. Don't..." his voice broke in two, "...don't grow up on me just yet."

"I'm not trying to grow up. I'm trying to go down to the baseline and help the guys prep the field." I tried to smile, but my fear—that he'd try to take this away—stopped me.

"He slept with a player's wife. Don't think he'll behave around you." Our dance of avoidance stopped, the issue front and center.

"You're giving my beauty way too much credit. I came from your ugly stock, remember?" I reached down and hefted my heavy backpack onto my shoulder, because he *would* let me go, he had to. So help me, if he didn't, I'd turn into every other hellacious teenager that slunk through this stadium.

"Tyler." Just one word from him, but it said so much.

"Dad."

We stared at each other for an eternity, one long stretch of silent communication where I begged, and he countered, where I screamed and stomped my feet, and he hugged me. It all passed through our eyes, his stance unchanging, and I knew I had won when he finally moved, pushing off the fence and dropping his hand.

"Fine."

"I love you." I reached out a fist. "Spikes first?"

He reluctantly met my fist in the air. "Spikes first."

Ty Cobb once spoke about sliding into base. Something about how his foot was coming up fast, his spikes out, and if the baseman happened to get in the way, oh well. Shit happened. Dad first told me that story when he was teaching me how to slide. I was eight, and still stubbornly clinging to the concept of dolls and dresses, and the thought of intentionally getting dirty was terrifying. It had been early February and hot, my cleats stained red by the dirt of an Orlando practice field. We had battled on that field, he and I. I hadn't wanted to learn to slide, the entire lesson stupid, one I would never use, and he had insisted on it, one of the rare moments in those early years when he had put his foot down. The Ty Cobb story had made me smile, mostly because Dad's retelling of the story included the word 'shit,' a forbidden curse that gave me a shot of glee.

On that day, on that field, I had gotten dirty. Even though I wouldn't admit it, I enjoyed it. Afterward, we'd gone to a sports store, and Dad had bought me some sliding shorts, a few T-shirts, some pants. That day had been the first crack in my little girl veneer. And from then on, *spikes first* had been our code. Our mantra in life, the thought that you dove full force into confrontation, damn the repercussions to others, should they be too dumb to move out of the way. Sometimes you made it there safely. Sometimes you didn't, the enormous effort a waste. But if you had the opening, you had to try.

I said *spikes first* in that bullpen to remind him of that. To remind him of the girl he'd raised. She wasn't the type to go home when there was a game to be played. Chase Stern be damned. Naked bodies be forgotten. I was here for one reason, and it wasn't lust.

 **22**

Pregame, batting practice. I didn't know what idiot created the standard baseball uniform, but they were terrible. Almost canvas in their thickness. Stiff with starch. Scratchy. Hot, even in our mild summers. I leaned forward, resting one hand on a knee, and wished, for the thousandth time in my life, for a pair of loose cotton shorts. The batter swung, and I jerked left, sprinting for his ball, my glove reaching out and falling a few inches short. I bent, scooping up the ball as I ran, and threw it in.

"Distracted?" Lucas, one of our outfielders, asked with a wink.

"You think you could have got that?" I shot back with a smile.

He scoffed, clapping a fist into his glove. "All day long, baby."

I stabbed the grass with my cleat and let out a controlled breath, my fingers flexing in the sweaty confines of my glove, a new form walking slowly up our dugout steps, the sun glowing off his white uniform, his arms flexing as he worked a hand into a batting glove.

I had decided, that morning, that I would hate him. Based it on the cockiness in his tone when he'd spoken to me. The way he didn't bother to cover himself when standing before me. The laughter that had been in his eyes.

Hating him would make everything easier. Cleaner.

But I couldn't. I stood there, lost in far left field, and watched him reach for a bat. Watched him run his hands along its length. I watched him step up to the bag and push the batting helmet hard onto his perfect head.

And before he even tightened his grip, before that first swing that cracked open our future and sent the ball high over my head…

I was already done for.

 **23**

The girl in left field had an arm on her. Chase watched her launch a ball from the fence, barely an arc on the delivery to second base, her jog back into place casual, as if the throw had been nothing. He turned to the hitter next to him, nodding a head to the girl. "Not a bad cannon for a girl."

"Who, Ty?" The guy let out a hard laugh. "That's Rollins's kid. She should. He's had a ball in her hand since she was old enough to pull on her own uniform."

Rollins's kid.

"He's my dad."

The girl from the locker room.

He stared at her figure in the field, and tried to connect her to the girl he had met yesterday. In the locker room, she'd looked meek and skittish. Out on the field, she was confident, a grin stretched over her face, her shout at another player done with ease, as if she was an equal.

"Rollins only have one daughter?" He tried to mold the two images.

"Yep." The guy reached for a bat and looked over, his eyes hardening. "She's seventeen. Just in case you had any stupid ideas."

Chase held up his hands in innocence. "Just complimenting her arm."

"Right." The man held his eyes for a long moment before strolling toward home plate, his bat gripped with both hands, one last glare given before he stepped up to bat.

Chase took off his hat and wiped at his forehead. Letting out a controlled breath, he turned his back to the field, no need to see anything more.

So she was a ball girl. For the team. A seventeen-year-old ball girl. Heaven help him if she traveled with them, too.

 **24**

4:48 AM. I counted out eight pairs of underwear. Two bras. Two pairs of jeans. Ten shirts. I stacked everything in the suitcase, grabbing an extra pair of Nikes and my toiletries bag. We spent nine months a year on the road. Packing had lost all creativity.

I could have grabbed my cute tops. Some footwear that was sexier than Nikes. My makeup. I thought about it, my hand drifting across the hangers, hesitating, but I didn't. There was no point in courting trouble. And with makeup, when I made an effort—I could be called pretty. I didn't want to be pretty to Chase Stern. I wanted to be invisible. He was God's gift to our team, not to me.

I zipped up the suitcase and yanked it off the bed. Pulled it down the hall and into the dark great room. I rolled through the kitchen, past the commercial appliances, white granite countertops, the photos of Dad and me stuck to the fridge. I opened the door to the garage, and heard the hum of Dad's truck, the early morning breeze crisp.

"About time," he griped, holding out a juice.

"Bite me," I countered, shaking the container before taking a sip. "We're five minutes ahead of schedule."

"Your schedule. We should be leaving by four-thirty."

I rolled my eyes and buckled my belt, his truck making the turn onto the main Alpine street, everything empty and still. "We'll be the first ones there. Like always."

He flipped on the radio, and I shifted lower in my seat, resting my sneakers on the dash. And, as always, I was asleep before we even hit the highway.

Our games were played in series—three in a city, then we'd move to the next, our play coordinated to reduce travel time and expenses. This trip would last eight days and hit Detroit and Dallas.

I adjusted the shade on the window and smiled at the flight attendant, taking the blanket she offered. The jet was full, with the exception of one notable member. Chase Stern. A man who could bat .340 but couldn't seem to get to an airport on time. I heard the travel secretary on her phone, trying to get ahold of his driver. When he jogged toward the plane, a leather bag in one hand, Dad leaned over. "We should have left him. Let him fly commercial to Detroit. That would have taught him."

He was right. We'd left players before. Hell, it was a regular occurrence, happening two or three times a season. When you tried to get thirty guys to show up at a certain time, shit happened. So they got left. Except him, apparently.

When he walked down the aisle, stepping over outstretched feet, murmuring apologies to anyone who'd meet his eyes, I looked away, out the window. I had managed, for his first two games, to avoid him completely, a difficult feat. Now, in the tight confines of the airplane, his presence felt huge and unavoidable. Especially when he paused just past our row, and I felt the push of my seat, his tall frame moving into the spot just behind me, his voice low and right there as he leaned forward, his hand gripping my headrest, brushing the top of my head. "I'm sorry."

"It's fine," I managed, not looking up, busying myself with my headphones, pulling the big Bose headset over my head. I relaxed slightly when the pressure against my seat relaxed, his body in place, and started my playlist, trying to drown out the sound of his voice, the low apology, the way the vowels had hooked into me and held on.

"Like what you see?"

I could feel Dad's glance and curled away, toward the window, tucking my knees to my chest and pulling the blanket up to my chin. There, I tried to not smell the fresh scent of his soap. I tried not to notice the occasional bump of my seat. I tried to pretend like Chase Stern didn't exist.

She smelled like pears. When he bent down, gripping the top of her seat, he smelled her hair. It wasn't intentional; he wasn't burying his face in her blonde strands, he just got a whiff. A whiff strong enough to stick, to give him another puzzle piece to add to the Tyler Rollins enigma. When she leaned over to say something to her father, he watched her profile through the crack in their chairs. When her seat reclined, he imagined those long legs stretching out. Too bad she was in jeans; he'd noticed that on his walk down the aisle, his glance just brief enough to avoid suspicion, but long enough to see that she was in a Yankee jersey and jeans. A bag on her lap, open, headphones half out, her face turned away, looking out the window. Her hair down, tucked behind her ear. Young. She looked so young. So innocent.

"Like what you see?"

Such a stupid thing to say. To a seventeen-year-old girl, of all people. But he hadn't known that, hadn't even *considered* that. Still, it was done. And now, those words wouldn't stop taunting him.

**25**

Detroit

We all had our favorite cities. Detroit wasn't mine. Especially on days
like this, when the rain pelted the field, the tarp doing little to keep
the clay dry. I huddled under the west overhang, my uniform cold
and clingy, an itchy skin that I couldn't shed, not for a while. The kid
beside me, some Michigan local who'd won his place in some radio
station giveaway, looked miserable. I was sure his visions of the day
hadn't included sprinting across a soggy field, sneakers wet and
squishy, toes frozen, picking up forgotten balls. Now, with a break in
the downpour, I nudged the kid. "Make a run for the Tiger's
dugout." I nodded right, and he ran—short, chubby legs darting
across the grass.

I pulled my cap down low and crossed my hands over my chest, too
mature to run, my steps nonetheless quick as I crossed to the far end,
taking the back gate and walking down the ramp and toward our
visitor locker rooms. I could hear the hum of voices, the men pent
up inside, everyone itchy, ready for the game to either be called off or
played, the inactivity excruciating.

It'd be an extra late night, the two-hour rain delay pushing back our
bedtimes. I shivered in the empty hall and walked faster, rounding
the final corner toward the locker room and running smack into
someone.

Someone with a hard body.

Tall, the bill of my hat hitting his chest, my hands instinctively
coming up and pushing against his stomach, nothing but hard abs felt
through dry uniform.

Uniform. My throat went dry; I stumbled back, my wet cleat slipping against the painted concrete, out from under me, and my hand tightened against his uniform, holding on, his body reacting, and suddenly I had his hands on my hips.

His hands were on my hips. I tried to process that thought, the feel of his fingers tightening, his body bent forward, over me, as I tilted back. I frantically moved my feet, my shoes sliding, legs spreading, and I finally came to a halt, one shoe stopped by the wall, his grip tight on me.

"Don't move," he ordered, both of us in danger of falling if I continued my leg windmill. My face was tucked into his chest, an intentional move I had made milliseconds earlier because keeping my chin up would have put us in a Hollywood dip of sorts, and that was quite possibly the only thing that would have made this more embarrassing.

His uniform smelled *good.* Some sort of cologne, unless he rolled out of bed smelling like a medley of forest and ocean. Dad wore Old Spice, which was the most unsexy, spicy scent on the planet. This ... I didn't want to let go. I wanted to yank off his shirt and wrap it around my head, surgically affix it to my face, and smell just that, forever, even if it made me an elephant man freak in the process.

Don't move, he had said.

I didn't. I stayed in place until he pulled me up, my feet almost lifting off the ground, and his hands stayed in place until he was certain I was firm on my feet, our bodies parting, my hands releasing their grip on his shirt, nervously moving to adjust my baseball cap into place, to pull at the front of my wet shirt, releasing the cold material from my skin.

"Thank you," I muttered.

"You should get into dry clothes."

"I'm fine."

"Your teeth are chattering." His hand reached out and was suddenly at my jaw, fingers gentle in their brush over my lips, and I ground my teeth, my eyes moving, shock pushing them up, past his touch, and to his face for the first time.

A mistake. This close, our bodies just a foot apart, his touch soft on my lips ... I was unprepared. Unshielded.

There was a line between his eyebrows, a hard pinch of skin. His eyes deep and soft, no laugh in them today, no cocky tilt of that mouth. He pressed his lips together, his jaw tight, skin golden, and it was pure beauty before me. I couldn't look away—not when our eyes met, not when his hand slid to cup my face.

He let go of me then—the moment his fingertips slid into the dip behind my earlobe, wrapped under the line of my jaw. He pulled away, his hand fell from my waist, and we both stepped back.

"I'm sorry." He rubbed at his mouth.

"It's a blind corner. No big deal."

"No." He coughed. "I'm sorry about the locker room. What I said— it was stupid."

"Oh." I could feel the blush, hot and prickly through my cheeks. "It *was* stupid."

He laughed in response, the sound loud and unexpected. "So you *didn't* like what you saw."

I stared at him, my eyes widening, no coherent, logical response coming to mind. "No!" I finally said, and it was five heartbeats too late.

"Really," he challenged.

I couldn't respond to that and stepped around him, moving down the hall, my feet quickening. I was desperate for an escape, for room to breathe, desperate for *anything* but another word of conversation.

"You always run, Little League?" his call rang down the hall, slamming into the back of my head.

I stopped. Turned. Met those eyes across twenty feet of nothing. "You always bunt?" I called back.

He snorted. "Bunt?"

I shrugged. "That's what it felt like to me." My lie came out strong, the words mixing his brown eyes into something darker.

"Grand slams aren't typically called for, in this situation."

"What situation is that?" I couldn't shut up. It was like I was running full force to the edge of the cliff, but my legs wouldn't stop.

"Untouchable women."

Women. Not girls, not children. Had I ever been considered a woman? *Was* I a woman?

"And it wasn't a bunt," he added, before I had the chance to formulate a response.

"It wasn't?"

He took a step back, turning away and tossing a response over one perfectly sculpted shoulder. "Babe, I haven't even stepped up to bat."

He was around the corner before my brain processed the words. Before I could form the question that followed the receipt.

Hadn't stepped up to bat? Meaning ... he hadn't even been interested? Or ... was that heart-stopping moment just a scratch at the surface of what Chase Stern could unleash?

It was probably good he left. I didn't think anything positive would come from a further explanation.

That night, the game was cancelled, and I went back to the hotel, my uniform still wet, my mind still wound.

When I closed my eyes in bed, all I could see was his stare, and all I could smell was the phantom scent of his cologne.

 **26**

Dallas

Chase Stern stepped off the bus, shifting his bag higher on his shoulder. Moving forward, he ignored the shouts from fans, their line of bodies packed in on either side, hands reached out over the barricade fence, balls and notepads thrust out, an undulating wave of obligations. A pair of tits caught his eye, and he slowed, stretching and taking a Sharpie from the perky blonde. "What's your name?" he asked.

"Kristin," she beamed, and when she leaned forward and adjusted the hem of her shorts, he could see everything.

He scribbled her name on the jersey she held out, glancing backward, his eyes connecting for a brief moment with Ty, her step off the bus quick and no-nonsense, her eyes moving off his, her face unchanging.

"My number." The blonde tried to hand him a piece of hot pink paper.

"I'm good." He waved it off, capping the marker and handing it back.

"Just take it," she insisted, still holding it out.

He took the next pen and scribbled out another signature, ignoring the paper, which seemed to make the blonde more insistent. Giving another two autographs, he stepped back, waving a hand to the crowd and avoiding the eyes of the blonde.

He didn't analyze his actions. Didn't wonder why his overactive sex drive seemed to have suddenly gone on hiatus. It was probably about time he stopped screwing around—especially with the Yankees, a team that frowned on scandal of any sort.

He stepped toward the building, following the line of players who had passed, his eyes finding and resting on a figure, shorter than all the others, one blonde ponytail bobbing among the men.

27

Tampa

11:14 PM. The Marriott. At an alcove at the end of the twenty-seventh floor, I stood and stared at the vending machine choices, chewing the edge of my cheek. I had my strengths. A killer curveball. Mad karaoke skills. The ability to finish off a Slurpee in five minutes flat with no brain freeze. Decision-making was *not* my strong point. Especially when faced with a well-stocked vending machine.

"Big thought process you got going on there."

I didn't look over. There was only one person who owned that voice. I held up the dollar. "Limited funds. I have to choose wisely."

"Go with the Milky Way."

That line of idiocy earned him a grimace; the gesture aimed in his general direction before my eyes were held hostage by the beauty that was a shirtless Chase Stern.

Navy pajama pants hung low on his hips, and I'd bet my dollar right then that he had nothing on underneath. No shoes. Bare torso, cut and lean, with enough muscle to rip homers and make any teenage girl come apart at the seams.

My seams twitched, along with my eyes, which pulled from his abs and to his face. I was still frowning, and his eyebrows rose in response. "Not a chocolate fan?"

He leaned a hand on the Coke machine, and the new pose popped unique muscles and pushed at the limits of my control. I fought to maintain eye contact. "Not a Milky Way fan."

"Then what's the big debate?"

"Starburst or Twix." I shouldn't be talking to him. Three conversations were three too many. On the other hand, it wasn't physically possible for my feet to walk away. They refused, rooted deep in the hotel carpet.

He straightened, reaching a hand into the pocket of his pajamas. The dig slid the waistband lower, and I looked away, hearing the low scrapes of a chuckle. "Here." He spoke, and I looked over, seeing his hand outstretched, cupped around a stack of change. "Get both."

"You don't have to do that."

"Shut up and take the money. Otherwise I'll be here all night waiting on you to make up your mind."

I twisted my mouth at him and held out a hand under his, the exchange of coins managed without any physical contact.

He said nothing as I inserted my dollar and the change, my fingers quick as they jabbed at the buttons. The moment grew uncomfortable, and I bent over, pushing the drawer open and reaching in for my candy.

When I straightened, I caught his eyes on my ass, and they darted, guilty as sin, back to my face. I ignored it, nodding politely to him as I lifted the candy in parting. "Thanks." I stepped around him and walked toward my room, trying for a slow and leisurely stroll, when all I wanted to do was sprint.

"What are you doing now?"

I stopped, glancing back at him. "Going to my room."

"You share a room with your dad?"

I narrowed my eyes. "Does it *matter?*"

He shrugged, pushing his hands in his pockets, his shoulders cupping forward. "I can't sleep. Thought I'd walk down to the marina. You been?"

"Yeah."

He chuckled, as if that was funny. "Want to go again?"

"You want *me* to go down to the *marina* with *you?*" I turned fully around to face him, my mind too slow to comprehend.

"Yes."

"Why?"

"Jesus, Ty. To talk. To get to know each other. It's not an orgy invitation."

"I'm not supposed to talk to you."

"Why?"

"You know." I waved my hand in his general direction. "Your reputation."

"It's a walk." He glanced to the machine, dropping in some change and punching at a button. "But whatever. Enjoy your night." The machine rumbled, and he crouched, pulling out a Gatorade.

I hovered, my candy in hand, and weighed my options.

I knew what I should do. Trot back down the hall and to my room. Lock the door, crawl into bed, and order a movie.

Instead, I stepped toward him, his eyes on mine as he twisted off the Gatorade lid and lifted it to his lips. "A short walk," I countered, stopping before him.

"Fine." He shrugged.

I smiled despite myself, and there, in the quiet hallway of the twenty-seventh floor, he smiled back.

 **28**

The hotel towered over the marina, both of them stuck on the edge of the Tampa Bay. We said little in the elevator, the silence uncomfortable, and I relaxed a bit when we stepped out the back doors and into the night air. It was late, the restaurant closed, few lights on, and our walk to the dock went unnoticed. My dad was probably sleeping, our goodnights said an hour before, his room quiet when I'd slipped out to get a snack. Still, I felt nervous. With every person we passed, I held my breath, worried about another teammate, or a coach, a media hound, or even a fan.

A breeze broke up the balmy night, and the tension in my shoulders relaxed a bit with each step farther into the dark, away from the hotel. When we reached one end, a mammoth yacht beside us, he crouched down, swinging his feet out and sitting down on the edge, looking up at me. "Sit down."

I did, leaving enough space between that we didn't touch. Before us, a gap between the boats, a twinkle of city lights lined the top of dark water.

He was a quiet guy. He sat there and said nothing, his Gatorade occasionally lifting to his lips, his strong profile lit gently by the yacht's lights. I didn't speak. Ten years with my father had gotten me accustomed to stretches of silence. I opened my Starburst package and pulled out a yellow cube. Unwrapping it carefully, I sucked the gummy candy into my mouth and leaned back on my palms. Against my bare legs, the night breeze tickled.

"You normally do this? Come on the road with the team?"

I rolled the candy in my mouth. "Yep."

"Must make a social life hard."

I turned and looked at him. "It's the same schedule you've been on for three years. Doesn't look like it's cramped your style any."

"I'm not a teenage girl. Don't you guys have sleepovers and—"

"—pillow fights?" I cut him off. "No." I reconsidered the question. "At least I don't. Friends aren't something I have a lot of." *Any of.*

"Why?"

"I don't know. Lack of options?" I didn't look at him. "No one else travels with the team except a few wives. And I'm home schooled so…" I lifted a shoulder. "My dad and I are close. And the guys on the team keep me company."

"No boyfriend?"

I risked a look at him. The darkness shielded most of his face, dim hints of his beauty peeking out at me. But I could see him looking back at me, the eye contact I was so scared of right there, his face expectant, his question hanging in the dark.

"I don't think you can ask me that."

"Why?"

I stuffed another Starburst in my mouth. "I don't have a boyfriend." I rushed out the words, the response barely audible through the candy, my cheeks burning.

If I expected a response, I was disappointed. He tilted back his Gatorade and took a long sip. I tried to think of something, a change in subject, but couldn't find a single question that didn't border on inappropriate.

He broke the silence. "I hate traveling." He screwed the lid on the bottle and flipped it into the air, catching it with one hand. "Why don't you stay home? Be a normal teenager?"

I set down my candy and tucked my hands under my thighs, swinging out my feet. "Dad tries every year to keep me home. He doesn't succeed."

"Most wouldn't give their daughter a choice."

"I think he just wants to make sure that I really *want* to be here. He argues, I fight back…" I shrugged. "Then the next season starts, and I'm back on the bus."

"But this is your last season, right?"

I turned to him, one eyebrow raised.

"Someone said you were seventeen," he explained. "I figured you were a senior."

I nodded slowly. "I am."

"So … what will you do after you graduate?"

I turned my head and met his eyes. "You ask a lot of questions."

"None of the ones I want." His reply was so quick that it caught us both off guard, his eyes moving away, head dropping, his teeth catching his bottom lip and holding it in place.

"So ask." I suddenly felt bold, his hand near mine, gripping the edge of the dock, those strong fingers, that home-run-hitting arm tight as he rested his weight on it.

"Nah. Not now." He smiled, as if in apology, and lifted his chin at me. "Ask me something."

"Why did you sleep with Davis's wife?"

It was a wildly inappropriate question—one I almost took back, the words hanging uncomfortably between us.

"Wow." He rubbed his cheek. "You really dove in there."

"You don't have to answer it." But I wanted him to. I wanted to know how someone could be so incredibly stupid.

"She was there. I was bored."

I shifted uneasily. "Please tell me that's not the sugarcoated answer."

"It's the truth. I'm a man. Self-control isn't exactly my strong suit."

"So … you didn't love her?" I heard the way the question came out. Naïve. Young. I know people fuck without love. I'd seen, in ten years around players, a lot of stupid decisions. But, I still needed to ask, needed to know what kind of man sat beside me.

He laughed, hard and cruel. "Love her? No. I'm not entirely sure I even *liked* her."

I wondered how Davis's wife had felt about him. If she'd been the same, their sex just some lust-filled side project that had gone wrong. Or if he'd poured on false promises, wooing and abandoning her with one easy signature on the trade contract. I wondered if she was heartbroken and crying, all while I giggled at him in a hotel hallway and felt special because he'd given me seventy-five cents for a candy bar.

I was suddenly angry with myself and pushed to my feet, my cheeks burning.

"You're mad?" He looked up at me, the moonlight on his face, his expression wary. "Oh." He barked out a laugh. "You wanted the bullshit response I gave the press? You want me to be remorseful and blame it on alcohol or drugs?" I moved to leave, and his hand grabbed my bicep, and then he was standing.

"I knew what I was doing," he said, low and close to my ear. "I knew the risks. I didn't care. And look." He let go of me, holding his hands out from his body. "Look at what I got. A spot on the Yankee roster. Not bad."

I smiled, and he didn't understand, his cocky grin becoming wary. "You think you're the first asshole I've met?" I shook my head. "I've lived in a man's world for a long time, Chase. And I've watched men like you make mistakes like that over and over again."

"I'm not an asshole," he said quietly, stepping closer—and I didn't want that. I didn't want to be able to see the detail in his eyes when they softened. The way they begged. What was he wanting? "It was sex. Nothing more. For either of us."

"Her husband was your teammate. It's like … being a family. You don't do that to family." He shouldn't need me to explain this to him. He should know.

"A team isn't a family. If it were, that would make your father and I brothers. And if we were brothers, then I couldn't do this." He stepped forward, his fingers warm, tips of contact sliding under the hem of my shirt, around to the small of my back. His other hand touched my cheek, a soft brush as if testing to see if I was real. I didn't move, my mind struggling to think, to process. Was he about to—then, his head lowered, his hand fell away, and he pressed his lips to mine.

I didn't want to kiss him. My hand was suddenly on his chest, and I wanted to push away. I didn't want my palm to mold to muscle, for my fingers to dig. I didn't want my mouth to open wider, my tongue to give in. I certainly didn't want for this kiss, with this man, to change everything I ever knew about chemistry.

Our kiss had energy, it was a battle—one fought with gentle teases, exploratory touches, and passion—need pulling me forward even as I tried my best to push him away...

And then it was done, my feet stumbling back, his hands releasing me, eye contact the only thing left between us. Hungry eyes. They held me in place as he all but licked his lips. They should have scared me, but they didn't. They matched the staccato of my heart, the gasp of my breath, the tremble of my fingers. They were wild and young, and I saw—in the widen of them—a peek of vulnerability.

I took another step back and almost fell off the dock, my foot turning on the edge of the path, my arms swinging out as I regained my balance. I blushed, my visions of a smooth exit shattered, and glanced over my shoulder at the hotel, no one in sight to witness my stumble, or our kiss. "I'm going to bed."

I could still feel his lips on me when I looked back, Chase saying nothing, his eyes darker now that I was farther away, their hold lessened, and I turned. I stepped down the dock, flip-flops flapping against the boards, and listened. But he didn't call out, didn't follow, silence the only sound behind me.

He let me go and that, more than anything, stabbed the hardest.

When I got back to my room, I turned off the lights and walked to the window. Pulling aside the curtain, I looked down at the marina. Chase was still there, his back to me, hands in his pocket, standing where we had kissed, his eyes on the water.

I leaned against the wall, my fingers absently touching my lips. The kiss should never have happened. If my father found out, if *anyone* did, it would be disastrous.

Together, we would only bring chaos.

 **29**

He didn't know what it was about her. How she managed to get under his skin. He'd sat next to her on that dock and wanted to wrap his arms around her. Sit there until morning and unwrap every layer, every story, every nuance of her soul.

That was a stranger talking, a Chase Stern who hadn't been around in a long time. A stranger who needed to stay hidden, especially around a minor. If there was one thing worse than fucking a teammate's wife, it was screwing one's daughter. Even *he* realized that. He thought of her question about Davis's wife, how she had gone to the jugular, his harsh response not scaring her away, the strength in her eyes only glowing brighter when she'd stepped to the plate and called him on his shit. That had done something to him, snapped some piece of his armor off.

He never should have talked to her. Not in that locker room, not in that tunnel, and definitely not buying her candy and luring her outside. Talk about creepy behavior.

The kiss ... he couldn't regret that. Wouldn't. There would never be another moment in life worth more of a risk. The quiver of her mouth, like her heart was beating so hard it would jump out of her chest. The tentative press of her tongue against his. The hungry way she had clawed at his chest, wanting more. The taste, the connection, the energy. Men had been killed over kisses like that. Careers had been lost. Hearts had been stolen.

He needed to stay away from her. Focus on his game and forget everything else. He had gotten here, to the place of his dreams. Hell if he'd mess it up now. Hell if he'd survive another kiss like that.

JUNE

"It turns out that Rachel Frepp had attended a couple of Yankee home games that 2011 season. But it took years for them to know enough to even *look* for that connection. When she died, no one thought it was because of the Yankees. It's a big city, with a lot of pretty blondes who die. No, it took a few years for NYPD to tie it all together."

Dan Velacruz, *New York Times*

 **30**

New York

I nodded my head to the beat, Jeremih and 50 Cent pumping as loud as my Beats would allow. Wiping down bats, I sang along to the lyrics, my rhythm interrupted by Big Lou, who tugged on the cord of my headphones, speaking to me in a string of Spanish. I obeyed his request, pulling out the headphone jack, my phone blasting "Down On Me," the beat hitting hard, the Dominicans laughing at my music before nodding their heads in time. I beat-boxed with Frank, dancing in place as he rapped out a line, his version ten times dirtier than my clean mix.

I spun, my hands raised, a laugh spilling out, and saw Chase. He stood in the doorway, a towel over one shoulder, his V-neck shirt dirty with clay stains. I looked away, before our eyes met. Laughing at Frank, I stepped back to the bats, focusing on the task, the beat continuing, everything continuing, but everything, as it always was when he came near, was different.

 **31**

She was laughing, her head back, smile big, her blonde hair fanning out as she lifted her hands and turned.

It might have been the most beautiful thing he had ever seen.

 **32**

Beneath my feet, the slight vibration of travel. Above my head, my seat light shone down on the pages of my economics textbook. When the ball of paper dropped from above, a gentle tap on the page, I stared at it. Tightly crumpled, the size of a grape, it looked innocent, coming to rest in the gully of my textbook. A silent, deadly foe. I glanced around, my dad sound asleep in the next seat, the same fate hitting the two men across from me. I glanced back, the Yankee jet dark behind me. I unrolled the ball of paper carefully, stretching it out.

check underneath your seat

The handwriting was terrible, slanted and sloppy. I didn't have to study the lines of it, didn't have to turn around to identify its thrower. In this plane, it could only be from one man.

I didn't want to dig under my seat. I wanted to be the stubborn, proud woman who tore up love letters and moved on to the next great event in her life. But I wasn't that woman, and this wasn't anything close to a love letter. This was bait and at three in the morning, it was infinitely more exciting than the power of the euro in economies of scale. I reached under my seat, my hand closing around two distinct objects, and I smiled before I even pulled out the Starburst tower and the Twix.

I unwrapped the Twix, halfway into my first bite, when the second ball of note hit my lap. This time, I didn't hesitate, my fingers fast in their work.

Quit hogging the only candy on the plane. The hot guy five rows back is starving.

I almost laughed, my lips clamping down as I glanced quickly at my dad, a well-timed snore coming from his sagged chin, his cap pulled over his eyes. I finished my chew and contemplated my choices. There were really only two—stay in my seat or don't.

I didn't. I got up slowly, as quietly as possible, laying my textbook on the seat, and stood in the aisle. My eyes tried to adjust to the dark, scanning the rows of sleeping athletes. He waved, six or seven seats back, and I stepped toward him, stopping by his seat, his lazy smile tilted up at me.

I looked at him in mock confusion, holding up the wrinkled scrap of paper. "This says…" I squinted at it in the dark, "a *hot* guy." I looked up from the paper in time to see him tilt back his head and laugh. I didn't think, prior to that moment, I'd ever found a neck sexy. His was. Half-covered in the dotted texture of stubble, thick and strong, leading to that jaw, then that *mouth*. I tried to remain unaffected, to not think about what it could do, how it could taste.

"Sit down, Little League." He patted the empty seat next to him—a window seat. I looked down at his long legs, stretched out, the crawl over one that would be impossible in any sort of a lady-like fashion. He saw my predicament and leaned forward, standing up, towering over me in the small space, our bodies too close for comfort. "Sit," he whispered, right against my ear.

I sat, his return to his seat giving me the vague feeling of being trapped. This was a bad idea. I should be back at my seat, finishing my work, not surrounded by sleeping giants, holding out my candy to the worst one in the bunch.

He took the candy, breaking off a piece of Twix before handing it back to me. There was a pause, and I wondered what on Earth we were going to talk about.

 **33**

"That doesn't make sense," I argued, pulling my hair into a messy ponytail. "It's selfish." New fact learned about Chase Stern: he had a family. A mother and father, still married and living on five acres in Ohio. His mom worked as a paralegal, his father an electrician. They wanted him to be a lawyer, and still wondered when he would 'stop this ballplaying and settle down.' He hadn't mentioned any siblings. We'd gotten distracted at the mention of Casper.

"How's that selfish? It's my dog."

"It *was* your dog. Then you decided on a career that put you on the road. You can't play baseball *and* have a relationship with your dog."

"A relationship?" he coughed, shaking his head as he finished off his water. "It's not a relationship."

"It *should* be," I pointed out. "The strongest bond on Earth … man and his dog…" I waved away his skepticism, plowing forward. "You can't take the dog away from everything he knows and bring him to New York. It's wrong."

"He doesn't exactly have Wednesday coffee dates with his friends," he said. "He plays in the yard with a Frisbee. He can do that in New York. I'll get a yard. Besides, he's *mine*." He reached out and stole a Starburst.

"Your mom wants what's right for him. She's the one who's taken care of him for the last four years. I agree with her." I shrugged. "Here he's going to sit at your house, all alone, and be miserable."

"You can come over and play with him," he offered.

"Ha."

"Seriously. I'll hire you. You can be his new best friend."

"No. And his owner is supposed to be his best friend."

"You can teach me."

"I don't know anything about dogs."

"Ha!" he said loudly, and I gripped his arm in warning. *Swoon.* So strong, I felt the tendons move when he turned toward me, my fingers instinctively tightening, wanting to feel every pulse, every seam of his body. He glanced at my hand, and I let go.

"Shh," I hissed, and his eyes lifted to mine. Our seats suddenly felt too close, the side of my knee against his.

"You just said you don't know anything about dogs," he whispered.

"So?"

"So stop telling me what I should do with mine."

"He belongs at your mom's house," I whispered back, our eyes still connected, our arms now touching as we hunched together, over the center console.

"Do you have any idea how beautiful you are?" he said, the words husky, his hand moving forward to cup—

I leaned back, needing air. Possibly a soda. Maybe I was dehydrated. Something was wrong; I was too flushed, too hot in this space, my skin jumping against itself, the twist and pull of right versus wrong, kissing him versus not ... we couldn't do this again.

"Were you about to kiss me?" I accused, my whisper forgotten, my voice too loud, and he looked around in warning.

"Watch it," he snapped.

"Were you?"

"I don't know." He sat back in his chair. "What if I was?"

"You can't kiss me again."

"Why not?"

"I just..." My eyes darted front, my dad in shouting distance. "Don't."

"You know, most girls, if their dad tells them to stay away from someone, they do the opposite."

"And most guys avoid jailbait."

"I'm avoiding you."

"Doesn't seem like it."

He watched me closely, his direct eye contact something that twisted my stomach into knots. "We're friends."

Friends. I didn't have a lot of experience with friendship, but I was pretty sure this wasn't it. "You kiss all your friends?"

The corner of his mouth turned up. "When they have a mouth like yours."

I snorted. "Please." *Did he mean it? Had he been as affected as I was by our kiss?*

He kept his eyes on me. "You think you know me, Little League?"

I considered the question. "I know enough."

His mouth twisted in a mocking smile.

"I do," I pressed. "Honestly. It's embarrassing my level of Chase Stern trivia." I waved him on. "Go ahead. Quiz me."

"You know what's been written about me. That's not me."

"You love to do interviews. That tells me something." Dad never did press, despite every attempt by the Yankees to push him into the spotlight. Nineteen years in the Majors, and I'd never once seen him sit down with a reporter. Chase had them trailing him like groupies. Dad once said that a man who sat down and spilled his soul to strangers didn't have much of a soul to protect.

"I have a brand. I feed it." He tossed up the ball and caught it. "Try again."

I jabbed harder. "I know you make some stupid decisions."

He scowled. "Life is a series of stupid decisions interrupted by luck."

"Poetic, but completely wrong."

He spun the ball on the center console, the red stitches blurring, the ball wandering toward the edge. "You can't always recognize stupidity, Ty. Most of the time it takes years to see your own mistakes."

I caught the ball when it fell off the edge, squeezing it hard, my fingers at home in their grip. I looked up from it and into his face. "What's the biggest mistake you've ever made?

I expected him to say the Davis affair. Or the DUI he got rookie year. Or the two years he wasted at Stanford. I was wrong.

His answer took everything I thought I knew about Chase Stern and scattered it to the wind.

 **34**

"Emily."

A girl. A small part of me, the one that still drew hearts and flowers around the words Ty Stern in my notebook, wept. *His biggest mistake was a girl.* I swallowed hard. "Was she your first love?"

"My only." A new look crossed his face—somber. It haunted his eyes and closed off his features—his jaw tight, mouth hard. "You ever think you could love someone too much?"

I hadn't. But in a way, a seven-year-old girl's way, I had. There was a reason I never thought about my mother. A reason I avoided women, their perfumes and hugs, their kind words and motherly gestures. Some things were too painful to mourn. My love for her had been too great for my little heart to handle. "Yeah," I said softly.

"Emily was ten." He reached over, pulling the ball gently from my hands. "She was my little sister."

I said nothing. I couldn't ask, couldn't bring myself to voice a question he wouldn't want to answer.

When he finally spoke, his voice was wood, no life in its syllables, no movement in his eyes. "I forgot to pick her up from gymnastics. I had practice; it ran late. She walked home. Didn't make it." His mouth tightened, voice growing thin. "It was getting dark. She didn't look, ran across the road toward our house. A truck..." he stopped.

I reached over, covering the ball with my hand, his fingers moving, reaching for mine, our hands looping together around the ball. "I'm so sorry," I whispered, leaning into his chest, his other arm wrapping around my shoulders, pulling me tight.

We stayed like that for a long moment, the tension leaving his body slowly, one muscle at a time, his fingers still tight through mine. When the jet started its descent, the sun peeking over the New York coastline, I got up slowly, carefully crawling over his legs, my fingers gentle in their pull from his grip, his body still curled around the space where I had been.

I felt off balance, settling back into my seat. So many of my impressions of him changing, his skill on the field fading in my mind, the details of Chase Stern emerging as everything I felt about his blurred. I had thought, with all of my fandom, all of my research, all of his stats and interviews and press, that I knew him. Maybe I didn't. Maybe there was more than talent and ego stretching those veins.

 **35**

Chicago

Knives clinked against china. Gold-press wallpaper and black velvet curtains held in the loud conversation—twenty hungry bodies pulled close to the table. I chewed on a piece of filet and half-heartedly listened to Dad's discussion with Fernandez about immigration reform. Across the table, a few bodies down, was Chase. Our eyes had met once. I had given a small smile, then hadn't looked back. I could feel him watching me. It was uncomfortable, but I craved it, the scratch to the itch that wouldn't stop crawling across my skin.

To my left, Mr. Grant wished me a happy birthday. Asked about school. Told me Tobey was coming to the Cincinnati series next week. I nodded politely and remembered our kiss, grabbed in those shadows of their mansion, right before the news of Chase broke.

"You should hang out with him," Dad said, his bony elbow poking me in the ribs.

"Sure." I smiled politely. "Maybe we can grab a matinee."

"You don't have to work the game," Dad offered. "Take the night off. Celebrate your birthday."

"We already did." And we had, in high-style. Road trip up to Maine. Two days stuffing our faces with lobster and crab, our shirts stained with butter, smiles big. Dad sang karaoke in a dive bar in South Portland, and I won twenty bucks against bikers in Portland. I hadn't needed friends, and watching a chick flick with Tobey a week after my birthday wouldn't come close.

"I know Tobey would love to see you," Mr. Grant pushed.

I coughed out an uncomfortable laugh, pinned between the two of them. "I appreciate it, Dad, but I'll work the game. I've never—"

"—missed a game. I know. Just know the offer is there."

I met his eyes and narrowed my own. It was no mystery that my father loved Tobey. Five or six years ago, when Tobey wanted to be a pitcher and Dad had spent the better part of a winter coaching him— they'd bonded over Revolutionary War history and the Steelers. Since then, Dad and Mr. Grant had been scheming, trying to put us together. But he should know better than to think I'd give up a game to prance around the mall.

I pushed on the edge of the table and stood, flashing a regretful smile at the two matchmakers. "Excuse me, I need to use the ladies' room."

I sidestepped down the table, my eyes sliding forward, past the row of men hunched over their food, each engaged in conversation or busy eating. All except for Chase, who sat back, one arm draped over the back of a chair, his expression impossible to read, his stare dark and penetrating and locked on me. I tried to look away, but couldn't, holding the contact until I reached the end of the table and was free, all but tripping in my heels in my haste to exit.

I stared at myself in the bathroom mirror, trying to find a reason he'd stared. Spinach in my teeth? *Nope.* Giant zit on my face? *None.* I flipped the handle, was washing my hands under hot water, when my cell buzzed. I grabbed for a paper towel and reached for my phone, a moment of confusion at the text.

Grant's son? Didn't realize your Yankee loyalty went that far. Oh. And Happy Birthday.

I leaned against the counter and sent back my best attempt at coyness. *Who's this?*

Guess.

I didn't need a guess. I hesitated, then had a moment of evil inspiration. Holding back a smile, I replied. *Please stop. We were a one-time thing. Get over it. It wasn't even that great.*

I sent the red herring into cyberspace and waited, smiling. Let my new 'friend' stew over that. I watched dots of activity appear, and then stop.

Ty?

I waited an appropriate length of time, leaving him hanging, then set the hook. *Who's this?*

Chase.

Oh. Nevermind. I thought you were someone else.

I didn't wait for a response, my high note hit. I stuffed the phone in my purse and tried to compose myself, to hide my smile, before I stepped back out. The man needed to be taught a lesson, needed to learn to mind his own business. It'd do him some good to stew over my mythical team boyfriend.

 **36**

What the…? Chase looked down at his phone, rereading the lines of text, the conversation taking an entirely different direction than he had anticipated. When he'd gotten Ty's number from one of the ball boys, he'd planned to have it for emergency purposes only. Then … after overhearing that attempt to push her toward Grant's silver spoon of a son, he couldn't help himself. He had planned to rib her a little, poke out a little fire. He hadn't expected to uncover *this* bomb. He texted back, his fingers fighting against common sense, the words out and sent before he could bring them back.

Who did you think it was?

There was a flash of blonde, and he locked the phone, sliding it into his pocket, watching her as she reentered the private room, her dress navy and short—too short for a place like this, one filled with men— her smile the only feminine thing in the room. She was a blur of tan legs and tight material, her long hair swinging as she settled back into her chair, her smile easy as she responded to something her dad said, her phone elsewhere, along with her concern. His text would be unread, would sit out there, insecure and abandoned, for who knew how long.

He shouldn't have sent it. It was pathetic. He shouldn't have messaged her at all.

He picked up his knife, his cut into the steak rough and hard, his irritation mounting as he stabbed the piece with his fork. Chewing, he glanced down the long table and wondered who, of the men present there, she had mistaken him for.

 **37**

Cincinatti

Maybe it was because I'd skipped lunch. Or maybe it was because Forte had left his gold chain at the hotel and I had to get a driver to take me there, then back, missing batting practice, all so he could put that nasty thing around his neck and *still* error. It hadn't been 'right on the dresser' like he'd said. It'd been in the shower, coiled up next to a used bar of soap with various old man hairs stuck in it.

Whether it was due to hunger, or Forte's errand, I was grouchy. We were also down by two, which made me jittery, my palms sweating as I hung off the dugout and watched Fernandez whiff.

"Ty."

His voice was low, but I heard it, pushing off the fence and turning to Chase. He sat on the metal bench, his hat pushed back on his head, one hand rubbing at his mouth.

I said nothing, just raised an eyebrow.

He lifted his chin, nodding his head back. "A few rows up, the brunette in the tight red shirt."

I fought to keep my expression level. "Yeah?"

"Get her number."

I glanced back, Fernandez still at bat. An oh-and-two count, two outs on the board. I could tell you, without even seeing the pitcher's curl, what was about to happen.

There was the smack of a ball against leather, and Chase leaned forward, coming to a stand, his hand working into his glove. "You got a problem with that, Little League?"

It wasn't the first time I'd been asked to scout girls from the stands. It was practically part of the job description. A player saw a girl they wanted, they sent one of us over. It had never bothered me before. But now, after his kiss, after our talks, it burned. It burned hot and red and made me want to *launch* myself at him, fists swinging. *I shouldn't have sent that text.* I'd thought it was cute. Witty. I'd thought it would make him more interested. Instead, he'd just moved on.

"She's a Reds fan." I spat out the response that I should have kept to myself.

"So?" he shrugged. "I like the forbidden." He grinned at me, and I looked away, the dugout suddenly crowded, traffic moving both ways as we took the field.

"Brunette. Red shirt," he reminded me, his smile wide, grabbing a ball from the stack and tossing it my way, my catch of it automatic.

"He bothering you, Ty?" The hand that clapped on my shoulder was big and strong, and I turned to meet our catcher's eyes, ones filled with protective concern.

"No," I managed. "I'm fine."

"You sure?" He climbed the steps and paused, one foot on the field.

"I'm sure," I said, more conviction in my words. "Now go and shut this shit down."

He laughed, bright white teeth shining out from his dark skin. "You know it, baby." I watched him jog off, the crowd on their feet, stomping and cheering.

Swallowing a groan, I moved to my bag and grabbed a pen and pad of paper.

I like the forbidden.

A Reds fan. Talk about terrible taste. I took whatever warm and fuzzy feelings I had about Chase Stern and let them flutter out, caught by the wind, into the night sky.

 **38**

"Really? Chase *Stern?*" Any chance the mystery girl wouldn't be interested drowned in her giant stadium cup that I'd bet twenty bucks was spiked with liquor. She bounced up and down in excitement, letting out an unladylike squeal.

I tried to smile. "He'd like your number," I repeated, this time a little slower, but she was too busy freaking out to listen.

"Your number." Her friend poked her, stopping the mess of brown curls from bouncing any higher. "Give the girl your *number.*"

"Can I get a picture with him really quick?" the girl whined, holding out her phone as if I might inspect it. "Just right now, super fast?"

"They're in the outfield," I said dryly. "So, no."

"I can wait. Just right down there, by the rail thingy."

I smiled again and contemplated knocking the drink out of her hand. "If you could just give me your number, you can take all the pictures you want with him after the game." Chase was an idiot. Meeting fans during the middle of a series. He should spend tonight focused on the next game, not doing God-knows-what with this giant-breasted Barbie doll.

When I walked back down the steps, her phone number tight in my hand, I looked out to the field, my eyes finding Chase. He lifted a chin, I lifted her number, and our gaze held for a minute.

Then there was the crack of the bat, and our eye contact broke. I jumped the dugout railing and contemplated throwing the number in the trash. I didn't. Instead, I was a good little ball girl, putting it in Chase's helmet, right where he wouldn't miss it, a location that eliminated any need for follow-up conversation.

Maybe I was getting too old for this job.
Maybe I *should* call Tobey.

 **39**

Our traveling secretary liked to put the team all together on one floor. And whenever possible, she put me in a room adjacent to Dad, a proximity that allowed him to sleep better at night. I didn't used to have my own room, that change coming the summer I turned fourteen. I'd gotten my period for the first time, Dad suddenly got uncomfortable, and when we'd landed in Seattle, I'd unexpectedly had my own room key. That first night, I stayed up until four in the morning watching reality TV. The next night, two. Three years later, I was a boring old woman typically in bed by midnight.

Typically. But tonight I was squashed against my door, a book in hand, waiting for Chase to come home. We'd passed him in the hall earlier, Dad and I coming back from Moe's, takeout containers in hand. Chase had stepped aside to let us pass, he and Dad exchanging a curt greeting. I'd looked away, but I'd noticed everything.

The smell of him. Different than before—cologne.
He'd been dressed up, a stiff button-down tucked into slacks.
His phone stuffed into one pocket as he'd moved past, toward the elevators.

He had been going to see *her*—a possibility I'd stewed over since we'd left the field. It'd been an afternoon game, putting us out early—early enough to allow for a date, should one asshole of a player feel up to it.

Dad and I had eaten our dinner in his room, watching the Devil Rays play, little said until the fifth inning, when he'd turned his chair toward me.

"Stern ever hit on you?"

"What?" I coughed, his timing right during a sip of soda, the liquid confused when I jerked, catching in the wrong pipe. Dad just sat there as I struggled between life and death, my eyes watering by the time my esophagus figured out the issue.

"Has he?" He muted the TV, and it was suddenly a serious conversation, the telltale signs beginning to emerge. Awkward silences. A stare you couldn't avoid. The chasing of a subject until it died a slow and painful death. The Sex Talk, executed one year earlier, had been just like this. I didn't know who Dad thought I was going to have sex with, but he'd seen some TV special about teenage pregnancies and had stumbled through a forty-five-minute lecture about STDs and pregnancy and condoms. I'd interrupted him around the time he got to death via labor with a clear proclamation that I was a virgin and had <u>no</u> plans to change that so could he please, thank you very much, turn on ESPN.

"No, Dad. He hasn't hit on me." I managed the words, unsure if they were true. He <u>had</u> kissed me. But since then, he'd gotten that girl's number. Was on a date with her right now.

"Anything I need to know?"

"About Chase Stern?" I shook my head. *"He's just another player."* A laughable statement. He would never be just another anything. It wasn't in his DNA to be normal. He was a superstar, the best in a sea of greats, and that was what my soul struggled with the most. Because as much as he may be a slut or an ass, all it took was him swinging that bat against a fastball, or his impossible leap into the air after a line drive, and I was lost. Watching him play poured steroids into the bloodstream of my want. It wasn't fair to give one man so much, to put him in pinstripes, and on the greatest stage on Earth, and then ask me not to notice.

"He's a good looking guy," Dad pointed out awkwardly. *"He—"*

I laughed, grabbing a pillow off his bed and throwing it at him, my accuracy deadly, his duck slow. *"Stop, Dad. Just stop worrying. Please."*

He tossed the pillow aside. *"Go out with Tobey. For me. Just a movie or ice cream, something to get the Grant family off my back."*

I wrinkled my nose. "I don't know."

He stood and held a hand out for my trash. "Go. I'm forcing the issue. He's a nice guy. If you aren't in love with him, that only puts my mind more at ease."

I passed him my burrito wrapper, taking a final sip of soda before handing over the cup. "Fine," I grumbled. "I'll call him."

"Be back by eleven," he added, his interest in matchmaking apparently limited in scope.

"That won't be a problem." I glanced at my watch, the time just after seven, and headed back to my room with every intention to call Tobey.

Only I didn't. I went back to my room, took a shower, and pulled on a jersey and some underwear. Redid my pedicure. Read an entire Cosmopolitan *and was left with the mental task of committing '85 Ways to Make Him Moan!' to memory. I stared at Tobey's number. Went back and reread Chase's texts. Went back to Tobey's number. Decided I had no interest in being set up by my father. I'd been there, tried Tobey. If we were meant to be, I wouldn't be trying to talk myself into calling him. So I hadn't. I'd raided the minibar of snacks and grabbed my book.*

And now I was here. Squashed against the door, pretending that it was the most comfortable place in the room to read. It was, really. I liked a cramped back and sore shoulder.

Just after nine, there was a sound, the elevator landing, and I dropped the paperback, shooting to my feet, my hands flat on the door, my eye glued to the peephole.

It was Chase, his hand at the back of his neck, rubbing the muscle there, his walk down the hall slow and—thank God—alone. I relaxed against the door, keeping my eye in place, treasuring the moment of uninterrupted voyeurism. He was just out of sight, his walk past my door slow, when he stopped. Backing up a step or two, he turned to me. I flinched, lifting my eye off the peephole, before I realized he couldn't see me. He lifted a hand and rested it on the doorframe, his head hung, and there was a long moment of nothing. I didn't breathe, didn't move, just stood there and waited. What would I do if he knocked? What if Dad heard him knock? What if he pounded on the wood, and then Dad opened his door, and I opened mine and the three of us were standing there?

He lifted his head, and I got a full, front row view of beauty. Even in my warped peephole view, he was gorgeous. Heartbreakingly so. Terrifyingly so. I stared into his face and tried to figure out what he was thinking. Why he was standing there, and what his next move would be.

It turned out to be to his pocket, his hand reaching in and drawing out his phone. He turned away from my door and hunched over it, his fingers moving, and I jumped in surprise when my phone buzzed, loud on the desk. My eyes darted back to the view, Chase facing my door again, his head down, looking at his phone.

My steps were quick, my hands fast when I grabbed my cell, the text on my screen simple and demanding.

Open your door.

I didn't try to think of a witty response; I didn't fight with what to do. I went against all reason and reached down, twisting the knob and pulling open the door.

"Ty." His eyes held mine.

"Yeah?" I didn't move, didn't breathe. Realized, watching the fingers of his hands curl around the edge of the doorframe, that he was mad. Shaking mad, his body tight, like it was being held back. Or maybe not mad. Maybe just upset. Or—

My hypotheses ended when he lunged forward, his hands rough in their grab of me, walking us backward, his foot kicking the door shut as soon as he was inside.

I didn't fight it. I wrapped my arms around his neck and let his kiss crash into me.

 **40**

Chase had tried. He'd tried and fought it as long as he could. Two nights without sleep would drive a man wild. Two days of watching every man on the team and trying to figure out which one had touched her. Two days stacked on two months of seeing her face, her smile, her body ... and a man could only retain so much self-control. He'd tried to end it, sending her up into the stands, toward a strange girl. He'd wanted to test her reaction, to try and push some space between them. It had worked, on some weak scale, until he'd seen Tobey Grant.

The asshole had been downstairs. Drinking at the bar, two friends with him, idiots who cheered him on and laughed too loud. Given the hour, given the slur in Tobey's speech ... Chase had only wanted to warn Ty. Tell her about the drinking, maybe dissuade her from seeing him that night. But then she had opened the door, wearing what appeared to be nothing but a jersey. Hair down, cheeks flushed, she had smelled of soap and fucking innocence. She stood there in that doorway and studied him, and so help him God, he couldn't stop.

He had stepped in, reaching for her, his touch too rough, his control shot, and had a moment of worry, hearing the slam of the door, feeling the tremor of her body—that he was forcing himself on her.

Then her arms had wrapped greedily around his neck, her mouth opening for his, her body soft against his ... and it was official.

He was screwed.

 **41**

I suddenly got it. I understood why women cheated on husbands, why teenagers screwed in the backseats of dirty cars, why naïve girls let men like Chase Stern into their hotel rooms late at night. Our mouths met, our kiss fed, and I couldn't stop. I wanted to touch him everywhere, pull him closer, inhale his scent and never stop breathing. His hands slid to my waist and lifted, my feet coming off the floor, and my legs were suddenly around him, my mouth frantic, his kiss deep, my fingers digging into his scalp, pulling his hair, wanting a hundred more moments and terrified that he would stop.

My butt hit the desk, my legs around him, his hands yanking up my jersey, the brush of fingertips against my sides surprising, my mouth gasping off his as he pulled back, his hands lifting the jersey higher, mine quick to grab it and hold it down. "Wait," I panted, his hands stopping, his head lifting until our eyes met. "Wait," I repeated, both of us breathing hard, his hands trembling as he released my shirt. "Leave the shirt on."

"Okay." He swallowed, putting his hands flat on the desk, one on either side of me, the motion lowering his head next to mine. "Is this okay?"

I rewrapped my legs, bare skin against the smooth fabric of his pants, and pulled him closer to the desk. "Yes," I whispered.

He ran his lips slowly down my neck, nuzzling the skin, pushing aside my hair with his nose, his hands still flat against the desk. His mouth opened, and I shivered, the scrape of teeth against my shoulder, then the hot, wet flick of his tongue. "Is this okay?" he repeated.

"No." I said, bolder, my hands running up his sides, coming across the front of his shirt, my fingers pulling at the top buttons of it. "I need more."

He growled, the sound low in his throat, and I felt the twitch of his thumb against the outside of my left thigh. He shifted, keeping one hand flat, and lifted the other, sliding it softly up my thigh, his fingers spreading across the skin, his head dropping to watch its journey, my breath losing a beat when his fingers hit the edge of my jersey, gently tracing the fabric before slipping underneath it.

I could feel every single finger and its movement, the anticipation heightening the arousal, my heart hitching as he whispered my name, his kiss suddenly soft as it landed on my collarbone, then the hollow of my neck, then my jaw. I tried to prepare for it, tried to stay still, tried to contain the sound in my throat, but I whimpered, unable to hold it back, his fingers now moving along the edge of my panties, the gentle scrape of his nails, and then he gripped them, pulling slightly on the cotton, the boyshorts cutting in between my legs and my arousal turned the corner of insanity.

I had never known this. The pulsing need, the urge to grind against something, *anything*, my legs trembling, body crying, every thought reduced to the primal instinct of wanting more. Everything. Anything. I sat on that desk before him and opened my mouth and begged, the word *please* slipping out, over and over, my hips twitching against the desktop, needing more friction, my hands clawing at his shirt, pulling at the fabric, reaching for the belt, my actions instinctual, the consequences be damned.

He twisted his hand, pulling the panties tighter, the cut of them in between my legs almost bringing me off the desk. I closed my eyes, and dropped my head, completely at his mercy.

"Good lord, Ty." He groaned the words, and his other hand was suddenly there, tight and rough in its grip of my opposite thigh. "Look at me," he rasped out. "If you want more, I need you to look at me."

I opened drugged eyes, his face coming into focus, his eyes tight on mine.

"There, Ty. Look at me."

I tried. But then his clench on my thigh was gone, and he ran his fingers across the tight stretch of my panties, a brush that did something inside of me, something that broke down any last stronghold, something that made my legs collapse, my thighs fully spreading for him, my chin trembling. His fingers brushed back, then took on a new life, slipping down, between my legs, pushing and rolling across the soaked fabric, my head falling back again, eye contact difficult as I tensed beneath his touch.

"That..." One of my hands was suddenly on his shoulder, my nails digging into his shirt, holding on for dear life. "Don't stop."

"Look at me, Ty. Stay with me, baby."

"I—" I whimpered out the word, not sure where it was going, his eyes reading me well, one of his fingers pushing past cotton and dipping inside of me.

Holy shit. If I thought that ... whatever that had been, was amazing, his bare finger, pushing inside of me, *bending* inside of me ... it was, in an instant, the sweetest, purest pleasure I had ever known. I cried out his name, twisting before him, my hands clinging to him, crazy sounds of nonsense pouring out of me, everything in me focusing on the maddeningly perfect touch of his.

I broke under his hands. I might've cried. I definitely swore. In those moments, his eyes on mine, his touch pushing inside, I climbed into heaven and fell back down a different woman.

 **42**

He couldn't. Never again, not with anyone else. Nothing would ever, after that moment, compare. Not with her cry, not with her reaction, not with her kiss. A woman shouldn't be created in such heartbreakingly beautiful combinations. A woman shouldn't, in fifteen minutes, have the ability to ruin him for life.

 **43**

When I woke up, the room was dark. I rolled over and reached for him, my hands finding nothing, the bed empty. I sat up far enough to see the clock. 1:02. When I'd fallen asleep, I had been on my side, he on his, my body under the blankets because he'd said he couldn't take the temptation, his body on top, six feet of gorgeous stretched out, his shoes kicked off.

"Tell me about Ty Rollins," he said, his gaze on me, his hand gentle as it tucked a bit of hair behind my ear.

"Not much to tell. My mom died when I was seven. I joined Dad on the road. Been a clubhouse brat ever since." I smiled, and his eyes softened, dropping to my mouth.

"Tell me about your mom."

My smile faltered. "I don't remember a lot."

"Was she a baseball fan?"

I shook my head. "God no. I remember them fighting. That was really all I knew about my dad. That he'd be gone for long stretches of time, then he'd show up and they'd fight. About money, about his job…" I winced at the memory. "I was terrified when he picked me up and took me on the road."

He rolled onto his back and looked at the ceiling. "There was no one else you could have stayed with? Grandparents or an aunt?"

"Sure." I snorted. "But he was stubborn. And for whatever reason, he wanted me with him. I hated him for it at first. I wanted to be home, with my friends, back

in Pittsburgh."

"*Not on the road with a bunch of old men?*" *He smirked.*

"*Exactly.*" *I mimicked his pose, rolling onto my back, his body scooting closer, his arm lifting around me, and I rested comfortably in the crook of his arm. I'd never been in that place before, my chest rising and falling next to another, my face close enough to turn my head and kiss his neck. "But ... you know ... it was the best thing to ever happen to me. Not my mom dying, but coming on the road with him. Once I got over it all—the guys, the team—they became my family." I curved a little into him, my hand resting on his chest. "And I wouldn't change anything about it now.*"

"*Anything?*" *His voice held a bit of hope, and my heart had lifted despite myself.*

"*Maybe I'd change one thing,*" *I conceded, thinking of all of the places this conversation could go. A relationship talk? Was this what we were about to have? Or was it still too early for that? In baseball, I knew everything. With relationships, I knew nothing.*

"*Yeah?*"

"*Yeah.*"

I didn't give him anything more, was too shy to put myself out there, and our conversation moved to baseball's greats, then movies, then spring training and our favorite stadiums. We'd talked until we were hoarse, then we didn't say anything for a while. At some point, the room had blurred, my eyelids too heavy. At some point, he'd left, turning out my light and going back to his room. Room 724. He'd thrown that out at some point, lifting his eyebrows suggestively, my eyes rolling in response.

Room 724. I moved out of the bed and brushed my teeth. Staring into the mirror, my hair was loose and wild, my lips bruised from his kisses, the faint burn of a hickey on my neck. I pulled my hair back and stared at it in the mirror, fascinated. *A hickey.* I'd never had one before. I let my hair fall back into place and examined my reflection, a stranger's reflection, that of a wild woman.

Room 724. I rinsed my mouth and flossed. Walked back into the bedroom and found my phone. Plugged it in and checked my texts. Three from Tobey, one from Dad. Nothing from Chase. I crawled into bed and stared at the ceiling.

Room 724.

My body knew before my mind. My feet moved quickly when I finally stood, my room key pocketed, pajama pants pulled on underneath my jersey. I opened the door and was careful in my shut, glancing toward Dad's room, the door closed without incident, then I was headed down the hall, with no clear game plan in mind.

I was such a stupid girl. Running to a man's room in the middle of the night. A man who I thought I shared something with. A man who had left my bed for something a little more mutually beneficial. I realized my mistake as soon as she swung open the door, her hand to her nose, her eyes swinging a little before they landed on me. Her boobs had grown since the game, pushed huge and out of a corset top, a beer and cash in one hand, her smile wide, Chase seen dim in the background, his back to me, a second girl hanging on him, the glimpse of her the last thing I saw before I turned, muttering *wrong room*, and ran down the hall, tears blurring my vision, to the safety of my room.

When I rounded the curve, almost there, I was stopped, strong hands grabbing me, my name said as I looked up through the sting of tears and into a familiar face.

 **44**

"Ty."

It was Tobey, and I almost pushed away, my mind conflicted, escape my primary goal. What if Chase came after me? What if Tobey saw? What would he say? What would *I* say? Stupid, stupid, stupid. A shot of anger coursed through me, and I straightened, finding my footing, my hand wiping at my face.

"Are you okay?" His face, so concerned, so *not* Chase. From down the hall, there was the sound of a door banging against something, and my urgency increased.

"I'm fine. Where's your room?"

"Right here." He held up a key, a beer in his grip, and I grabbed it, tilting it to my lips, the liquid cold and sour against my freshly-brushed teeth.

"Easy, Ty." He laughed, reaching for the bottle, and I held it away, nodding to his room. "Open it." I chugged the rest of his beer, liking the way his bleary eyes followed my throat, settling on the open neck of my jersey. My first sip of beer—it was weak and watery, cold and a little bitter. I swallowed and wanted more. Wanted to be someone different, a girl who didn't care about Chase or our night or...

the girl, her back to me, her lips against his bare shoulder, her arm reaching around him...

Why had they been in his room? And why did he give me his room number if he was going to do that?

131

Tobey's door was open, and I stepped through, the empty bottle tossed toward the trash, my feet bee-lining for the kitchen of his suite, my hand pulling at the door of his fridge. Empty. White lights illuminating clean shelves.

"What's wrong?" Tobey was right behind me, so close that when I turned, I bumped into him, my hand pulling at the bottom of my jersey.

I tried to smile. "Got any more beer?"

"No." His voice was wary, the response stretched out, and he stepped back slowly, my hopes of erasing this night with alcohol dimming. Then he crouched, fumbling open a cabinet, and my eyes dropped, the door open, a row of mini bottles shining from the dark depths. "But I have these." He smirked up at me, and I stepped forward, my hand held out, mind replaying too many things.

We were so good together. I twisted the cap of the first tiny bottle, something clear, and I swallowed a huge gulp of coconut fire, my throat burning, my eyes tearing as I took the juice Tobey handed me and chased down the liquor.

I thought he'd been different. Different than the mistakes I had read about, the stupid decisions of his past. I'd thought, in just the way he'd looked at me, that I was healing. Fixing him. I took another bottle, Tobey unscrewing a duplicate and holding out mine, our tiny bottles clinking together, and then more was going down, another burst of bitter fire, this one golden, this one worse, both of us coughing at its end.

Tobey smiled at me, appreciation in his eyes. "Damn, Ty. I didn't take you for a hellion."

A hellion. I liked it, liked the look in his eyes, that wary pride. Liked the way his gaze stuck to my chest when he reached back into the minibar.

I thought we were special. Another clear bottle, and the room spun briefly, then stopped, the world back in focus, just as ugly, but Tobey tugged at the end of my hair and said something, something funny, and I laughed. He pulled my hand, leading me toward the couch, and I didn't move, pointing back at the minibar, wanting just one more.

I was a hellion.
I was strong.
I was wild.
I could not be hurt.

I'd been falling in love. Wasn't that how love felt? The connection that was impossible to fight? The unique tie between two souls that changed lives forever? This one didn't burn going down my throat— it soothed, it warmed. I smiled at Tobey and realized, in an instant, how handsome he was. Rugged. He held out a soda, and I pushed it away. He pulled at the front of my shirt, and I stepped, or fell, into his arms. He pushed hair out of my eyes, and then we kissed.

Then we were on the couch.
Then he was above me.
Then everything that had once been pure, was gone.

I'd heard that it'd hurt the first time, but it didn't. I hardly felt anything. And I didn't, in the minutes before I stumbled back across the hall and into my own bed, think of Chase at all. I returned to my empty room, no sign of my father, my phone silent, no missed calls or texts. I hadn't thought, in my night of recklessness, of Dad, and the possibilities of being caught. I crawled into bed and fell asleep with one bit of comfort, that he would never know what had happened.

Another dumb thought. One of so many that night.

Fuck Chase. And fuck being eighteen. So far, it sucked.

 **45**

"Was it your guy?" Chase turned, finding the girl in the TV's light, her approach closer, his eyes watching the blow of her hair as she moved, individual strands fluttering through the air.

"No, but he's coming." She bent over the table, doing a line. Chase felt sequins move against his hand and turned his head, laughing softly at the girl, kneeling by him, her hands on his belt. He pushed at her gently, and she tumbled back, a string of curses shot out. It didn't matter; nothing mattered. Not for this tag-along. Not for the other girl, both of them here for the drugs. Drugs they weren't providing, this tiny taste worthless. He watched her finish the line and snapped his finger, gesturing for the mirror, her pass too slow, his eyes narrowing.

At least she was brunette. Watching Ty sleep, her hair tangled against the pillow ... it'd been so soft and white. So much like Emily's. He shouldn't have told her the stories, memories that had made him smile, but so painful in the aftermath, once she was asleep, once the room was dark and it was just her sighs and his thoughts. Too many thoughts, especially tonight. *June 21st*. The night he could never forget. The night always the hardest to get through. It was no coincidence that he'd gotten a DUI three years ago today. It was no coincidence that right now, he was here, surrounded by these idiots, craving an escape. Another few lines would do it. Then he'd be able to forget.

There was another knock, and he watched her stand, grabbing the cash, her move to the door unsteady on her heels. This visitor was right, a man's voice heard, and he finished off his beer, sitting in the chair, anticipation pushing hard through his veins.

Soon, he'd forget. Soon, the anniversary of Emily's death would be the furthest thing from his mind.

 **46**

I didn't want to see Chase Stern ever again. I didn't want to see the smooth arc of his body as he jumped for a catch. I didn't want to see the hug of his ass in baseball pants, the muscles beneath his uniform when he lifted his hands to adjust his hat. I didn't want to see the twitch of his smile when his eyes met mine.

When he came on deck, I stayed in place, his slow and lazy climb passing up the steps to my left. I held my breath as he passed, my chin resting on my crossed forearms, my eyes stuck on Rodgers, who took a step off second. Chase stopped in the dirt before me, right in my line of vision, his practice swings slow and perfect. I straightened, my irritated huff subdued as I moved left, leaning against the dugout wall.

"Grab me a new bat?" My eyes flicked to him, dropping to the bat he held out.

"What?"

"I want to hit with something else." His mouth did that thing that I didn't want to see, where it twitched, as if we shared a secret.

"You always hit with that bat."

His eyes flickered at my tone, and he stepped closer. "I'll try the Marucci."

"Why?" This was stupid. He'd hit with a Louisville Slugger all season, and *now* he wanted to try something new?

"Is something wrong?" Dad was suddenly there, next to me, his eyes hard on Chase.

"No," I muttered, grabbing Chase's backup bat, another Slugger, and thrusting it out to him, my eyes daring him not to take it.

He did, flipping the old bat toward me, the exchange wordless, the weight of Dad's eyes stifling. Then Cortez hit a single and Chase was up, his glance at me unreturned, my actions brisk as I wiped off his original bat, sliding it into place, my back to him when he swung hard, the Louisville Slugger sending the ball high into the cheap seats, the home run adding three runs to the board.

Try a Marucci bat. Guess I wasn't the only one walking around with a head full of stupid.

"What's wrong?"

I froze, bent over my tennis shoe, my final knot of laces slow as I bought an extra second before standing. I looked up to the front of the locker room, where he stood, his hand on the doorway, an edge to his voice.

"Nothing." I grabbed my jacket and shrugged into it.

"You're not staying for the second game?" His gaze skated over my jeans. We were into the first inning of the second game, today a long doubleheader day.

"Just running up to the box, got a message for Heston's wife." I held up the folded piece of paper, a note I already peeked at, the sexual promises in it stopping my snoop three sentences in.

"You're acting weird."

I pulled the end of my ponytail out of my jacket, avoiding his eyes. "I don't feel well."

"This have anything to do with last night?" He stepped closer, and I moved back, grabbing at my phone. I wasn't going to cry. Not here, not in front of this asshole. "It does." He sounded surprised. "I thought you were okay with all of that. It wasn't..." His voice softened. "I didn't mean to push, if you weren't ready—"

I cut him off before this conversation got more off track. "It wasn't that."

In the stadium, there was a cheer, something happening. I felt a sear of panic. "You need to go. You'll be up soon." Someone could come in at any moment. Our staff. The Reds' staff. Another player. Someone could come in and we'd—*this*—would be caught.

"Did I miss something?" He moved, blocking my exit, and gripped my shoulders with both hands. I finally looked up, a mistake. He looked so innocent, so sincere, his brow furrowed over those gorgeously dark eyes. Eyes that I had fallen into last night. Eyes that I had seen a future in, some ridiculous imaginary future. "I thought..." He swallowed. "I thought last night was pretty great."

Ha. Fury boiled in me, images burned in my soul pushing to the surface, the heave of cleavage, his bare back, the run of a girl's hand down it, her mouth reaching for his face... "It was great," I spit out. "Until you left. Until you went back to your room and—" I couldn't finish. The words stuck in my throat like bile.

He let go of me. "You went to my room? Last night?"

"Yeah."

He looked down, rubbing the back of his neck. "And what'd you see?"

It was the wrong thing to say. Not a confession, just a request to know how deep his grave was dug.

I shouldn't have answered. I should have pushed for more, pinned him until everything came out. But we were in the middle of the game, and our time was short. "Girls." I swallowed hard. "Kissing you."

"They didn't kiss me." One of his hands was back on my arm, and he was guiding me, until my shoulders hit a locker, and his stare was impossible to escape from. "Look at me."

I was looking. I couldn't *not* look. I was staring into his eyes, and I believed him when he spoke.

"They had a connection. They got me some coke. They were there, they snorted it with me, they left. Nothing happened."

"Coke?" I whispered. "*Cocaine*? Are you *stupid*?!" I yelled the word, shoving at his chest, but it didn't give. I glared into those eyes and saw shame.

"Yeah." He gritted out. "I was. And I was weak. And I'm sorry."

"Don't be sorry to me!" I exploded. "If you get tested—"

"It's out of my system in three days. And I'm not going to get tested. You know they don't test for that unless I give them a reason—"

The door at the end of the locker room banged open, and a ball boy squinted at us, Chase caging me against the wall. "Mr. Stern?" the teenager called out, some Cincinnati local.

"Yeah?" Chase didn't turn his head; he stared at me, eyes begging for understanding that I couldn't give.

"You're in the hole."

Shit. There would be talk. Speculation. The door slammed shut, and we were alone again.

"I like you," he said, and there was never more simplistic beauty.

"You hurt me," I accused and felt tears come. Tears at a terrible time, our team's needs imminent. "You're stupid," I repeated. *Drugs*? I hadn't believed the rumors, too many of them swirling around these men. I'd thought he was above that. I'd thought he was stronger than that.

"I'm sorry," he said, and he leaned forward, his lips gentle as they pressed against my cheek, underneath my eyes, my tears kissed away. "Forgive me. Please. I need it."

I didn't know if I could. His need for drugs had led to too much. What I had given up in Tobey's hotel room … it hadn't felt valuable then, it hadn't felt major. But now, looking into his eyes, I wanted it back. I wanted Chase to hold me and love me, and I wanted to have that to give to him. I hated him for ruining that. And I loved him for his regret—regret that matched my own, my heartbeat echoed in his eyes.

Both of us had made mistakes. He had confessed his. I couldn't begin to bring up mine. Instead, with precious seconds ticking by, I ducked under his arm. "You've got to go," I called over my shoulder, heading toward the door.

I was almost there when I saw the handle turn, my jump to the side barely in time before it flung open, in my direction. I flattened against the wall, hidden by it, and heard the bellow of our manager. Chase had been following me, almost running into Don, and I watched his fingers wrap around the edge of the door, keeping it away from me. "I'm coming," he gritted out, his eyes darting to me, and I mouthed the word *GO*.

He didn't move, and I gave him the only thing I could, a smile. It was small and hesitant, but his eyes grabbed at it, his fingers leaving the door, and he reached for me, the pads of his fingers brushing over my cheek for a brief moment, and then he was gone, the echo of his cleats bouncing off the walls as he followed Don to the field.

That night his disappearance was the talk of every sports show, our own team giving him hell, his bathroom excuse bought by most but not by all. Maybe it was just paranoia, but I felt my dad's eyes, boring into me, past the laughter and the ribbing. I focused on the glove I was oiling and didn't look up.

That night, he texted me and asked if he could come by.
That night, by the time he gently knocked, I had my mind made up.

 **47**

"You can't do drugs anymore." I cracked the door and spoke quietly through it, scared to give my heart more than a sliver of a view. I'd be the first to say that I was naïve about a lot of things. Young in the world of experience. But drugs—I'd seen them destroy too many players. Their marriages, their careers, their reputation. He had too much at stake. Not just with me, but with life.

"Okay." He tilted his head at me, and I eyed the freshly shaved jaw, the damp hair, the cornflower blue polo cleanly tucked into the top of his jeans.

"I'm serious." I wet my lips and saw his eyes drop to them. "No coke, or weed, or heroine or—"

He pursed his lips at me. "It's just coke—*was* just coke," he amended. He held up his hands. "But no more. I promise." I didn't know him well enough. I didn't know whether his promises were gold or tinfoil. He glanced both ways down the hall. "Please let me in before someone sees me."

I rolled my eyes but opened the door wider, ready to table the discussion for another time. "Scared of my father?" I asked.

"Terrified." He grinned at me and stepped forward. I shut the door behind him, and quietly flipped the latch.

"We can't stay in here all night." He stood at the window and looked out, the Cincinnati skyline glittering out of the dark.

"Why not?" I spun in the chair, watching him. He turned his head, looking at me for a long moment, his eyes traveling up the length of my legs before he chuckled, shaking his head, saying nothing. "What?" I pressed.

"Nothing." He looked back out the window, and I stood, walking over to him.

"What?"

"A man only has so much control, Ty. I'm in a hotel room with you, alone. No one watching, no one to see. No one to stop me from kissing you." He looked at my face. "And from doing a hell of a lot more."

I took a step back, still shaky from my mistake with Tobey. The mistake I'd decided to never think of again. I wasn't the only one regretting it. I'd passed Tobey in the hall that morning, and he'd practically broken his neck trying to avoid eye contact.

Chase's eyes followed me, the dark arousal in them fading. I could see the thought process and spoke quickly, before the conversation turned serious. "So what do you suggest?"

His mouth broke into a grin, and he glanced down at my pajama pants. "Got anything else to wear?"

 **48**

He didn't know why she trusted him. Especially after whatever she saw that night. She shouldn't. He was fucked up in more ways than one. Drugs were just the side effect of the bigger problem: a broken heart, one too afraid to love and too wary to trust. What happened with Emily proved that the greater the love, the deeper the pain.

He walked down the hall toward the stairs, thinking of the look on her face when she'd stepped away from him. It had almost been fear. It had certainly been cautious. In his mind, everything had changed when she'd turned eighteen. He needed to remember that, for her, it was just another day on the calendar gone. It didn't change her outlook on things. It didn't make her ready for something that his cock was frantic for.

He could be patient. He could wait.

He stepped into the stairwell, and leaned against the wall, the door settling closed behind him.

She shouldn't trust him.
He should have the strength to stay away.
There was no way any of this would end well.

The door creaked open, and the most gorgeous blonde on the planet stepped quietly through, a backpack on her back, hair down, smile peeking wide below mischievous blue eyes. "Ready?" she asked.

And there was no way this *wouldn't* end well.
For that smile? He could be a better man. He would be a better man.
And everything would be okay. It had to.

 **49**

Twenty-seven flights of stairs was a bitch; it didn't matter who you were. Well, unless you were a Major League freak of nature who barely wheezed while the blonde beside him struggled to stand. Not that I was wheezing. Or had sweat dripping down my cheek (I think they had the heat on.). Just hypothetically speaking.

We left the hotel through the stairwell door, coming out in a back parking lot. Chase grabbed my hand and pulled me toward the street. I gave one last glance back at the building, then followed.

I had told my Dad goodnight, in those minutes before we left. Same as I did every night, his voice tired and sleepy, the light under his door already out. He wouldn't know about this, couldn't, but I still worried, my phone tucked into my back pocket.

"What if someone recognizes you?" I hissed. They would. His face was too beautiful not to notice, too famous to forget.

"We're not going anywhere that I'll be seen."

And, thirty minutes later, he was right. It'd taken three phone calls, five hundred dollars in cash and a photo op with two security guards, but we were standing in the one place that no one in a city of millions, would see him. The Newport Aquarium, at eleven o'clock at night.

Before us, glass stretched to the ceiling, a thick divider between us and a million gallons of salt water. Floating gently, lit bright blue, the biggest stingray I had ever seen.

"He's beautiful," I said quietly, watching his giant fins silently pass through the water. Chase nodded, crouching beside the tank and watching a group of seahorses bob along colorful grasses.

"Have you been here before?" I asked, lifting my chin and following the path of the ray as he soared above me.

"As a kid. Not at night. You?"

I came here as a kid also, my hand tight in Mom's. I had a small memory of a coloring book, purchased at the gift shop. And of holding a starfish. I remember those moments, but not the sight of her face when she looked at the fish. Or the sound of her laugh. I was too fixated on the things that hadn't mattered. It seemed unfair that I'd remember those and not her. I told him so, and he pulled me to his chest, his arms wrapping around my shoulders, pinning me to him. I looked up into his face and memorized the line of his nose, the dent of it where a break once occurred. The thick brush of his eyelashes, framing eyes that searched my soul. I dropped my gaze to his mouth, his lips pale and smooth, tilting toward me as he softly brushed them against mine. I stayed still, the delicate skin of our lips against each other, and vowed never to forget this moment. I smelled the faint scent of chlorine, and his cologne, and felt the tighten of his hand, our lips parting, tongues meeting, and held onto each detail desperately. I would not forget this moment. I would never forget this moment.

I laid in the backseat, my head in his lap, his fingers in my hair, absentmindedly playing with strands. The SUV, a fleet car from MLB, drove slowly, bumping over occasional potholes, the driver clueless to my identity and highly-paid to ignore Chase's.

We passed over a train track and the clatter made me think of my mom. Of the sounds in the kitchen when she cooked. Pots clattering, the scrap of metal spoons against a pot. Funny how odd things can take you to new places. I looked up, into his face.

"My mom was a great cook."

"Yeah?" He ran a soft finger over the lines of my ear and waited.

"Yeah. I remember sitting in the kitchen and drawing as she cooked." I could picture the coloring book perfectly—my favorite—one with Belle and Gaston and all of her relationship drama. "Is it bad that that is the only thing I can remember?" Not the scent of her perfume. Not the sound of her voice. I just remember that damn coloring book and the smell of spaghetti cooking.

"It's not bad. I don't remember much from that stage of my life. And you don't have to remember her to still love her."

"I know." I turned my head, watching the shadows as they moved across the leather. But did I?

"What happened to her?"

"She was having surgery. Something went wrong with the anesthesia." I'd been home with a sitter. Dad had been in Colorado, playing. Neither of us there when she died.

"I'm sorry. Is it hard to talk about?"

I looked away from the shadows and up into his eyes. "No. But you're the first person I think I've ever told." I think he was the first who had ever even asked. When I was younger, people brought up my mother a lot. Nothing worse than a heartbroken girl being innocently asked where her mommy was. "My dad did a good job of stepping in," I said quickly, my loyalties fierce. "A great job."

"Are you going to tell him about us?"

I opened my eyes. "Us?"

"Well, yeah."

It was a question worthy of sitting up, and I did, turning to him, my equilibrium off for a moment before I found my bearings. "I didn't know there *was* an us."

"I'd like there to be." His voice was low and steady, like we weren't having the biggest conversation of my life, like he wasn't CHASE STERN asking me to be his girlfriend.

"You want to be my boyfriend." Clarification was needed because this was huge, and if I was wrong, if I was misreading this, then I needed to reel my heart in before—

"Yes."

"Exclusively."

"Yes."

I looked away from his eyes for a moment. "That means no other women."

His mouth twitched into a smile. "Yes. I know what it means."

"I'm not ready to have sex." *Again.* I wanted to add the words, to give him some hint that I had, unfortunately, done that before, but couldn't. Adding that would lead to questions. Answering those questions would mean facing my mistake head on. It was easier, especially in this new world, one where Chase wanted to be my *boyfriend*, to pretend that it never happened.

"That's fine." He reached for my hand, and I pulled away.

"No. You say that's fine, but I've lived in a world of men for ten years. And I've seen almost every one of them cheat. There's too much temptation—it's not fair for you to be with someone like me, someone—"

"Ty." He cut me off, his hand pulling at the back of my neck, bringing me forward, his mouth hard as it kissed the top of my head. "Shut up. I'm a big boy, I can handle some celibacy. Just please don't tempt me too much." He lowered his mouth, bringing it to mine, and we shared one long kiss, a kiss that had my heart pounding and nails digging into him, the muscles in his arm tight under my grip.

When the kiss ended, we were both breathless, and I pushed my hair back, trying to find my composure, my sanity in all of this. "I can't tell my dad." Not yet. Not when his opinion of Chase was lower than garbage. Not when I was barely eighteen, and Dad was finally giving me space. "If he knows, he won't let me see you. I mean ... not like this." There would be curfews and limitations. He'd watch me like a hawk, and question me to death. Assuming that he didn't forbid it altogether. I may be eighteen, but I was a Yankee employee. And I was his daughter, his world. For the moment, my life, and my decisions, weren't exactly my own.

He studied me for a moment, then nodded. "It's your decision. Just let me know when. But I'm yours. No other women. No drugs. I promise."

I nodded. And when he pulled me onto his lap for another kiss, I felt his conviction in his touch, his taste, his reverent whisper of my name.

And just like that, five blocks away from the Marriott Marquis, we were official. Officially together.
Officially committed.
Officially screwed.

JULY

"Even once they made the Yankee connection, Ty wasn't compared to the victims 'til the fourth girl died. Then some criminal behaviorist finally made the correlation between the hot blondes and Ty. *That* was really when the investigation started to break wide open. And that's when the protection detail started following Ty. For all the good they did."

Dan Velacruz, *New York Times*

 **50**

Cleveland

I hid my yawn behind my glove, the motion still caught by Higgins, fifteen yards away, in left field.

"Tired Ty?" he called out, reworking the glove onto his hand.

"Nope." I scoffed, earning a laugh from him, his head turning as the hit went high left. Foul. Five innings in, and we were up by two. The remaining innings were crawling by, my eyes heavy, a nap calling my name. I'd been dragging all day, Dad all but pulling me out of bed that morning. My body wasn't built for 3 AM bedtimes, a habit that my secret relationship with Chase was fostering. Last night we'd driven to his hometown, a quiet suburb forty-five minutes out of Cincinnati. He'd given me the grand tour, the final stop his high school.

The ball shot through the dark toward me, and I reached out, catching it barehanded, grateful for his light toss. Behind him, the dark lights of the stadium, the high school barely visible across a sea of grass. I stepped closer to him and threw it back, the toss short, him only fifteen feet away.

"It's so odd," he said. "That you've never been in high school."

I shrugged, glancing over my shoulder. "I didn't miss it." I held out a hand, ready for his throw, but he turned, tossing the ball back to the dugout. I watched as he came closer.

"High school's pretty great." He looped an arm around my shoulders and steered me around, heading for the bleachers, his first step up on metal loud in the

deserted dark. "I had some great moments here. I hate that you missed it."

We sat halfway up, the metal hard and cold against my upper thighs, and I looked toward the buildings, a fortress of red brick that looked more like a prison. "What was so great about it?"

"It's hard to explain." He leaned forward, rubbing at a spot on his palm. "There's this energy in high school. A sort of magic." He looked over at me. "I see it in you, sometimes. The way you smile when you see something new. The excitement you get over something dumb. How your breath hitches when I lean toward you."

"That's not high school. That's just … being young." I hated that I was five years younger than him. I wanted to have this conversation on an adult level, one where we were equals.

He leaned back, resting his elbows on the row behind him. "I would have loved to meet you back then."

"When you were in high school?" I wrinkled my nose. "You would have ignored me."

"No." He sat up, tucking some hair behind my ear. "I would have fallen for you the minute I saw you. You would have been the star of our softball team, and I would have stayed after practice and offered to help you with your batting."

I snorted. "And I would have told you where to stick it."

"Nah." He shook his head. "I was a stud in high school. You might have tried to play hard to get, but you would have been all over me."

"You know … you're still a stud." I looked over at him, his eyes lifting off the field and back to me. "I think you're probably more of a stud now than you were here."

Something in his eyes dimmed. "High school's funny. It builds gods out of those who don't deserve it. Makes them feel invincible just because they can hit a ball, or score a goal."

I heard the catch in his voice and knew he was thinking of Emily. Of the late practice and distractions that had cost her life. And I distracted him the only way I knew how, throwing my leg over his and straddling his lap, my hands settling on either side of his face. "What would you have done, if I had let you coach my swing?"

He ran his hands slowly up the back of my thighs, caressing the skin before he got to the edge of my cutoff shorts, his fingers carefully sliding under the edge of them, hot points of contact that squeezed my ass. "I would have gone to first base."

"Which is?"

His hands pushed further, and I lost my breath, his mouth lifting to mine as he pulled me down, harder on his lap, the rough fabric of my shorts almost painful as he lifted his hips and pressed against me. His mouth was greedy, his kiss ragged and deep, my hair falling around our lips as they battled. His final kiss slowed the tempo, his hands sliding out of my shorts and I panted, my body craving his, craving more, and never wanting to stop. "That's first base?" I asked. It felt enormous for something so minor, yet nothing between us had ever felt ordinary.

"A Chase Stern first base." He smiled at me and swept my hair behind my shoulder, his hand on my neck as he tilted it back and kissed the delicate skin there.

"Would you have tried for second?" I closed my eyes, his hold on my neck comforting, his mouth on my throat the most sensual thing on the planet.

"With you, I'd have tried for anything."

I pushed gently on his chest, his lips leaving my neck, and pulled at my T-shirt, the thin material stretching over my head, everything Yankee gray for a moment before it was off, and he was staring at me, and if I could have taken a photo of his face right then, I would have saved it for eternity.

"Don't even think about third," I said. Then, I reached back and unclasped my bra.

He hadn't tried for third. He'd been a perfect gentleman, even when I could feel him rock hard in his jeans, his expression painful when he went to stand. I had reached for his jeans, ready for more, but he'd stopped me, his hand firm on my wrist, his voice solid when he'd spoken. Now, in the light of the next day, my arousal calmed, I was glad he'd had the strength when I didn't.

I yawned again, forgetting to cover my mouth, and heard Higgins chuckle. "Shut it," I snapped, both of us straightening to attention when there was a pitch—strike. The third strike. I pushed off the wall and joined Higgins, both of us jogging for the dugout. I caught Dad's eye from the pitcher's bullpen and waved.

"Want to come out with us tonight?" Higgins offered. "Shawn and I are hitting the local casino. Watching us win at blackjack might wake you up a little." He threw an arm around my shoulders and squeezed.

"Nah." I smiled up at him. "But thanks. I'm gonna head to bed early."

We approached the dugout, and he motioned me ahead, my eyes quick as I came down the stairs, scanning the bench, looking for anything that needed to be done. Behind me, a wave of men took the stairs, the area filling up quickly, spirits high, the air rough with masculinity and competitiveness. Still, I knew the minute Chase walked past. I felt the soft touch of his fingers as he brushed them against mine. I felt his presence, then ached for it as soon as he was past, as soon as his butt hit the seat of the bench, and I had only his eyes—burning contact that I had to avoid, had to look away from, lest we get caught. I turned toward the field, stepping up to the fence, and watching the outfield settle into place, but couldn't stop my smile.

 **51**

New York

"Chase, baby, how is life?" The fast crone of his agent took him right back to Los Angeles, to that big glass office full of ambitions and regrets.

For a rare moment when speaking with the man, Chase smiled. "Life is good, Floyd."

"Really?" The skepticism was high, and Chase had to laugh. "The Yankees are treating you well?"

"I think they're still warming up to me, but the home runs are helping."

"How many COC lectures you gotten?"

Code-of-Conduct. The Yankees were big on everything, especially image. No facial hair, other than mustaches. No fighting. No drunk-in-public behavior. Nothing that would flutter the perfect hair of Maxine Grenada, the PR tycoon who kept the Yankee's reputation squeaky clean. Chase winced. "A few."

The man lowered his voice. "I really want you to think about stopping any powder. Every stupid thing you've done—"

"Already ahead of you," Chase interrupted, opening the sliding glass door of his hotel room and stepping onto the balcony.

"Meaning what?"

"I've stopped. I could piss in a cup right now and be good to go."

"Keep that up through the season, and you'll make me a happy man."

"I'm done with that shit. Permanently. Like you said, it gets me into trouble."

The man was silent for a long, suspicious minute. "What about girls?"

"I'm dating someone." The thought of her made him, for the hundredth time that day, smile. "Exclusively. So stop worrying. I'm behaving, I'm happy, I'm playing like God."

"Who's the girl?" His agent wasn't happy yet, four years with Chase turning the man into the worst kind of cynic: a suspicious one.

"You don't know her."

"I need details. She a stripper or a saint? Where'd you meet her? No offense, Chase, but you're batting zero when it comes to picking the right women."

"She's a bat girl for the team. She's eighteen," he added quickly.

"What are the Yanks doing with an eighteen-year-old bat girl? That's asking for trouble." The man's voice was quicker, wheezing through the phone line.

"She's been with the team a long time, since she was a kid."

"Jesus Christ." The man caught on, a heartbeat of pause before he continued, "You're talking about the closer's kid. Frank Fucking Rollins's daughter? Please tell me you're kidding."

"She's an adult," he defended, his hands tightening against the balcony railing. "She's five years younger than me. This isn't—"

"Rollins makes *one* call to anyone, and you are *fucked*. The Yankees will drop you before the ink dries on the statutory rape press release. You'll be done with MLB—shipped to Canada or Japan to play. And I don't care if she's eighteen. They'll accuse you of cumming in her teenage panties. You think they're not gonna care—screw that. They're going to throw a fucking *party* over this story. You think Nancy Grace is gonna let this slide? She hasn't had a Caylee Anthony or a Natalee Holloway in *years*. She's gonna ride your ass right to a ratings high, and convince every person in America, and in the Yankee organization, that you're a pedophile." The man took a deep, shuddering breath. "You think I'm *happy* you're exclusive with this girl? Do me a favor and find another girl. Hell, I got a stable of them on call. Just tell me hair color and measurements and I'll send ten of them over."

"You can't replace her, Floyd. Ty, she—"

"Stop talking right now. *Don't* be exclusive with this chick, in fact, don't even go *near* her. I'm tempted to call up Thomas Grant right now and tell him to yank her from traveling with you guys."

"Listen to me very carefully." Chase turned from the view and stepped inside, closing the sliding glass door and speaking clearly in the silence of his room. "You can try to paint this however you want—the press can paint this however they want—but there is nothing wrong with our relationship. It's the purest thing in my life. She is saving me. And I don't expect you, in the twisted world you live in, to understand that. But you know this industry and that's the only reason I'm still on the phone with you right now. I need this to work. I need her in my life. And I need you to tell me how to make that work."

There was nothing between them on the line for almost a minute.

Then, with a heavy exhale, Floyd started to speak. And, for the first time in his career with him, Chase actually listened.

 **52**

Toronto

At night at Woodbine, the horses ran. Million dollar muscles bunched underneath slick coats, spotlights illuminating colorful silks, wide eyes and the spray of dirt kicked up by hooves. We made it to the last race of the night, having to wait until after ten to leave, my father's bedtime now a nightly waiting ritual. A car took us to the VIP entrance, hidden from press and onlookers, but there was no need. In Canada, Chase Stern's face didn't carry the same weight, his low-pulled baseball cap the only disguise needed. We sat at the rail, my arm looped through Chase's, and bent over the program, my fingers rolling down the list of horses. *Kirby's Moonshot.* The name stood out, as if in bold, and I tapped it excitedly, turning to Chase. He smiled when he saw the name.

"You think he's the one?"

"Definitely."

"He's a longshot," he pointed out, running his hand over, past his name and to his stats. "Hasn't won a race all season. 14-1 odds."

"I like the longshots." I beamed at him and something in his eyes changed, a look that I was starting to see more and more. Awe was too strong of a word but close. It was a look that made me feel a million feet tall. And it came at the most unremarkable times. Like this. He leaned over and kissed me, a soft press of lips that he followed with another, then another, our kisses turning to laughter as I almost fell sideways from his enthusiasm. "Stop," I giggled, pushing him back. "Now focus. We only have a few minutes."

"Moonshot," he said, pushing to his feet. "I got it." He held out his hand, and I surrendered my savings, forty-three dollars scrapped from my stipend fund. We had decided, on the drive over, that I would be the primary investor of this evening. He had wanted to cover it, but I had been greedy with the possibility of winning, wanting full ability to pick my own horse and then be obnoxious with all of my excess cash. "You want it all on him? Win-place-show?"

"Just win," I said confidently. "He can do it."

He raised his eyebrows skeptically, and I gestured at him to hurry. I watched him go, my eyes following until the last minute when he stepped through the doors. They returned to the page, my finger running over the horse's name. Yes, he was a longshot. But that didn't mean he couldn't come out on top.

He didn't come out on top. Kirby's Moonshot struggled through the first corner, fighting for a third place position before hitting the first straightaway and getting left in the dust. *Literally.* I almost lost him a few times in the cloud of dirt created by the horses ahead of him. I was dismayed, Chase laughed, his mouth finding mine at every opportunity, my lost fortune blatantly unconsidered.

I insisted that we find the horse, to give him a consolatory pat, something for his harrowing journey. Chase remarked, with worrisome sincerity, that we might walk in on him being put down, the racer's performance less than ideal. My steps quickened at that possibility, my breath held until the moment I rounded the corner and saw him being hosed down, his head hanging low, mouth munching contentedly on something. Surely they wouldn't bother to wash a horse destined for death. And surely they didn't do that anymore, the glue factory a mythical thing designed to torture the minds of small children trying to happily paste school projects.

I approached the horse and dug in my bag for the apple—one I had snagged from a welcome fruit tray in Dad's room, the bright green skin catching the eye of a handler, who stopped me. "Can't give him that, ma'am."

Chase stepped in, and there was a moment of celebrity fandom, one where the man smiled brightly and hands were shaken and photos requested, and my fingers itched to sneak the fruit into the racehorse's mouth. He flapped his lips at me, his big brown eyes watchful, and I inched closer.

There was a negotiation of sorts, tickets to tomorrow's game mentioned, and then Chase waved me on, the apple allowed, and I stepped up to the horse, holding it flat in my palm, my fingers running along his face as he crunched into the apple, half of it gone, the other half quickly taken, my palm wet from his contact. I had a horse once. One winter. Boarded fifteen minutes away. I had memories of standing in our kitchen, in front of the blender, a concoction of apple cider, carrots, and oats in the blender. I poured it into a thermos, and Dad and I went to the barn on her 'birthday,' pouring the dubious mixture into a bucket, my excitement mounting as she ate it all. There were winter days where schoolbooks were pushed aside, and I climbed upon her back, riding her bareback through the ring. But then there was spring training, those months in Florida and far from her. And then there was the start of the season, and somewhere along the way she was sold, and I barely noticed, my world dominated by pinstripes, little time for anything else. Suddenly, with my hands capturing the racehorse's muzzle in mine, his breath huffing against my palms, I missed her.

On the ride back to the hotel, I told Chase about her. Her name had been Rosie. She'd been an Arabian, fiery and ill-mannered. "Like you," he said, and I made a face. He reached over and took my hand, pulling it to his mouth. "You are never allowed to pick winners again, Ty Rollins."

"It wasn't my best moment," I conceded. "But in all fairness to Moonshot, I think he was robbed. There was clearly some unfair jostling at the start."

He raised a brow at me. "I saw no jostling."

I shrugged. "You're old. Your eyes are getting weak."

Then he laughed and leaned over the center console. "I'm falling in love with you," he said softly.

I swallowed hard, my eyes lifting to his. They were steady on me, sure and unwavering, as if he spoke an absolute certainty. My smile began, a runaway train out of control, no force able to stop its spread. "Okay," I whispered, unsure of how to respond.

"I just wanted you to know."

"Okay," I repeated. "That's good to know."

And it was. It was, actually, great to know. My smile grew, until the moment that he pulled me forward and kissed it away.

**53**

It felt like everything was moving too fast, yet time was also standing still. It'd been three weeks and six cities since that night we broke apart and then fell back together. Only 24 days, yet ... when every evening was spent with him ... it felt like a year. There were just over sixty games left in the season. Then, I would have a decision-filled offseason. The biggest question that weighed me down? Whether to tell my father about Chase.

"We don't have to do this." He gasped into my mouth as his hand yanked at my zipper.

"Shut up," I pulled at his shirt, my nails skidding across his back in my haste to get it off, to expose that torso, the perfect lines surrounding each muscle, his abs a ripple of beauty.

"Are you sure?" he asked as his fingers dug under the waist of my jeans, pulling them over my hips, his mouth on mine as soon as the question left it.

"Third base," I shot out, in between frantic kisses. "Stop arguing with me and do it."

He gripped my waist and pushed, then I was on his bed, my jeans skinned off, flip-flops tossed somewhere, and he was pushing me back, crawling on top of me, his weight gently on mine, the press of him hard and hot, in between my legs.

It was strange how so many points of our body could touch, from foot to shoulder, the length of him atop me, his weight supported by his hands, his mouth on my neck, marking his territory, and yet the only thing I felt, right then, was his cock. It was hard, in his boxer briefs, between my legs, his cotton underwear against mine, my legs wrapping around his hips, and when he gently ground against me, I almost lost my mind. Suddenly, I didn't want his mouth on me; I didn't want to go down on him. I only wanted him to pull it out and push it inside of me. I wanted him to own that part of my body, to replace any memory I ever had of Tobey, to thrust inside and teach me how it was done. This time would not be a rushed affair, with no phone calls, total silence afterward, both of us running back to our normal lives. This time, with Chase, would be done right, sex filled with love and passion and the promise of a million more times. I begged him for it, and he silenced me with his kiss.

"Don't ask me for that, Ty. Please." His voice rasped on the beg, his hips shifting, dragging his arousal over me, each pump of his hips sending me to a new level of delirium. He pushed up on his hands, looking down between our bodies, my panties sticking to me, his bulge extended, and he slid one last painful time across me, my back arching off the bed with the need of it all. "You have no idea how badly I want that," he groaned. "But right now, I want something even more." He sat up, pulling at my legs, unwrapping them from his waist, and pushed at my knees, spreading them apart, his body sliding down the bed before I realized what was happening.

"Wait!" I called out, reaching for him, propping up on my elbows and trying to stop him, my hand on his shoulder, pushing him off. "I changed my mind. We can just skip this base."

He pulled at my thighs, dragging me to the edge of the bed, his head lifting to look at me. "Skip it?" I felt the stretch of my panties and then they were gone, pulled down and off my legs, the last barrier between his mouth and me, and I'd never felt so exposed in my life. Thank God the lamps were off in the room, the only light coming from the bathroom. Thank God he couldn't see my blush in the dark.

"Skip it," I whispered, suddenly too shy to take this step, to have his mouth on my most private place, a flood of doubts and insecurities taking over.

He didn't skip it. He ignored me, leaning forward, and then his mouth was on me, and it was different than a kiss, different than his touch, different than anything I had experimented with on my own. I pushed against his head, resisting, scared and insecure … then he moved his tongue, a soft flick of it across my clit, and I groaned, my hand twisting in the short length of his hair, the sound from my mouth one that I had never made. My toes dug into the bed, my knees pointed at the ceiling, and I lost everything. Every conscious thought, every worry, every understanding of what was pleasure and what was right. I watched his eyes close, felt the slow, beautiful movement of his tongue, and finally understood what the giant fuss about sex was all about.

His hands gripped my legs, his mouth gently made love to my clit, and my heart, after two months of struggle and a few minutes of ecstasy, finally stopped its fight.

There was no stopping this. There was no more resisting. Damn any of the consequences, damn any future heartbreak. I clenched my legs, I gripped at the bed, and I cried out his name in the moment that my soul broke open.

I was his.

 **54**

"I love you." He said the words so softly I almost missed them, my groggy mind too sluggish to comprehend. I was tucked under his arm, lying next to him in bed, my hand playing over his stomach, my lazy mind trying to work up the courage to drag my fingers lower, down the lines of his abs and toward the edge of his underwear.

My mind repeated the words, trying to sort them from background noise, trying to understand if I really heard them or just imagined it. "What?" I finally said, rolling toward him and propping myself up on his stomach.

"I love you." There were pillows underneath his head, angled toward me, his eyes clear, his face strong and confident. He should be confident. I'd all but worshipped him in the last hour, my voice running wild, comparing him to God All-Mighty as I had bucked underneath his mouth, two orgasms stolen from my body before he finally stopped.

"Why?"

"Why do I love you?" There was a smile in his voice, as if it was a dumb question.

"Yes."

"That's a hard question."

I made a face. "Ugh." I pushed off him. "You fail."

"Wait." He stopped me, his arms strong as he held me in place. The same arms that had held down my legs as he had tasted between them. The same arms that swung a bat and brought millions of Americans to their feet. I lifted my eyes from those arms and to his face. "It's not easy to answer. I love you because you look at me and see more than just a baseball player." I went to speak, and he stopped me. "I love you because your smile does something to my heart. I love you because when I see you, I can't stop staring at you. And when you're away from me, I can't stop thinking about you. I love you because right now, there's nothing more tempting in life than to pull you on top of me and push inside of you. And I love you because you're the first woman on Earth who I've wanted to wait for. Who I've treasured enough to be patient. I could wait a hundred years for you because the thought of doing anything that brings you pain makes my heart break. You are the most complex woman I have ever met." I made a face, and he shushed me. "I'm serious. You are like a guy in so many ways—the way you call me out, the things you know, the way you swear, the arm on you that would put a hundred recruits to shame … you're my best friend, Ty. And I haven't had a best friend in a really long time. But…" He shook his head. "You're also the most feminine creature on Earth." He ran his fingers slowly down my side, over my hip, his fingers spreading as he placed a warm palm against my skin. "Your face, your body—the way you laugh, how you smell—hell, just the way you *walk*. It's intoxicating."

I held my breath, watching his eyes search mine, his hand soft as it ran through my hair.

"The end," he finally said, and I smiled, his mouth turning up in response, his hand moving from my hair and gently rubbing over my mouth. "That smile right there," he murmured. "You have no idea what it does to me."

I crawled up his stomach, my bra dragging along his chest until we were face to face, my hair a curtain around our faces, his chin lifting up as he met my eyes. "I love you too," I said softly, and even through the veil of my hair, I could see his smile.

"I'm going to marry you one day, Ty Rollins," he said softly, gently tucking my hair behind one ear, and my heart stopped.

"One thing at a time," I said, leaning down and pressing my lips to his, a soft brush that became a fire, his hands tangling in my hair, his lips turning desperate on mine.

I stayed by his side until the sun rose, pink sunlight tentatively pushing through the open curtains, my name a beg off his lips when I finally rolled out of his bed, pulling on my jeans, sneaking barefoot down the hotel hall and back to my room.

I undressed in the dark of my own room, crawling into my bed, my phone plugged in, and fell asleep quickly, my heart soaring, a smile stretched over my face.

It was perfect.
More than I'd ever dreamed of.

 **55**

New York

Wish u were coming home with me. You still need to see my place.

I stretched in the hall, my bag at my feet, eyes on my phone, halfway through a response, when the hand landed on my shoulder. I jumped, lifting my eyes off my cell, and stuffing it in my back pocket, the text from Chase still open on it. "Mr. Grant," I said with a smile. "Good game."

"*Great* game." He beamed. "I can smell the playoffs now."

"Me too."

"What are your plans this week? Tobey's at the house, and we'd love to have you over for dinner. Maybe Tuesday?"

The door to the locker room opened, and the owner of my heart stepped out. I kept my eyes on the man before me, the act heroic in its struggle. "I'll check my schedule. Dad keeps me pretty busy when we're home."

The soft smack of shoes on wood, Chase slowly wandered closer, the hall too thin, my control too weak, and I met his eyes despite myself, my mouth curving into a smile. Mr. Grant followed my eyes, his mouth breaking into a smile, and he clapped Chase on the shoulder. "There's our star! Man, am I glad that we got you in pinstripes, boy."

"I just score the runs, sir." Chase nodded to me. "Her dad's the one keeping them off the board." And Dad had done a great job of it, closing the last eight games without a single hit.

"While you're here," Grant said, gripping Chase's shoulder and turning to me. "Convince Ty here to take a few days off. I'm trying to get her over to our house for some home cooking that will fatten up those bones of hers."

Chase smiled at me, and I could read everything he was thinking in those eyes. My return smile was less enthusiastic, a hard pit forming in my stomach, as I hoped, prayed, that he wouldn't take this conversation any further, wouldn't mention—

"Is she the prettiest thing you've ever seen or what?" Grant peered at me alongside Chase, and I shifted, reaching down and picking up my backpack, my stomach tighter.

"I won't argue with that." There was too much feeling in his voice, and I looked up in warning, my eyes sharp, Grant catching the inflection and turning to him with a laugh.

"Now easy there. Don't go getting any designs on her. You may not know it, but you're looking at my future daughter-in-law." My stomach dropped even further and I felt suddenly hot, stars appearing in my vision, and I didn't realize that stress could make you physically sick.

"Is that so?" Chase's voice was low and steel, and all I wanted to do was escape.

Instead, I tried a laugh, the sound almost strangled. I reached out, patting the older man's arm. "Did you see the Marlins' highlights?" I babbled. "Grio batted 4 for 5."

The man brushed me off, turning back to Chase. "Have you met my son yet? Tobey's at Harvard. He's smart as a whip and has had eyes for Ty here since she first joined us."

"I was twelve," I interjected. "I don't think Tobey liked me then."

"Well," he conceded, "maybe not then. But those two…" He smiled big, turning to me with a wink. "They're destined to be together. I just know it. So, what do you say Ty? Dinner with us Tuesday night?"

I almost swayed, the need to vomit growing stronger with each shade darker that Chase's face grew. "Let me check with Dad," I promised Grant. Then, gripping my backpack tightly, I turned tightly on my heel and all but sprinted down the hall, hitting the bathroom and bending over the toilet.

I didn't vomit. Maybe all I needed was to escape the situation. Maybe wiping my face down with cold water helped. What didn't help was the bathroom door opening, Chase entering, and staring at me with a face of fury. "What was that?" he bit out. "You're betrothed to that prick?"

"I was being polite," I yanked at the paper towels and pointed to the door. "You're not allowed to be in here. It's the women's bathroom."

"And you're the only woman within a hundred feet. And it didn't sound like you were being polite. It sounds like you're childhood sweethearts with this guy."

"I wasn't. I'm not," I shot out, my phone buzzing in my pocket, probably my Dad, looking for me.

"Have you ever dated him?"

"No. Not…" I amended. "Not ever a relationship. Just isolated things."

"Things?" he pressed, stepping closer, caging me against the sink. "Like what?"

"You know. Dates," I managed, and this conversation would be a thousand times easier if I hadn't *slept with Tobey*.

"And?"

"And what?" I exploded. "I haven't done anything wrong!" But I had. Even if it was fresh off the heels of seeing him with those girls. Even if I was mad, and we weren't exclusive, it had all been wrong. From the minute I stepped into his room, it'd been wrong.

"Have you kissed him?"

I flushed. I could literally feel the heat on my cheeks and watched his face pale, his features tighten. "You have," he said, the words carefully controlled.

"I've known him a long time," I said. "We've kissed before. It's not a big deal." Now was the moment I should tell him the truth. I knew that, yet it seemed the stupidest decision ever.

"Just kissed."

"No." The word was a rough exhale from my lips, and he closed his eyes in response, his fist flexing and unflexing, the motion one of bare control. I was almost afraid to continue, this side of Chase one I'd never seen. "I slept with him." My mind begged, silently, for him not to ask questions, for him to take the information and leave, for this to be a brief fight that would continue later. Instead, he asked the one question I hoped he wouldn't.

"When?"

I looked down at my shoes, my weight heavy against the sink, my voice small when it came. "The night we first … when I saw you with those girls in your room." I lifted my head. "When you had left me alone in the room and went to do drugs." The final sentence had fight in it, and his eyes flared.

"So … you told me no. You *stopped* me. And then you went to *him*?

And let him do *that?*"

"We weren't … us … then. We weren't anything then." I sobbed the words, my heart breaking as he looked at me in a way I'd never seen, like I wasn't the person he loved, like *we* weren't in love.

"I loved you…" He stepped back from me, his voice gruff, cracking on the syllables. "I loved you from the minute I saw you. I thought…" He brought his hands to his head and turned away from me. "I thought it was the same for you."

I did. It was. I never had a chance to respond. He pushed on the door, and, before I could get a word out, was gone. I sagged against the sink in the empty room, my hands gripping the edge of cold marble. Unable to control myself, I burst into tears.

I should have chased him. I shouldn't have worried about anyone seeing, or anyone hearing, and just run after him. Tugged on his arm and told him everything that I felt. How much I regretted that night with Tobey. How little it had meant to me. Instead, I let him go and cried, alone in that bathroom stall.

I should have chased him, but I didn't know. I didn't know that it would be the last time I would see him.

56

Each step away from her was agony and relief, all at the same time. His chest tight, he rubbed at it, unsure if it was physical symptoms or just heartache. He didn't understand how she could do it. He'd have sworn, having her in his bed, that she was a virgin. From her reactions, her hesitancy. He'd thought that everything they were doing was special, had taken his time with her, had thought of her virginity as this precious fucking gift that they were preserving, her first time one that would be done right, and only when she was really ready. The concept that, less than a month ago, she'd been in Tobey Fucking Grant's bed, had him *inside* of her, was mind blowing, and against everything he thought about her, every way he looked at her.

He breezed through the exit door and toward the employee lot, two security guards standing at his approach, one tipping his hat at Chase before holding out a hand for his pass. He yanked at his bag, pulling out the card and passed it to the man, who held it at the card reader. It lit red, and something inside of Chase snapped. He took a deep breath, watching the man scan it again, the same result produced.

"You know who I am, just let me through."

"Mr. Chase, if you could just step to the side." The man had an attitude, the tone one used on misbehaving delinquents, and it pushed tacks into the thin skin of his self control. Any minute, Ty and her dad would come outside. Any minute she'd be feet away, her eyes on him, those begging eyes, and he would lose his mind.

One of the guards stepped to the phone, his eyes on Chase, and who the fuck could he be calling, why the fuck were they keeping him here, and they needed to fix their machine and open the damn gate.

He pushed forward, past the man and reached for the handle, the man shouting a protest, and when hands closed on his arm, the final thread of his self-control snapped.

A little known fact about Chase Stern: At fifteen, he was an amateur boxing champ, a career that could have brought him much success, had he not instead focused his fast hands and hand-eye coordination on baseball. It didn't take much to drop the three-hundred-pound security guard. One right cross on the man's left jaw did it.

One right cross that changed everything, instantly, for them.

 **57**

"This isn't like you." Dad was worried, I could hear the strain in his voice. I pushed open the door to the bathroom and came face-to-face with him. I ended the call and dropped it in my bag.

"I wasn't feeling well," I lied. "Something I ate. You know. Diarrhea." It was a crude but effective answer, his face relaxing, though worry still pricked his eyes.

"Want me to get the team doctor? He can give you—"

"Oh my God," I interrupted him. "I am *not* going to Dr. Z about this."

"It's a long way home. Do you think you'll make it?"

"I'll be fine." I nodded to the door, ready to get out of here. "You ready?"

There was a commotion at the end of the hall, a group of security guys hauling someone away, and his eyes flickered to that before returning to me. I swallowed, hoping that all traces of my cry were gone, the last few minutes spent fixing my makeup. "Okay," he said slowly, suspicion lacing his words. "Let's go home."

We rode home in silence, the only break when he asked me, twice, how I was feeling. It felt wrong to lie to him. But on the other hand, I'd been lying to him for a month. But those lies hadn't been so blatant. They'd been lies of omission, me telling him goodnight and then walking out of my hotel room. He'd never asked me, the next day, if I had done anything other than go to bed. He'd had no reason to.

But now, the air in the truck thick with distrust, I felt the pain of lying, the guilt of everything I had kept from him. I hadn't told Chase about Tobey, and look where that had gotten me. Chase stormed off, and I couldn't even call him and properly apologize. Not until I got home and had some privacy. Dad wouldn't storm off if I told him about Chase. But he would be disappointed. And hurt. And would probably never let me stay in my own hotel room ever again. The thought of going on the road and not spending time with Chase … the concept was a physical ache in my chest. Before, I had loved our life on the road, Dad and me, the team, the life. But love had dulled that. Love had made everything brighter, my smile bigger, my days longer. Every secret smile from him, every stolen touch, had been a shot of happiness. Every night we'd spent together had been a step deeper into our friendship, a cut deeper into my heart. I should have told Dad. Right then, before anything else happened. But I couldn't risk ruining the remaining weeks of the season. I couldn't risk a moment away from him.

After the season. That was when I would tell Dad.

At least that had been the plan.

When I got home, I called Chase, but his phone went straight to voicemail. I didn't leave a message. I washed my face, brushed my teeth, and took a quick shower, washing off the clay and dust of the game before putting on pajamas and getting into bed. I tried to call him again, with the same result. I opened a text and struggled with the words, part of me still stubbornly mad, a month after that night, about what I had seen in his room. We hadn't been dating, so I hadn't, technically, done anything wrong, especially not after what I had seen.

But I knew where his hurt and anger lay. In the lost opportunity. I knew because I felt the same way, I hated myself for not giving that moment to him, to us. I hated that I'd lost my virginity through anger and resentment and not in a night of love and passion. I hated that it had been Tobey pushing into me, and not Chase. I hated the look I had seen in Chase's eyes. The loss of some bit of reverence that he had had for me.

I turned on the TV as a distraction, something to keep my mind off him. Instead, with a somber Scott Van Pelt speaking into the camera, I watched our fairy-tale summer shatter.

58

The facts known were little, a few sentences that the newscasters discussed on repeat, each flip of the channel bringing the same maddening three sentences.

Chase Stern was involved in a physical altercation with a member of the Yankee organization.
He was not arrested.
The Yankees have not issued a statement at this time.
We have no further information.

I'd been in the walls of that stadium long enough to know what would happen if this information was true. A member of the Yankee organization? Was it a coach? Another player? A member of the crew? Who it had been wasn't really crucial to the outcome. This wasn't Los Angeles, where it took punching a fellow teammate after fucking his wife to get a rise out of management. This was New York, where every person on the NYY payroll was family, and we protected our family. We loved our family. We fought for our family. And we fought against any discord in our locker room, in our stadium, in our family.

My fear was confirmed at 2:17 AM. I was bleary eyed, my fingers numb from pushing buttons on the remote, from redialing his cell and getting voicemail. I was exhausted, both mentally and physically, my psyche raw and brittle, when an update finally happened, one thin line of text scrolling across the bottom of the screen, mid-commercial.

UPDATE: Chase Stern traded to the Baltimore Orioles.

Seven simple words that brought down everything we had.

The phone dropped from my limp hand, and I fell back on the bed, my eyes closing in defeat.

 **59**

I couldn't stop crying. At first it was small leaks coming out at inappropriate times, my hands wiping at my cheeks while stirring Carla's spaghetti sauce. Then it was giant, gushing sobs, impossible to hide, Dad's wide-eyed confusion not helping. I locked myself in my room, not eating, not working, not talking to anyone. The week ended, and then the next, and then the Yankees were back on the road, Dad leaving for Chicago, his knocks on my door unanswered, his calls to my cell ignored. I was in bed when he kicked in my door, the frame splintering, my head turn too slow to suit him, my quiet study of his flushed face one that seemed to make him more upset.

"Talk to me, Ty. I'm not leaving until you do."

I rolled away, pulling the comforter over my head. "There was a key to my door in the kitchen junk drawer," I mumbled. "You didn't have to break it down."

The comforter was ripped from my grip, the aggressive move bending my fingers, and I yelped, bringing my injured hand to my chest. "Ow!" I yelled. "That hurt!"

He bent over the bed, his fists biting into the sheet, his glare matching mine, twin sets of Rollins-bred anger. "What's this about? What happened?"

I rolled back, my knees curling against my chest, needing the cover of a blanket, something to hide me. "Nothing."

He walked around and knelt beside my bed, his face there, in the narrow view of my peek. "I'm not leaving until you talk to me."

"You'll miss the flight," I mumbled.

"I don't care."

"You'll get in trouble."

"You've never missed a trip before." I knew it would cause a red flag. Even more than my fits of tears. I didn't miss games, this last week an oddity in itself, an argument every time Dad left for the field. I had blamed a stomach bug, then the flu, and Dad had called bullshit on both. He'd yelled, I'd cried more, and he'd stared at me, bewildered. Rollins didn't cry. We cursed, we fought, we punched walls and said hateful things. He didn't understand a teenage girl whose face became hot and whose voice broke. Hell, I didn't understand that girl. I had become a walking mess of emotions at a time when I should be making plans, calling Chase, fighting for our relationship, our future life.

I love you.

He'd meant it, hadn't he? Even if I had fucked up, even if I wasn't the virgin he'd assumed me to be, he had loved me.

I'm going to marry you one day, Ty Rollins.

True Love didn't give up because of a hiccup. Or a trade. True Love stood together and fought. But I wasn't fighting. I was being, in the worst way imaginable, like every emotional girl I had always ridiculed. And I couldn't seem to find a way to stop. I couldn't find the energy to call him again. I couldn't find the strength to meet my father's eyes and tell him the truth.

"I'm old enough to stay here."

"You've never *wanted* to stay here. That's the problem. Is it the Stern trade?"

Fresh tears leaked weakness. "Why would you say *that?*" He knew.

He *had* to know. Or maybe he didn't.

"It's convenient timing with this breakdown."

"It's not a breakdown." I sat up and sniffed, a glob of mucus thick down my throat.

"Then toughen up. Whatever it is. Either talk to me about it, or stop crying and get the hell over it."

I twisted my mouth, holding back a burst of angry words. I was mad at him, and for no good reason. We had always talked, often no one else around to bounce things off of, and his treatment of me as an adult was one I valued, my attitude and silence for the last week uncharacteristic. I didn't blame him for being confused, or for being sharp. He wasn't at fault in all of this. Chase was. Who punched a security guard over a slow key machine? Who told a girl he loved her, and then moved to Baltimore without saying goodbye?

"Pack up. Get on the plane. Let's get to Chicago and you'll feel better. The game has helped me through a lot of hard moments. Pull on cleats, smell your glove, run on the field … it'll help with whatever you're going through."

It was tempting. For the first time, I considered leaving the house. Moving on. Returning to life. But how could I walk on a field and not think of his jog across it? Sit on a dugout bench and not remember his slouch against it, his eyes on me? Walk down a tunnel and not think of our collision? Every memory, every piece of my life was now tainted with him. I couldn't turn on ESPN without hearing his name. Couldn't go through our schedule with every Orioles game looming, eight more games left this year. Eight times we would share the field. Eight times he would stand on the dirt, just steps away.

I just wasn't ready to smell the leather of a glove or to walk into an empty hotel room. I couldn't handle any memories of Chase right now. But eating … maybe *that* I could do. I swung my feet off the side of the bed. "I'll stop moping. I'll try." I gave him the best smile I could muster.

"And you'll pack? Come with me to Illinois?"

I shook my head. "Next week," I promised.

That was enough, and he held out his hand, pulling me to my feet and wrapping me in a hug. "You stink," he murmured into my hair, and I laughed.

"I'll shower too."

"And eat something. Carla just made your favorite: chicken pot pie."

I nodded, the smell of her cooking coming through the open door. My stomach woke up, churning to life, and I pulled out of his hug, his arm keeping me close, and he bent down to press a kiss on the top of my head. I suddenly felt hot, the scent of food overwhelming, my shove against him harder than I intended, my sprint to the bathroom barely in time, the door slamming against the wall, my knees hitting the tile, hands on the seat, my stomach heaving.

I wheezed, the action painful, each lurch of my stomach bringing up little, my forehead dotted with sweat by the time I collapsed against the wall of the bathroom, my legs weakly falling open, my eyes traveling up my father's body and to his face. He watched me, concerned, then paled, turning ashen. Seeing it cemented all of my fears, his hand dragging over his face in the moment before he pointed a shaky finger toward me.

"You're not … not…"

I swallowed hard, more tears threatening, barely held at bay, my mind counting over the last few weeks, trying to remember when I'd last had my period. "I think so," I whispered. "I'm pregnant."

I didn't end up going back on the road.

I didn't go to another game that year.

The next time I walked into Yankee Stadium, it was through the owner's entrance, my journey by private elevator and surrounded by security, until I was seated in the skybox, my dinner order taken by a tuxedoed waiter, my ring shining in all the glory that seven carats brought. I sat up there, ate crab cakes, sipped hot tea, listened to my fiancé talk, and watched my boys play.

With every single play, I thought of him.

With every single play, I died a little more.

FOUR YEARS LATER
2015 Season

JUNE

"Rachel Frepp was the first. She died on September 28th, the last day of the 2011 season, when the Yanks lost to the Rays. A jogger found her, stabbed, early that next morning, in the alley behind her apartment. That's how all the girls died, and they were practically carbon copies of each other. Single blondes on the Upper East Side, all in their twenties. All in love with the Yankees. I guess those were his favorites."

Dan Velacruz, *New York Times*

 **60**

When I woke in the morning, the sun barely peeking over the park, I thought of the dead girls. Rachel. April. Julie. Tiffany. Their names had almost blended together in my mind, one long word that ran on repeat. RachelAprilJulieTiffany. *RachelAprilJulieTiffany.*

I used to wake up and think of Chase. I'd roll over in this bed and want to cry, the need for him was so strong. As the years had passed, my memory of his smile had faded, the sound of his voice grown weaker, the taste of his kiss almost completely gone. I almost missed those painful mornings. Thinking of him would be better than crime scene photos and guilt.

RachelAprilJulieTiffany. With each day deeper into the season, their names got louder, the pressure grew stronger. I couldn't take another name. We couldn't shoulder another death.

I closed my eyes and willed sleep to take me back.

"Mrs. Grant."

I didn't move, the blanket warm and smooth against my skin, layered with two sets of the best sheets money could buy. Sleep was still close, my mind not fully awake, the sink back into nothingness—

"Mrs. Grant."

I gave up and cracked open an eye, the room coming slowly into focus, warm light streaming in the windows and onto the bookshelves, the fireplace, the leather rug. From the angle of the sun, it was late. "Yes?"

"Mr. Grant is on the phone." One of the house attendants, Paula, primly held out the phone, her free hand cupping her stomach, a pose I hated.

"Thank you." I took the phone and sank back into the bed, before rolling onto my back and staring at the ceiling. *RachelAprilJulieTiffany.* "Hey."

"I'm sorry to wake you, but Caleb's school called me. He's in the nurse's office, got a bug of some sort." Tobey's voice was strong, one that spoke of hours of productivity. To the outside world he was charismatic and patriotic—the perfect man to lead the Yankees. No one knew of his inner struggles. No one knew of the brittle layer beneath his façade of strength. *He was a good man, one who loved me.* I avoided the girls by sleeping late. He avoided them with coffee and work, both of us sprinting uselessly down a treadmill of avoidance.

"I'll pick him up." I craned my neck, glancing at the silver clock on our bedside table. "What time did you leave?"

"Five. I know you told me to wake you, but you were sleeping so hard."

"I'm glad you didn't." I glanced toward the door, where Paula was making a quiet exit. "Paula? I'm leaving in ten."

She nodded, shutting the door behind her, and I sat fully up, pulling back the covers. "How long are you staying?"

"I'm not going with them to Kansas City. I'll be back Friday. Trust me, I need a vacation more than you right now."

"I believe that." I reached over to the bedside table, grabbing my ring and sliding it on. "Have you gotten tonight's lineup?"

"I texted it to you. Doc says Gautte's shoulder still isn't ready."

"Damn." I smiled. "You're on top of it."

"Trying to be. I got big shoes to fill."

"Don't get too comfortable. I'll drag your sister out of the hospital myself if she stretches this into next week."

He laughed. "I love you."

"I love you too. Keep me posted."

"I will."

I ended the call and tossed the phone onto the bed. Five minutes later, jeans and a henley on, I laced up my boots, grabbed a leather jacket, and jogged down the staircase, smiling at Paula, who held out my coffee and a bag with breakfast. "Thanks."

Our elevator was waiting, and I had, in the quiet of the ride down, a moment to collect myself.

Margreta Grant—Tobey's sister. A bottle blonde in the hospital for a procedure I strongly suspected to be another breast augmentation, but she was insisting otherwise. I should be in Tampa with the team, one of her socialite friends holding her hand through this harrowing experience, but it turned out fake friends sucked at real obligations, and sisters-in-law were expected to step up in their stead. I stepped out of the elevator, into the garage lobby, and nodded at the driver, taking a long pull of my coffee.

"Good morning, Mrs. Grant."

"Morning, Frank. We're picking up Caleb from school, then swinging by the hospital."

"Yes, ma'am." He opened my door, and I stepped into the warm car, tossing my bag onto the floorboard, my phone out and against my ear by the time we pulled onto the street.

Dad answered on the third ring, "Hey Ty."

"Hey Dad. How's Florida?"

"Terrible. Nothing but sunshine and bikinis."

I laughed. "Stay there. New York hasn't gotten the memo that summer is coming."

"Surprised you guys haven't flown south."

"We'll be in Aruba this weekend. I can defrost then."

I opened the bag from Paula, pulling out a muffin, my phone put on speaker and set aside, conversation between us easy as I ate breakfast and tuned out the outside world. It wasn't until Frank coughed that I realized we were at the school.

"Got to run, Dad. Drink something with an umbrella in it, and give Carla a hug for me."

"Done and done."

I ended the call, stuffing the rest of the muffin in the bag, and stepped out of the car and into the brisk wind, my walk into the school quick. Dad had retired two years ago, three weeks after summoning the courage to ask Carla to dinner. They'd married last year and bought a place in Key West, dividing their time between that home, and our old place in Alpine. It was strange, after so many years, the two of us against the world, that we were now separate, each with a spouse, each with our own lives. Part of me had been happy when he'd retired, the man deserving of a vacation, of a life outside of the strike zone. Another part of me had hated it. His job had been the last tie I'd had to the field. After he left, my relationship with the team as an old ball girl, as a teammate's daughter... all that had died and I had moved fully into the role of Mrs. Grant. Mrs. Grant, who sat in the skybox. Mrs. Grant, who did "stuff" in the main office and wore suits and heels and was a stranger to everyone but the oldest uniforms on the team. The new guys were stiff, smiling politely and shaking my hand after games. They didn't know me, and they didn't care to. In the game of baseball, owners were the high maintenance afterthoughts, something I knew well, even if Tobey didn't.

I stepped into the sophisticated interior of the prep school and saw Caleb, sitting miserably in a seat, his feet swinging dully, his eyes on the ground. I cleared my throat, and he looked up, his eyes lighting, sick legs working just fine in their sprint across the room, his small body colliding into my arms. "Aunt Ty!" he cheered.

"Hey buddy." I squeezed him tightly and enjoyed, for one heart-breaking moment, the smell of little boy.

 **61**

I lost the baby at five months. After four years, I still couldn't talk about it without crying. Funny how something I hadn't wanted, became the only thing I'd lived for.

I wouldn't depress you with the details. One day I was pregnant, our nursery ready, plans and possibilities in place, the next I wasn't.

I'd given up so much for that baby. And he never came.

JULY

"Ty practically bled Yankee blood already. She should have been
ecstatic, marrying into the Grant family. But that first year of
marriage, she wasn't. She seemed shell-shocked. Almost like a trauma
victim. She smiled, she said all of the right things, but there just
wasn't any light behind her eyes."

Dan Velacruz, *New York Times*

 **62**

"Tell me what I can do to make you happy."

I rolled over onto his chest, and looked up at him. "Trade Perkins," I said, without hesitation.

Tobey laughed. "That's it? Your key to lifelong happiness?"

Lifelong happiness? A concept given up years ago. "He's dead weight. His knee is shot," I pointed out. "And he smokes. If he doesn't care enough to quit, he doesn't care enough about his job."

"Some things can't be quit, Ty." His eyes darkened, and his hand, the one wrapped around my waist, slid lower.

"Like chocolate?" I teased, laughing when he moved on top of me, kissing my neck, his hand tightening on my butt and pulling me into place.

"Sure," he mumbled, pushing my legs apart, wrapping them around his waist. "Go with chocolate."

Then he yanked at my panties, pulling them aside, and I stopped thinking about Perkins and chocolate. I wrapped my arms around his neck, I opened my mouth to his greedy kiss, and I gasped out a sigh when he thrust inside of me.

He loved me. Fiercely. Unselfishly. For most women, it was all they needed in life.

But me, I needed the curse to stop.

I needed a year to pass without blood marring our pinstripes.
I needed a World Series win.

 **63**

"We're looking at nineteen million, paid out within the first eighteen months. A three-year term with the rights to the sneaker for perpetuity. You'll get a five-percent royalty on the shoe, and you're giving Nike an exclusive on footwear, but nothing that will affect your Under Armour sponsorship." His agent tapped the table with each point, an incredibly annoying habit.

Chase flipped over the page, reading the words carefully, the contract boilerplate, the fifth signed in the last three years. When he was finished, he initialed each page and scrawled his name across the bottom, sliding the papers across the polished wood table toward Floyd. "Here. Anything else?"

"You could hold back your mountain of gratitude."

Chase shrugged, tossing down the pen. "It's money. At some point, I'm going to run out of time to spend it."

"That's what kids are for." The man cracked a smile that went unreturned. "Sorry." He stood up, leaving the contract on the table and buttoned his suit jacket. "Want to hit Scores while you are in town? We can—"

"No," Chase said shortly. "There's a jet waiting at JFK."

The man studied him for a minute, then nodded, holding out his hand. "Thanks for making the trip. It was important for Nike to have the face-to-face."

Chase stood, and they shook hands, his exit through the agency done quickly, a car waiting for him up front. He ducked into the backseat without a word.

"JFK, sir?" the driver asked.

"Yes. Hurry." He put on headphones and unwrapped a piece of gum, his jaw working overtime as he closed his eyes and tried to, during the drive, ignore the city around him. The city she lived in, towered over, the air filled with her scent, her presence. She lived on Fifth Avenue, just blocks away. Probably ran on these streets, ate at the restaurants they were driving past. Four years, and he hadn't seen her once. Not at Yankee Stadium, not on the Orioles' field. After his trade, he'd searched. Every seat, every inch of the dugouts, he'd expected to see her slim body encased in pinstripes, a hat pulled low on her head. But she'd been gone.

He should have answered her early calls. The ones right after the night he'd been charged with assault, and then promptly traded to the Orioles. In New York one moment, and gone the next, arriving in Baltimore just in time to suit up and play. His phone had rang several times that night, during the game, the phone buzzing in his locker, the missed calls not seen until later. He'd been too pissed to return her calls, or to even listen to her voicemails. He hadn't wanted to hear her excuses, or her apologies. She had ruined everything, including his trust, his spot on the team, his spot in her life. He'd ignored the calls, wanting a chance to cool off, wanting her to truly realize her mistake.

Only she had stopped calling. Just a week after his trade, his phone had gone silent. And when he'd finally broken down and tried her cell, it had been disconnected.

Then, the rumors had started, whispers about an engagement. He'd refused to believe it, had cut off Floyd's casual question when it'd came. It was *impossible*. They were in love. For Ty to run to Tobey … it just didn't make sense.

The final nail in his coffin was a damn *People Magazine*. Her smile had shone from the glossy cover, her eyes warm, a baseball glove covering her mouth. He'd stopped in the middle of the hotel lobby, and stepped into the gift shop, his hands trembling as he'd pulled the magazine off the rack, flipping through pages upon pages of junk until he'd found the article. They'd called her the Blue & White Baby and had played the Cinderella aspect of the story—a ball girl marrying the billionaire's son. It didn't contain any helpful details, just that they had known each other for seven years and had dated for "some" time. Whatever the *fuck* that meant. There had been a picture of her ring, an enormous diamond that she'd never be able to pull a glove over. And a photo of Tobey, the prick's grin big enough to piss off Chase.

He still hadn't believed it, expected her to pull out of the engagement, to show up, follow him to Baltimore, but she hadn't. She'd walked, three weeks after the article, down an aisle dripping with flowers. He'd drank enough whiskey to black out. She'd changed her name, moved into her new husband's house, and started a different life. One he'd known nothing about. He'd vowed to never speak her name again and turned all of his focus to the game.

It had hurt. *More* than just hurt. It had *destroyed* him. Almost as bad as Emily's death had. This destruction hit a different part of his heart. It'd stabbed him there and stayed, a constant ache that never left, her scent imprinted on his soul, her voice in his ear. He ran until his chest ached and thought of her. He threw balls until midnight and wondered where she was, what she was doing. He had sex with a blonde, then a brunette, then swore off women all together, each experience only bringing her to mind.

It'd been almost four years since he'd touched alcohol, drugs, or women. Four years since he'd last seen her smile, heard her voice. Four years of being a saint and focusing only on baseball. His reputation had soared, as had his stats, and his finances. But his sanity was still in question. Four years later, and he couldn't even bear to stay a night in the same city as her.

First loves were supposed to be flimsy and temperamental. They were supposed to burn bright and fade fast. They weren't supposed to stick. They weren't supposed to eat away at a man's heart, his capacity for life. The car slowed, the jet beside them, and he reached for his sunglasses, pushing them on and stepping out.

It wasn't until he was in the air, ten thousand feet above the city, that he could take his first clear breath. He had, at least physically, survived.

 **64**

On the night I had told Tobey about my pregnancy, I had been both tearful and emboldened, stiff and defiant when I'd uttered the words and waited for rejection, every pore of my soul ready to fight to the death for my child.

He had been silent, then he had sworn, a stream of curses punctuated by his hands tearing through his hair, his fall into one of their chairs heavy, mood black. I had watched without words. In that moment, I hadn't judged him. I had gone through a similar moment, everything in my world breaking apart, everything suddenly changed. I'd waited for him to come through it, to collect himself. To say the next thing, something that would tell me exactly what my baby's father was made of.

"You'll get married." His father spoke for him, stepping out onto the porch, his voice allowing no discussion on the subject, my own dad behind him in the open doorway.

"Dad—" Tobey's one word died, his head turned to his father, their eye contact held for a long moment before he turned away.

"You'll finish this semester at Harvard, and you and Ty will live with us until you graduate. You can get married at Thanksgiving. Grad school will have to wait."

Mr. Grant turned to me, his nod firm, the affection I'd always seen in his eyes still present, his excitement at the news almost worrisome in its glee. And with his declaration to Tobey, the decision was made. Tobey and my eyes met, and his face was that of a trapped man. I looked away, a fresh wave of nausea rising.

Maybe I should have protested. If I had, maybe the baby would have lived. Fate was funny that way; it had its own way of changing our lives.

AUGUST

"It was like the Curse of the Bambino, just bloodier. You see, the girls each died on whatever day the Yanks lost their chance at the World Series, be it the final game of the season or the playoffs. It was a brilliant strategy, if I can even say that. All of the attention, all of the pressure, went to the team winning it all. But every year, they fell short. And every year, another girl had to die."

Dan Velacruz, *New York Times*

 **65**

I propped a foot on the windowsill, all of Yankee Stadium stretched out before me. To my right, Tobey sat, his phone out, his finger moving. To my left, Dick Polit, the team GM and a world-class idiot.

"Shrimp cocktail?" the waitress offered, first to Dick, then to Tobey. She didn't say anything to me, the staff accustomed to my tastes, the first rule of thumb being that I didn't eat anything dignified during a game. Nachos, peanuts, and hot dogs were fair game. Beer was fine, soda preferred. I liked the massage girl if we were up by more than three runs, and could be downright hostile if we were down. My first days in the box, I adhered to the expected dress code, pairing a navy sheath with a white cardigan. As soon as I felt comfortable, I went native, ditching anything dry-cleanable for a jersey and jeans.

I watched Perkins closely, his step off second stiff. "See?" I elbowed Dick. "Watch Perkins move. He's favoring that knee."

"He's also batting .284. He's recovering from his surgery; it'll get better."

"It won't. He's a weak point. We could get some draft picks for him if we move quickly." I chewed on the end of my straw.

"If we move quickly, we'll have a hole in the outfield until the draft."

"Coach says Vornisk is ready to move up. I watched his footage last week. He's already better than Perkins." There was the crack of a bat, and we all watched in silence, my eyes focused on Perkins, his run to third more of a hobble. "See!" I pointed, nudging Dick again. "Look at him. That could be a run. Right *there*, he just cost us a run."

"I'm not trading an experienced player for a Minor League graduate." He leaned forward, talking over me to Tobey. "You want me to get rid of Perkins? Give me enough cash to get a real player in. We can't wait for the draft, and we can't bring someone up, not halfway through the season. If Ty has a point, and you know I hate admitting that, we need quality, experienced blood."

"I have a point," I grumbled through a peanut shell, an empty cup to my lips, the shell spit out.

"You've got the biggest payroll in the league," Tobey snapped, looking up from his phone. "Don't poor-mouth me now. Not after I just paid twelve-mil for that reliever."

"Hey, your wife's the one griping." Dick sat back in his chair.

I chewed on the inside of my cheek, staring at Perkins, working through the scenarios. "He's right," I finally said, turning to Tobey, ignoring the dramatic sputter of Dick. "If Perkins needs to go, and he *needs* to go, we can bring up Vornisk from the Minors, and he can step in. He'll be stronger than Perkins, and we can finish this season in a better place than we are now."

"I'm missing the place where Dick is right," Tobey said slowly, his eyes on mine.

"We'd finish the season in a better place than now," I repeated, "but it's still a waste of a season. We'll make the playoffs, but we won't win. And that's why we're *here*—to win. You've got three hundred million invested in this season for that reason—to *win*. And," I pointed to the field, "you can't do it with him. And you can't do it—not this year—with Vornisk. We need to stop fucking around and fix this. And an experienced shortstop, one with a strong bat, would do that. It'd put us where we'd need to be. It'd put the World Series in reach." I didn't need to mention the girls, the curse. It was there, unsaid, in the corner of every room, haunting all of our lives, especially since Tiffany Wharton. I blinked away the memory, *her lifeless eyes*, and focused on Tobey's face.

"How much?" he asked, the question directed at me.

"I think we could get—"

"Ty," Tobey interrupted. "How much?"

"Fifty," I said without hesitation. I could have said more. I could have said a hundred. But a hundred million put us in Chase Stern territory and—damn the curse—I couldn't stomach that possibility. Fifty million would give us a solid player. Fifty million would be enough to fix everything

"And you'd be happy?"

The corner of my mouth lifted, and I hid my smile behind another sip of my drink. "For now."

He leaned forward, pulling the drink away from me and kissed my mouth, the contact quick and hard. When he sat back, he nodded at Dick. "Fifty million. Get us the best bat and glove you can. But I want a promise, from both of you, that we'll be in the World Series."

"We will." I nodded, Dick less than enthusiastic in his guarantee. He shook the hand Tobey held out, and I settled back in my seat, my eyes leaving Perkins, my outlook considerably improved.

"You guys are the weirdest couple on the planet," Dick muttered. I laughed, Tobey's hand sliding over mine, our fingers intertwining.

He knew what I needed, how to make me happy. And in that moment, I was.

I didn't know. I didn't know that I had just signed our relationship's death warrant.

 **66**

"Good news," the voice rang through Chase's headphones, and he paused the treadmill, slowing to a walk, his heart beating hard.

"What?"

"Yankees want you back."

"What?" His hand jabbed the emergency stop, and he stepped off the end, ripping the earbuds from his head and lifting the phone to his ear. "Are you fucking with me?"

There was a long pause. "I thought you'd be happy," Floyd said cautiously.

"I'm not. You told me four years ago, very clearly, that I was—and this is a direct quote—'*dead* to them.'"

"I thought you were."

"I don't want to go to the Yankees." He pinched the bridge of his nose and let out a long, controlled breath.

"Are you serious? Stop holding a grudge and get *excited* about this. Remember when you were in LA, and obsessed with playing for them?"

He closed his eyes tightly. "Tell me it's not fucking done. Tell me that, Floyd."

Another long pause. "You don't have a no-trades clause. You *knew* that. Back then, when we signed the contract, you were so fucked up, Chase. We were lucky to get you any kind of contract."

"Tell. Me," he gritted out. "That. It's. Not. Done." He crouched, the hotel gym too small, the room closing in on him. He couldn't do it. He could barely survive four hours in that city, much less move back there. Put on her husband's uniform. Walk back into the world where they fell in love. What would happen when he saw her? Every emotion that he'd tried to bury, every piece that he'd tried to forget … it would all come back.

"It's done. They want you there tomorrow for the Red Sox game." All the excitement was out of his agent's voice, the words dead in their delivery.

"I can't," he said. "You gotta get me out of this, Floyd. You *have* to."

"There's nothing I can do." The man sighed. "I'm sorry."

Chase ended the call and sank to the floor, leaning against the gym's rubber wall, his mind trying to work through its knots.

New York. Tomorrow. He needed more time to prepare. But a lifetime wouldn't be enough. He'd never be ready to face her again. Not without pulling her into his arms. Not without refusing to ever let her go.

 **67**

"Chase Stern?" Two words I had promised myself, on the floor of a bathroom so long ago, to never utter again. "That's who you got?" My knees wobbled, and I gripped the edge of the doorframe, my eyes moving to my hand, watching in detached horror as my knuckles turned white.

"Go ahead," Dick mocked, from behind his desk. "Find fault with *that*."

I thought of Thomas Grant's funeral. Thousands of roses as white as my knuckles. The same blooms, identical in every way, to the ones that had blanketed our marriage chapel. I remembered hating that tie of his death with our union. I remembered thinking, if I ever wed again, that—I had stopped that thought right there, not allowing my brain to finish the thought. *There would be no other weddings.* I had my husband. And there, at that funeral, his father lowered slowly into the ground, my husband inherited my team. Our team, one which suddenly included Chase Stern on its list of assets. *Again.* Last time it had made me nearly scream with joy. This time, a scream once again threatened my throat, one birthed in an entirely different place.

I swallowed. "He's a leftie."

Dick laughed. "You say that like it's a bad thing." He was right; it was a stupid thing to point out. Getting a left-handed batter with Stern's fielding was like finding a unicorn.

"He doesn't fit our standards." A better argument. We were the only team in the league with appearance and ethics standards. It was part of our pedigree, our history.

He snorted. "Since when? Five years ago? He was a kid then. He's been squeaky clean ever since. A freaking priest."

Not five years. Barely four. Three years, ten months, four days since I last saw him. An obsessive statistic to know.

He leaned forward, resting his elbows on the desk. "You feel okay, Ty? I thought you'd be doing backflips over this news."

"She's not happy?" Tobey's voice boomed from behind me, his hand gentle in its clap of my shoulder. He moved past me and into the large office.

"I am," I said quickly, releasing my death grip on the doorframe. "I just wasn't sure Stern was the best choice. Who else is there?"

Tobey looked at me as if I'd grown a second head. "Who *else*? Ty, it's Chase Stern. The picketers can finally go home. Maybe the press will stop their shit. And most importantly, maybe that psychopath who's killing these women will finally stop." He let out a hard exhale, his hands flexing around a bottle of water as he unscrewed the cap. "What's the problem?"

I stiffened, crossing my arms in front of my chest. "Last time he was here, he clashed with the team."

"That was almost a decade ago," Dick argued, glancing at Tobey.

"Half that," I shot back.

"Were you balling when he was here?" Tobey turned to me, his brow furrowing, a look I knew well. He was trying to remember.

"Yes," I spoke quickly. "And he didn't fit in."

"Half those guys are gone." Dick shrugged. "And the trade is done, so you can stop analyzing it. You guys wanted the best, you got it. You can thank me in World Series bonuses." He grinned wide, and I wanted to crawl over his desk and punch the smile right off his face. This was not a smiling matter. This was a crisis.

"Ty?"

"What?" I blinked, realizing I had missed something—something Tobey had said—both of them looking at me expectantly.

"We're going down to the airport to meet Stern's plane. Give him the red carpet welcome and prep him before tonight's game. You coming?"

"No." I shook my head quickly. "I was going to visit Margreta and Caleb." For the first time, I was grateful for her high maintenance breasts and their lengthy recovery period, one which seemed unending.

Tobey glanced at his watch. "You're good. I'll call her on the way. Come on." He headed to the door, and paused, his eyes studying me.

I turned quickly, before he could formulate any thoughts, and grabbed my bag off the floor, my steps heavy as I walked through the door, Tobey's hand invasive as it settled onto the small of my back.

This. This would be a disaster.

 **68**

The jet landed into gray, a fog covering the city, thunderclouds in the distance, a setting fit for his entry into hell. Chase watched the ground approach, his eyes closing in preparation, his hands gripping the armrests until the bumpy landing was over. They taxied down the long runway, the travel assistant speaking as soon as the engines had quieted. "Mr. Stern, I've booked you a room at the Royalton until you get an apartment. We have a driver who will be on call this week, and I've texted you his number. Once we land, Mr. Grant and Mr. Polit are taking you straight to the stadium; they want to show you around before batting practice."

"Show me around?" he barked out a laugh. "I'm familiar with the stadium."

Her in the cramped equipment office, alone in the stuffy room; her head bent over a thick textbook; her foot resting on the bat cart, all long legs and concentration. Her eyes, looking up and catching his. Her cheeks flushing, a slow smile spreading before her gaze darted back down.

The woman fidgeted. "They'd like to show you around."

Chase made a face, looking back out the window as she rattled off a list of details that didn't matter. He watched the approach to the Yankee hangar, twin SUVs parked in front. As the jet approached, the vehicle doors opened, and two men stepped out. Then, the rear door opened, and the owner of his heart stepped out.

She was there to pick him up.

The view was terrible, the fog heavy in the air, her figure shrouded, but there was no denying it was her. She didn't move like the teenage girl he remembered, her steps strong and confident, the move of a grown woman used to heels. But the cross of her arms across her chest was familiar, a tell of nerves, and he leaned forward, trying to see her face. If he could see her face, he would know what she was thinking, and how she felt about this.

The plane came to a slow stop, and he stood, grabbing his bag, then moved down the aisle, suddenly anxious to get off the plane.

When the door opened, the stairs lowered, and he forced himself to move slowly, his hand coming out and shaking Dick Polit's, then Tobey Grant's. He looked each man in the face, offering a curt smile, suddenly terrified of the next moment. Tobey turned, waving Ty forward. "This is my wife, Tyler."

His *wife*. A reminder that would never be needed, the words clawing a fresh hole in his tender heart.

She stiffly stepped forward, a polite smile crossing her face, and held out her hand, her eyes slow to move upward, their gaze settling somewhere in the vicinity of his chin. "Nice to meet you, Mr. Stern."

He wrapped her small hand in his and tightened his grip, wanting to squeeze some emotion out of her, a flash of anger in those eyes, a glare ... something. But she only stepped back, withdrawing her hand, and then looked away.

"We've met before," he tossed out, a challenge in his voice, his tone hard enough to stop her turn, her body freezing in its exit. "Don't you remember?"

Finally, her head turned, and her eyes found his. An empty stare, with none of the warmth and fire he remembered. He had wanted to know how she felt about his return. But looking into her eyes, he suddenly didn't want to know.

 **69**

Did I remember? What a cruel question to ask. I stared into his eyes and held back every emotion I could, a hundred memories pushing at thin spider-webs of restraint. I smiled tightly, words finding their way out of my throat, properly smooth and cold. "Oh yes. My apologies, Mr. Stern. It's been so long." I tore my eyes from his, finding Tobey's, strength in his easy smile, his innocence, my clueless husband unaware of the raging war. Giving him a small smile, I walked toward the SUV, taking comfort in the strong click of my heels on the pavement, the sound of escape, of a woman tougher than myself, just four steps away from safety, then three, then two.

Then I was in the truck, the firm shut of the door buffering the howl of the outside wind—everything muted, everything safe.

Alone, if only for a brief moment. I let out a shaky breath, one traitorous tear leaking down my cheek before I hurriedly wiped it away. The men turned, heading toward the vehicle, and I looked away, out the window, my mask of indifference settling back into place. Four years ago, I would have broken down. Reached for him, damn Tobey and anyone else. Four years ago I didn't know how to hide my emotions. Four years ago, I let my heart dictate my mouth, and said what was on my mind.

"I hate him!" I screamed the words, pushing against my father's chest, not even sure where I was fighting to go. Baltimore? What would I do there? Show up at Chase's hotel room, another man's baby inside of me, weak apologies on my lips? I'd called him six times since his trade and couldn't even get a return call.

"It took two of you to do this, Ty." Dad's voice was dry and deep, a bit of his Texas upbringing coating the words. "You can't hate Tobey for all of it. But we

have to tell him. We have to tell them."

Them. The Grants. Was it a blessing that Rose Grant had passed away before seeing her son knock me up? Maybe. On the other hand, with both of us motherless, I would be the only female presence in this baby's life. A terrifying thought, the additional pressure unwelcome and I screamed from the sheer frustration of it all. There was a gentle knock on the door and Carla peeked inside, her face worried, eyes scanning over me. I clenched my hands into fists and straddled the thin line between another scream and bursting into tears.

I couldn't tell the Grants. I couldn't look at Mr. Grant's face, or Tobey's, and tell them that I was pregnant. The elder had so much respect for me, had pushed for us to date for so long, had bragged about what a good girl I was to everyone... I sank against my father's chest, his arms wrapping around me, and bit back a sob. And Tobey. He'd all but run from me that day after our sex. Hadn't so much as texted me since. Then, I'd been grateful, my heart belonging to Chase, no interest on my part for any more of that mistake. But now, I was furious. Maybe it was unjustified. I'd certainly had just as much part as him in the event. But my anger was there, hot and desperate, and it needed a target. And right then, in my bedroom, it was Tobey.

It had taken three days for me to get my emotions in check. For my heart to run the gamut from crying to screaming to crying to screaming. Dad had gone to his game, and I had stayed home with Carla, most of the day spent in bed, working through my hysteria. By the time he returned, I was calm. By the time we got in the truck and made the drive into the city, my mask was in place. Never once, in those first months with Tobey, did I let him see how I truly felt. I saved those outbursts for night, when I was alone in my room, our bedrooms not yet shared, and I had the privacy to cry.

It was one of those nights, when I was sobbing into a pillow, wishing for Chase, that Rachel Frepp died.

The first of the girls.

The beginning of the curse.

And I didn't even know. None of us did.

 **70**

Chase didn't know what he did in life to deserve the punishment of sitting next to this woman. To hear the soft huff of her breath and not kiss it away. Smell the scent of her skin and not bury his face in her hair. Watch the hem of her skirt, its rise up her thighs, and not run his hand up her skin.

He shifted in the seat and tried to look away, tried to focus on whatever the general manager was saying. Saw her, in his peripheral vision, tuck a piece of hair back. It was short now, a fashionable bob that ended just past her ears. When he gripped it, it wouldn't hang from his hand. When she rode him, it would fall into her face.

"We're heading to the stadium, where we can swing by the locker room and player facilities. We've redesigned a lot of it, and I'm not sure how much you remember from before." Tobey turned around, smiling at Chase.

"Everything," he answered, settling back in his seat and holding the man's gaze. "I won't need any reminders. I remember everything."

 **71**

"I remember everything."

I felt nauseated sitting next to him. The center console between us not wide enough, his elbow resting on the leather as if he owned it, his thighs spread on the seat, long legs stretched out. I hid behind sunglasses, sitting as close as I could to the door, feeling as if I was crawling up the glass. The desire to roll down the window and jump out was so strong that I squeezed my hand around the seatbelt strap to prevent the movement.

He smelled the same, the scent of him bringing a wave of unwanted emotions, my psyche instantly transported right back to the girl I used to be—that rebellious, stupid girl—one who wore her heart on her sleeve and drooled over such ridiculous things as batting averages and perfect bodies.

I was no longer that girl. I had grown up, found new priorities. I was chairwoman of the Boys and Girls Club for shit's sake. The first lady of the damn New York Yankees. I was married to a man who adored me, who spoiled me rotten, who listened to my opinion and valued it.

And Chase ... he wasn't the same man who had left me all those years ago. Better or worse, it didn't matter. We had moved down different paths, our fates parted, life possibilities killed.

He leaned forward, over the center console, and I stiffened, keeping my head turned to the window, willing him to stop whatever he was about to do, my composure too fragile for a poke.

"I like your hair." He spoke softly, but I heard every syllable, the words shouted in my mind, almost as loud as his last sentence. *I remember everything.*

"Thank you," I said stiffly, not looking his way, our earlier eye contact enough for a lifetime.

"Very ice princess. It matches your whole ... look."

I flexed my hand around the belt. "Thank you. Tobey seems to enjoy it."

He moved away, settling back into his seat, and I let out my held breath as subtly as I could.

I could do this. Play the correct part. Survive this hitch. Lock up my heart and protect it.

 **72**

It took me years to walk down the hallowed halls of our stadium and not think of Chase. It seemed unfair, with that scab finally healed, my ball club restored, for him to step through the double doors and ruin it all over again.

I walked next to Dick, Tobey, and Chase, the journey soon joined by our manager, John O'Connell. Their threesome stretched over the wide hall, both men speaking excitedly to Chase, their words floating back to Dick and me. Dick typed as he moved, his head down, phone out, no interest in their conversation. I walked in heels too high for this trek, my exit strategy planned as soon as we made our first stop.

Painfully enough, that first stop was the locker room. I held back, protesting, but John waved me in. "It's empty. No one's gotten in yet."

I reluctantly stepped through, lifting my watch as I checked the time. "Babe, I need to go," I said to Tobey. "Margreta—"

"She'll be fine," he said firmly. "We're having lunch up in the club, and I want you there." He turned to Chase, who dropped his bag in front of a locker already bearing his name. "Did you know that Ty was a ball girl for us for eight years?"

"Seven," I corrected.

"Wow," Chase drawled, turning slowly toward me. I looked away, focusing on a piece of something on my skirt, delicately picking at it. He stepped closer, and my heart cried for him. "You must have a lot of memories in this place."

"Nothing noteworthy." I raised my chin and met his eyes. "I preferred to be on the field." Those eyes. *"You ever think you could love someone too much?"* They were the same, just as beautiful, yet different. Colder. Sadder. They looked like I felt. How I'd felt every day for the last four years.

"She's got an arm on her," Tobey said proudly. "Gets it from her dad. She's—"

"Frank Rollins's daughter," Chase finished quietly. "I know." His eyes didn't leave mine.

I turned away, my arm looping through Tobey's, my eyes ripping from Chase's to look up into his face. "I'm starving. Did you mention lunch?"

Lunch was hell. A constant exercise in avoiding the one thing I wanted most in life. He cleared his throat and my eyes pulled to him. He answered a question and my breath caught, movement stopped, everything tensed to hear the way his words wrapped around syllables. His voice was different. Deeper. Older. From 23 to 27, and so much had changed. His shoulders were broader. His build was stronger. His hands, when he gripped the glass and lifted it to his mouth, those of a man. Every glance that I stole, he caught, each brush of eye contact another pin in the weak cushion of my heart.

Halfway through my lobster risotto, my cell rang. Finishing my bite, I set down my fork, bending and pulling my phone from my bag. Frowning at the screen, I excused myself, stepping away from the table to take the call.

I didn't answer it. Instead, I silenced the ring and held the cell to my ear, speaking lines of greeting to the empty phone. I walked through the empty lounge, away from our table, gave a polite smile to the waitress, and escaped into the hall.

Silence.

Air.

Space.

I continued, walking down the hall to safety, and stopped by the bathrooms. Leaning against the wall, I took a deep breath, trying to clear my mind, dropping my cell into my bag. *I couldn't be around that man.* Not next to him in the car, not sitting across from him at that table. Just being in the same stadium with him felt wrong. I had ended that part of my life. And now, after just an hour in his presence, I felt like I was holding the past with both hands, trying to keep it closed.

A hand locked on my arm, and I opened my eyes, everything moving, Chase a blur before me as he shoved open the bathroom door and pushed me inside. I didn't struggle; I sagged against the wall where he left me, watching him flip the lock, and then he was in front of me, his hand against the wall by my head, his eyes in line with mine, breathing hard.

"What are you doing?" he gritted out. "Bringing me here? Playing this game?"

"I can't be here with you," I said frantically. "My—"

"Husband?" he growled. "I know. You've mentioned him enough." He lowered his head, and then his lips were against mine, and my bag fell from my hand.

Almost half a decade since I'd kissed this man, and he still owned my mouth.
Explored it with more skill, more need, more passion, than anyone ever could.

I let him do it, let him ruin my future, his hand hard on my waist, pulling me off the wall and hard against his body. I sank in his grip, clutching at his shirt, kissing him back, the bathroom quiet as we dove into hell.

I felt him, his workout pants giving away everything, his hands on my ass, pulling up my skirt, against the hard length of his cock, a small whimper escaping me as my soaked panties dragged across his stiff ridge.

"Nothing noteworthy?" he rasped against my mouth, breaking from our kiss, my mouth hungry for more. "Is that what you said?" He dove back onto my lips, his kiss punishing, his fingers wrapping around my wrist, pushing my hand down, inside the waist of his pants, the fight leaving my fingers when he wrapped them around his cock. "Feel that?" he asked, thrusting against my hand, his voice angry. "You wanna look me in my face and tell me that's forgettable?"

I squeezed, unable to help myself. It was so thick. So hard. I should have dropped it, should have stepped away, should have smacked the confidence right off his face. But I didn't. I slid my grip up and down his shaft, my mouth greedy on his, my free hand digging into his hair, nails scraping against his scalp, the groan that slipped from him urging me on.

"Fuck me, Ty," he whispered. "Right now. Please." He pulled at my panties, and I almost moaned.

"No," I bit out, in between hot kisses, continuing the jack of his cock, his hands pulling the shirt from my skirt, the other squeezing my ass. "I can't." I quickened the speed of my hand and he all but shuddered, his grip on me tightening.

"I'm gonna come," he panted. "Shit, get me a towel."

I almost didn't. I almost dropped to my knees on that Egyptian tile and took him in my mouth. Thank God I didn't. It was bad enough that I reached over, pulling a stack of white custom hand towels, the team logo finely imprinted on their paper front.

I watched him come, his voice gasping my name, his hand pulling me to him and kissing me on the mouth, hard and desperate, his head dropping back when I shoved at his chest and walked to the sink, damp paper towels tossed in the trash, my hands furious in their wash, over and over, underneath water so hot I flinched.

"Stop thinking." His voice, broken and quiet, came from behind me. I looked up into his reflection, into his face. An impossible directive, my thoughts frantic in my mind. *I just cheated on Tobey.* I wasn't that woman, I couldn't be that woman and ... especially not with this man. This wasn't a one-time, dirty affair kind of guy. This was the man who owned my soul. This was the man who, despite the miles of separation, and the years, and the gold ring on my finger, I still loved. *Fiercely* loved.

"That was a mistake," I said quietly, fixing my blouse, straightening my skirt, my hands shaking in their attempt to right all of this wrong. "A mistake." I repeated the words because everything I was feeling ... the shame, the regret—it wasn't over my marriage. It wasn't over my husband, sitting at a table just rooms away. It was the shame of leaving Chase without explanation, of marrying Tobey and not driving to fucking Baltimore instead. It was the regret that I wasn't, right now, five steps closer, back in his arms, pulling off our clothes until we were skin to skin, heart to heart, future to future.

"It wasn't a mistake." He pushed off the wall and stepped toward me.

"Stop." There was enough strength in the word that he listened. "I can't think straight when you're near me. Please. Just ... just stay over there."

"I didn't want to come here, Ty. *Your* side is responsible for this. I was happy in Baltimore."

I shook my head, turning to him with a sad smile. "You hate Baltimore." He told me that once, back in 2011, over midnight milkshakes on a Baltimore street corner. A story of a terrible childhood visit, a discussion of our youth and how memories can taint cities. He hated Baltimore. I hated Pittsburgh.

"It feels wrong, hating the city where I lived with my mom." I leaned against him, resting my head on his shoulder, watching traffic roll by, the downtown street busy, even in the middle of the night. Occasionally, there was a horn, a shout, a fan who recognized him, their arms waving in excitement.

"But that's not why you hate it, is it?"

"It's just that … all I can remember from that time was being sad. All of it, the house, the park where I played, everything made me miss her more." I had been glad when we left. Glad to start fresh in New York, in a house that didn't have her furniture, in a truck that didn't carry old tubes of her lipstick in its glove box. It felt like when we moved, we left her behind. And now, every time we returned, the city felt dim, draped in sadness. Thank God the Pirates were in the National League, our paths rarely crossing, my memories in Pittsburgh fading away.

"There's nothing wrong with missing her. Or with being sad. You're sad because you loved her, and because you had great memories to miss."

"Do you still miss Emily?"

"I'll always miss Emily. She's a part of me." He took a sip of his milkshake, his arm tightening a little around my waist. "Like you."

I looked up at him, my face scrunching in disbelief. "Like me?"

"Yeah." He looked down at me, and there was a moment. One of those where everything stopped, where I saw dots of streetlights reflecting in his eyes, the tickle of my hair across my face, the warmth of his breath against my lips. I looked in his eyes and believed that I was a part of him. Just as I believed when he said he loved me. I believed it because I understood it. I understood it because I felt it too. "Come on." He pulled, swinging me around and nudging me in the opposite direction, away from the street. "Let's go."

"I hated Baltimore, but only because you weren't there. And now…" He ran both hands over the top of his head. "I'll hate New York because you *are* here. How fucked up is that?"

I said nothing, picking up my purse from the floor. "Don't touch me again, Chase."

"I can't promise you that. You aren't a girl anymore, Ty. It was hard enough to keep my hands to myself then."

I opened the door, and glanced back, memorizing the lines of his face, the clench of his jaw, the burn of his eyes. I gave myself one final drink. "Try."

Then, I stepped back into my world and closed the door.

"The second girl died on October 3rd, 2012. April McIntosh. She worked at a deli right around the corner from the stadium. Left work that Wednesday afternoon, and just disappeared. They found her a few days later, when a construction dumpster started to smell. She'd been a troubled girl. Got around a lot, partied a lot, that kind of girl.

Had a Yankee pendant around her neck, a nice piece. Gold and diamonds. But like I said, nobody noticed things like that back then. Not the timing, not the Yankee connection. Not 'til Julie Gavin's death, in 2013, did they connect those dots. Not that it was a stretch. Her death was a damn flashing billboard. Anyone who missed that didn't deserve to carry a badge."

Dan Velacruz, *New York Times*

 **73**

"Smartest decision I ever made." Tobey bent over, kissing me square on the lips, then reached and clapped Dick on the back. "You were right, Ty. God, were you right."

Dick cleared his throat with a smile. "Smartest decision *I* ever made. Let's not forget who picked this golden boy."

I sat between them helplessly, staring at the field, the seventh inning beginning, the stadium lights illuminating the truth so bright it hurt my eyes. *Chase had gotten better.* I'd avoided any mention, any highlight of him in the past four years. I'd boycotted Orioles games, inventing a lifelong hatred of them as my excuse. I'd stopped watching ESPN purely to avoid the mention of his name. And now, with his perfect body encased in our jersey, I had seen everything I'd missed. His footwork. His arm. His bat. Two homeruns already. Five different plays that had made Tobey swear in excitement. Solid grounding, incredible focus, and the speed of an eighteen-year-old rookie. No wonder he had dominated the MVP ranks. No wonder Dick had ignored Tobey's fifty million dollar number and gone to seventy. I was shocked the Orioles gave him up.

"Fine, you get the credit." Tobey laughed. "But don't let him go. *Ever.* I don't care if he smuggles drugs on the off-season, he's retiring a Yankee, got it?"

What if he fucks your wife, Tobey? The question rang so loudly through my head that I brought my hand to my mouth, worried it'd slipped out.

"Are you okay?" Tobey bent over me, concerned. Always concerned.

Always caring. I felt the true urge to vomit and pushed myself to my feet.

"Excuse me," I said quickly, with a tight smile. He let me pass, worry in his eyes.

I didn't vomit. My body didn't allow me that reaction of guilt. I dry heaved into the toilet, wanting it, hoping it would ease some part of what I did, but my stomach stayed calm, the step away from Tobey's love all that it had needed.

I could not be this woman—a cheater. Not to this man who loved me so much. Not to this man who had given me everything.

I opened the skybox vanity kit and took out a fresh toothbrush and paste. After brushing, I stepped out and back into place next to Tobey, the seventh inning stretch beginning, the stadium swaying before us in harmonic concert.

"You know how the seventh inning stretch began?" Chase spoke quietly next to me, his arm resting on the dugout rail, his eyes on the field, "God Bless America" floating down and over the dugout roof.

"Yes." I rolled my eyes.

"You do?"

I laughed quietly under my breath. "There are five or six stories, and I have heard them all, so whichever one you use to pick up girls in bars, I know."

There was a long pause from his direction. "At Manhattan—"

"College," I interrupted. "Brother Jasper. Got it."

"In the summer of 1869, The New York—"

"Herald published an article about the laughable stand up and stretch."

He turned his head toward me, my peripheral vision catching the action, and I glanced his way, his eyes challenging me. "A letter——"

"By Harry Wright. Also in 1869. Cincinnati Red Stockings," I shot back.

"1889."

"World Series. Someone stood up and yelled 'stretch for luck.'"

"1910."

I smirked, the final one too easy. "President Taft."

He grinned at me, the trademark cocky smile a little different. Softer. Sweeter.

"Well?" I challenged. "Please. Tell me all about your precious baseball history, Mr. Stern." I put on an innocent face, and he laughed.

"Ty!" The bark made me jump, and I glanced over my shoulder at the bench.

"Go grab some more Gatorade," Fernandez said, his glare on Chase.

"You got it." I flashed a smile at Fernandez, and he watched me warily, his eyes darting back to Chase.

Thank God we'd finally switched back to the seventh inning stretch's original song, our troops out of Afghanistan, "Take Me Out to the Ballgame" resuming its tenure. Every game, that stretch had mocked me. Every game, I had steeled myself for its chords.

Now, I looked at the empty field and thanked God that I wasn't down in that dugout. Up here, in our throne, I could almost forget his presence. I could definitely avoid his eyes.

Behind me, there was the loud pop of a champagne bottle, and I flinched.

 **74**

After those minutes with Chase, I suddenly couldn't stand Tobey's touch. I didn't feel worthy, not with his loving gaze already clawing through my skin. That night, when he pulled me to him, I winced, the brush of his fingers across my stomach prickly, my hand unable to stop in pushing him away.

"Not tonight."

"Do you feel okay?" He was worried, after my rush to the bathroom during the game. I'd had nausea during my first pregnancy. So maybe … always the *maybe*, floating out there. He didn't know about the birth control implant I had put in. I'd done it after the miscarriage, terrified of the chance of another baby, one that might chain us together forever. Now, four years later, our marriage was in a different, stronger place, one where love had grown from the seeds of friendship and circumstance. But even after the love, I didn't remove the implant. I told myself that I couldn't handle another loss. And I didn't tell Tobey. I'm not sure why, except that I didn't know how to discuss my motivations. How do you tell your husband that you don't want to carry his child?

"Just something I ate." I could feel the disappointment in his silence. He kissed the back of my neck, our bodies connected, torso to toes, and I closed my eyes, trying to relax against his touch. *The love of a man who had stayed.* It should have felt wonderful. Instead, it felt empty.

Funny how much things could change in four years. In the beginning, when we were first pushed into the engagement, Tobey didn't care about the team. It was my thing. Mine and his father's. Tobey was an occasional participant in team meetings, sometimes at games, his schedule as sporadic as our affection, our common ground being our impending parenthood. After we lost the baby, we were two strangers in a big, new house, avoiding the nursery, avoiding each other, neither sure why we were still in the union. The team was what pushed us back together, Tobey's father having his first stroke, stepping down from his role in the organization, and pushing Tobey to take the reins. I think the old man knew what he was doing; I think he saw our marriage falter and wrapped pinstripes around the two of us, binding us. Whether by design or fate, we stepped into Thomas Grant's shoes as one, splitting duties and decision-making, our stiff dinners becoming more of business meetings, everything focused on the team and its success. And success did come, both for the team and for us. We moved on from the baby. Had sex more, awkward conversation less. We became friends, grew to respect each other's opinions, trust each other's decisions. Tobey grew up from a spoiled rich kid, and I grew up from a tomboy. And from our friendship, grew a love. A love that I thought would carry us, and the team, until our deaths.

"I love you," he whispered against my hair.

"I love you too."

I loved him. I did. Anything that I had once had with Chase … it had to stay in the past. What had happened in that powder room—it could never happen again.

SEPTEMBER

"Julie Gavin … she died on September 29, 2013. A date that will live in Yankee history. Her death left the clues that everyone needed to start tying the girls together. For starters, she was wearing a Chase Stern jersey, one from the 2011 season. Add the fact that she was left at the stadium, and a giant red arrow couldn't have been any clearer. *That* was when the press started calling it The Curse of Chase Stern. *That* was when the detectives started looking at dates and for Yankee connections with each of the blondes. Julie Gavin, bless her soul, was the tie they all needed. Her blood's still there, on the pavement outside the west gate. They tried to hide it, poured fresh concrete over it, but it's there, a mark that will never leave that stadium."

Dan Velacruz, *New York Times*

 **75**

My entire life, I'd known security. The team, whether it was the Pirates or the Yankees, always had security, men in black uniforms that flanked the players as we traveled, local cops closing roads, opening pathways, and holding fans at bay. After a while, they faded into the background, just one more bit of wallpaper in my life.

As a Grant, our security was completely different. Our home was a fortress, a trusted team of security everywhere. It was stifling, when I moved in, the feeling of constant monitoring. It was why I loved our weekends at the Hampton estate, the security protocol there almost non-existent. We had only one guard, James. He sat at the front gate, three hundred pounds of muscle that discouraged gawkers. And inside the house, we were free. Free to wander down to the beach, swimsuits optional. Free to fall asleep on the couch, the windows open, the scent of the ocean strong. Everything about that house was an escape, away from the city, away from the team, away from the murders.

Until Tiffany Wharton tainted it.

After that, there was no escape. After that, there was no more running. After that, everything in our world narrowed into one focus: Winning. Our world became a prison, the World Series our key to escape. And my nights on the field? That was my prison time spent in the yard. A big yard, one where gods played. A yard with thousands of steps and halls, plastic and grass and clay. It was the most secure compound in the Bronx, and it was, at times, the only thing that held my sanity in check.

The parking garage was quiet, my Range Rover the only car present, the sound of the door echoing through the empty space. I stepped to the back of it, opening the hatch, Titan jumping to the ground beside me, his nails clicking along the concrete. When I shut the hatch, I set the alarm, dropping my keys in my bag. It might be a fortress, but this was still New York, still the Bronx. I hit the button for the elevator, glancing at Titan as he sat, facing out, at full alert. We got him from Germany, completely trained, his journey to the US accompanied by a handler, a short man who lived with us for two weeks and yelled at me a lot. Apparently I had needed a lot more training than Titan. But now, three years later, Titan and I worked together just fine. He protected me, and I snuck him table scraps when Tobey wasn't looking.

The elevator opened, and I stepped on, pressing the button for the ground level. As it descended, I picked up the elevator's phone, listening to the automatic ring. Somewhere, making rounds, were more security guards, four of them. When my miss of the field had become too great, when I decided to move my midnight workouts here, Tobey had worried. Not worried enough to accompany me, his early mornings putting him on a different sleep schedule than me. Initially, he'd had one of the house team escort me. But in the quiet of the night, the extra person had seemed invasive, as if I were being caged more than protected. So we had made an agreement. I'd bring Titan, and I'd check in with security when I arrived and departed. The arrangement allowed Tobey to sleep well at night, and I didn't feel smothered. Didn't feel *as* smothered. At some point in my life, I'd find the ability to live a life without pressure. At some point, I wanted a lack of expectations, and appearances, and decisions that affected lives.

Security answered and I cleared my throat, speaking into the phone. "It's Ty."

"Good evening, Mrs. Grant. How long will you be with us this evening?"

"About an hour. On the field and in the stands."

"Wonderful. Will you need us to open the locker facilities?"

"No, not tonight." The elevator shuddered, the doors opening on the ground level. "Thank you."

"Certainly."

I hung up the phone and stepped out, Titan beside me. All was dim, emergency lights bathing the halls in a soft, red light, and I flipped switches as we walked, bringing the hallway to life, my steps quickening as I got closer to the place where I was happiest.

I'd heard that cutters enjoyed the pain of their activity because it caused them to feel. I'd never understood that until the first night I'd stepped back out on this field, almost two years after Chase left. I didn't know why I first did it. Part of it was because I had ordered myself to stop mourning his loss, and was ready to take the first step. Part of it was because I'd thought I was ready, ready to reenter the world which my pregnancy, which my dad's retirement, which my marriage—had all taken away. The nights afforded me privacy, the late hours insuring no party to my pain. Each visit, the scent of the grass, the dig of cleats into the dirt ... each sensation brought back a flood of memories. Sometimes I cried, most nights I didn't. But I always felt.

At some point, I'd be able to replace his memories with new ones of my own—my midnight workouts with Titan an attempt to paint over the past. An attempt that hadn't happened yet. And now that he was back ... that goal stretched even further into improbability.

I grabbed a bucket of balls and pushed through the double doors, stepping from the hall and out into the night. I was climbing the steps to the field when Titan's body knocked against me, his body jumping the final two steps and planting, four feet in the dirt, his hair raised, a loud snarl spitting out.

 **76**

"Achtung."

The foreign command rolled off her tongue like silk, no hesitancy in the word, and Chase hoped to God it meant something other than *attack*.

"Easy." He stepped off first base, hoping some light from the stands would light his features, the dark field no help. That's what he got for lurking here, the last two hours of jogging, stretching, throwing—all an excuse to wait, to hope, for this.

"Ty never comes to the field?" Chase watched the skybox suite, the interior illuminated in the darkening night. Inside it, Ty gave a strange woman a hug.

"Mrs. Grant?" The second baseman spit on the dirt. "Not really. I heard she comes out here late sometimes, to run."

"Late?" Chase looked away from the skybox. <u>Mrs. Grant</u>. *The name turned his stomach.*

"Yeah. Security mentioned it once." He shrugged. "They say she used to help out on the field, but I've never seen her pick up a ball. Probably just rumors."

Chase said nothing, stepping back into place and leaning forward, his eyes watching the batter, poised for action.

The information had haunted him, dragging him here for the last week, each night a waste, the security guards barely glancing his way by the third time he pulled up. But it'd been worth it. Because here she was and here he was and they were on, of all things, a baseball field. The perfect setting for this, a moment of privacy, a moment without Tobey Grant lurking around the corner, a moment without anything but the two of them.

She was as beautiful as the week before, but more so, the Ty of his dreams. The one in shorts and sneakers, her hair pulled back, no makeup on her face, a t-shirt clinging to her shape. He didn't look for a ring, didn't want to think of anything but the girl he knew. The one who had been as loyal as she'd been fierce. The one who had loved him with a passion and fire that had clawed at his barriers and punctured his walls. The only girl he'd ever imagined a future with. The woman he'd forgotten to get his heart back from, before he left.

"Easy," he repeated. "You don't want to kill the Yankee's newest star."

"Step forward again, and he'll rip out your throat," she called. Beside her, the dog snarled, his teeth bared, every muscle ready.

He stopped, holding up his hands, warily eyeing the German Shepard. "I surrender." He surrendered everything to her. She'd destroyed him once before. And here, a fool three times over for nights wasted on this field, he could already smell his demise in the crisp night air. Just as before, she held all the power in those little hands. No longer a girl's hands, they were older, wiser. A married woman's hands. Ones that could crush him. Ones that could ruin him. Their time in that bathroom hadn't shown him anything other than her weakness for his touch. He'd wasted that opportunity, going after low-hanging fruit and not the important things. *Did she still love him?* How could he have not asked that question? *Would she leave Tobey?* A scarier question, one that he was afraid to know the answer to.

She was loyal. He knew nothing if not that.

But would she be loyal to their love? It was a love that hadn't been touched in the last four years. *Or would she be loyal to her husband?* That question, he was terrified of. That question he could barely form in his mind, much less off his lips.

"Platz," she said, and every muscle in the dog's body relaxed as he looked up at her with a disappointed expression, a low whine coming out. "Platz." He laid down on the dirt, his eyes on Chase. She took one step forward and stopped. "What are you doing here?" Her voice was guarded but not angry.

"Are you alone?" *Do you still love me?* He couldn't ask it. The words just wouldn't leave his mouth.

"Yes." Her eyes darted to the stands. "But there are security guards here. So don't—"

"I'm not here for that." And he wasn't, but it didn't stop him from wanting to pull her into his chest. To lay her onto the grass and make her whisper his name into the night.

"Then what are you doing here?"

"Working out. My hotel's gym sucks." He tested the dog and stepped forward, smiling at her, the lie rolling convincingly out.

"Security can get you a key to the gym. It's on the third floor. I can have them open it for you—" she stopped talking, his head shaking.

"I don't want a gym. I like the field." His fingers tightened on the ball and he forced his feet to stop moving, a few steps of separation between them. This close he could see her eyes. This close, he could almost smell her. This close, if she wanted to, she could crush him.

 **77**

God, I love him. The truth that I'd run from every day of my new life smashed into me like a fastball into a mitt, stinging in its impact, radiating through my bones. *I love him.* Before, in my heels, wearing my ring, my husband standing beside me, it'd been easier to lie. To protect. But now, on our field, I felt naked, nothing between him and I but the truth. It wasn't supposed to be this easy to destroy your life. There were supposed to be moments where you could divert, could pick new paths that would lead back to success. But in this, there was only one path, a giant vacuum that sucked me in, the end hitting my heart with a resounding thud that shook everything, down to my soul. *I love him.* Still. *More.* Impossible, yet true. Whatever asshole said that absence made the heart grow fonder was right. Before, I fell for him with a teenager's love, bold and passionate, no real obstacles to overcome, no real consequences to consider. Now, the wind tickling past my legs, I could see the full path of destruction this would cause. I saw it, and in that moment, I didn't care. I couldn't care. There was right, there was wrong, and there was love. And love trumped it all.

I said nothing, my silence a waste of space on a blackboard crowded with possibilities. *Take me from this life. I'll always be yours.* "Did you know I'd be here?"

He didn't answer, and I could see more of him now, my eyes getting used to the dark. He was in workout pants and a long-sleeved shirt, it fitting snug across his chest, his shoulders, his arms. A glove on one hand, no cap. He lifted his chin and met my eyes. God, those eyes. I saw in them a hundred secret moments, moments out of jerseys and away from spotlights, moments where he had just been Chase and not The Chase Stern. Moments where he had been all mine.

I love you because when I see you, I can't stop staring at you.

I blinked away the memory. "Did you?" I swallowed. "Did you know I'd be here?"

"I hoped." He shrugged, reaching down, the eye contact broken, his hand grabbing a ball from the bucket by his feet. "You didn't show the other nights."

"We've been out of town." The words shouldn't have been said. He didn't deserve an explanation. I wished I could take them back. I wished I could take this night back, put myself at home, before I realized that I was done for, that my world was over, that my heart was still his. I wished I could take it all back, yet I didn't wish that at all. *The other nights*, he'd said. *He'd been waiting for me.*

He tossed the ball toward me, and I caught it. He stepped back. "Got a glove, Little League?"

"You can't call me that anymore."

He punched the glove. "Do you?"

I dropped my bag on the ground. "Maybe."

"Still got that arm on you?"

I reached down, slowly pulling out my glove and working it on. It slid easily over my bare hand, my ring at home, in the safe. I flexed the leather and looked up at him. "Are you wanting to find out?"

He grinned at me, holding up his glove and asking for the ball. I tossed it toward him, and then, despite my better judgment, jogged out onto the field, Titan breaking into a run beside me, my heart beating louder than it had in years.

I love you because right now, there's nothing more tempting in life than to pull you on top of me and push inside of you.

We said little for the next hour, falling into an easy rhythm of catching, the ball arching through the air between us, lost in the night, then found again when it connected with the leather of a glove. I caught grounders for the first time in years, my movements rusty at first, then smoothing out, the flex of an old muscle enjoyable.

It was, out of all of my nights on that field, the most painful of them all.

"It was crazy, with the whole city involved—picketers at the game, media crowding the press box, every fan demanding Chase Stern's return—there were only two people, in that entire city who really knew what was happening.
And only one who could fix it."

Dan Velacruz, *New York Times*

78

When we got the call about Julie Gavin, her body left at the East Gate, Tobey vomited. I remember standing at the bathroom door, my hand on its surface, and feeling heartless. He was the man, the strong one. He was the one who climbed mountains and stayed dry-eyed during The Green Mile. Yet he was puking into the toilet and I was calm, uncaring. I remember analyzing my feelings, trying to find the root of my problem.

"Babe." I jiggled the handle, frowning when I discovered it locked, the sound of retching causing my brow to furrow. "Talk to me."

"What the fuck is there to say?" he snapped, the words almost drowned out by the toilet flushing.

"It's not our fault." I leaned into the door, putting my mouth by the crack, hoping my words would carry. "We did everything we could. The security—"

"It's a pattern, Ty." He interrupted. "That's what Harold said. She isn't the first."

Yes, our head of security had been clear on that. This girl, the one that showed up dead outside our gates, a detective had linked her with two other girls. Both also stabbed, and also on the last day of the season. The detective thought it was a World Series freak, someone pissed at the trade of Chase, and punishing the city every year we fell short of winning it all. "They might be wrong," I said. "Who would kill girls over that? It's—" I stopped short of saying crazy. Because of course this guy, whoever he is, was crazy. Sane people didn't murder. And sane people certainly didn't base murders on a baseball schedule.

"I don't think they're wrong." He had moved, to a different part of the bathroom, his voice echoing off the tiles, and I jiggled the handle, wishing he would just open the damn door already.

I hadn't argued with him, but I hadn't taken it seriously. I hadn't felt guilt. Or pressure. Not until 2014. Not until Tiffany Wharton.

I was the one who found her. I later wondered if it was planned, my discovery of Tiffany. If so, it was brilliantly effective. I'd paid attention to the deaths before; we'd met with investigators, donated money to memorial funds, made personal calls to parents. But her death, at least for me, changed everything. After her, the deaths ruled my life. There was no way to avoid a dead girl. No way to forget the blank stare of her eyes, the open gape of her mouth. I *still* see her face in my nightmares. I *still* can hear the scrape of gravel as I skidded to a stop in front of her body.

She was on the edge of our Hamptons' property, on the service road that led to our back gate. Her body was on its side, as if it'd been kicked from a moving car, no care made to lay her flat, her arms at an unnatural angle. She'd been more than a fan. She'd been a member of our staff, a Human Resources' admin, her face familiar to me.

Titan and I had come around a curve, his ears up, stance alert, and we'd almost stepped on her. I'd known, as soon as I'd seen her, that it was a message—one screamed through blonde hair and the dust of our property on her face.

In that moment, I understood Tobey's nausea. I understood his panic. I felt the pressure, the breath of this psycho on the back of my sweaty neck. Whoever the madman was, he had my attention. And from that moment on, he had all of my focus. We needed to win. The NYPD needed to step up its fucking game.

Time was ticking, and everything amped up. Our recruiting. Our training. Our pressure. Tobey changed, retreating into himself, short with everyone but me, his obsession with winning almost manic in its focus. And that day, I became the same way.

 **79**

"Hot Dog Day can't come before Hoodie Day!" Mitch Addenheim, one of our senior marketers, slammed his fist on the table like he was preparing for war. I stifled a yawn and drew my best impression of Mitch's hot dog on the edge of my agenda. It wasn't impressive. "I've got suppliers already lined up and committed, plus the calendar magnets printed."

I glanced at my watch as discreetly as possible, tuning out the argument between Mitch and the others, an issue with our hoodie manufacturer creating a mini-crisis of sorts. It was just after eleven. Forty minutes of hoodie discussions and I was over it. I cleared my throat and Mitch stopped mid-sentence.

"Keep the current scheduling. We'll hand out the hoodies that we have and issue vouchers for the rest. It'll give them an excuse to come back to another game." I waited a half-moment; no objections presented, and moved on. "What's next? Kirsten?"

The blonde stood, taking over, and I flipped the agenda over, skimming the remaining topics, my mind struggling to stay on point. Three days since I had seen Chase on the field. I hadn't gone back, the last two nights restless, my legs twitching, my eyes darting to the clock as each grew later. Titan had laid by the back door, too well trained to whine, his eyes following me every time I stood. Normally, during a home week, I was there every night. But not this week. Half of it was self-punishment. The other half? Self-preservation.

I was in hell. Going crazy with thoughts of him, with the anticipation. I couldn't pull through the stadium gates without searching the cars, wondering if his was there. I sweated through games in the skybox, every glance at him torture, his eyes up, on our box, the contact so frequent that I both dreaded and expected Tobey's mention of it. A mention that never came, the observation missed, everyone oblivious to what was being screamed, at top volume, for all the world to hear.

I thought women enjoyed affairs. I thought they got sparks of pleasure at the buzz of their phone, thought they ran around with a glow, their world suddenly on fire with new love. I thought they were women with terrible husbands and unhappy lives, an affair the first step in an eventual ending of their marriage. I thought that they were horrible, selfish women. I never thought that I would be one of them. I never thought that I'd be so weak. It turned out being the perfect wife was only easy when there was no temptation, no mistake haunting and overshadowing your marriage.

I loved Tobey. Another man shouldn't be able to tempt you when you loved your husband. But love felt like a flat emotion with Tobey, something that had grown with time, a winding of two lives, built on a foundation of friendship and respect. I was attracted to him. We had sex, a more active life than most couples. We had all of those building blocks that make a marriage strong ... yet one touch from Chase, and I'd crumbled. One moment of eye contact and I'd broken. One hour of throwing a ball with him and I'd been ready to pack up everything and leave my husband.

What kind of woman was I?

What kind of love did that?

Regardless of the reasons, or of my justifications, this entire situation was wrong. It was a black hole, each day with Tobey pushing me deeper, my claw to the surface, to the maintenance of my marriage, getting harder and harder.

I *had* to go to the fields that night. Not to see him, but just for a breather. I was a drowning woman, and needed my field, my grass, my dirt. I needed to pound up a flight of stadium stairs and stand in front of an eighty-mile per hour pitching machine. I needed a release, or else I just might go crazy.

 **80**

The ending of everything didn't come quickly. Pieces of my life flaked off, caught by the wind and scattered, too quickly for me to capture. It didn't matter; I didn't want to capture them. I stood in the wind, arms outstretched, and willed it to happen.

Maybe that made me selfish. Maybe that made me smart.

This time, I saw Chase before Titan did, his shape dark, way out by the bullpen. I could have left, gone to a different part of this enormous complex. Or called security and asked them to clear the field. I didn't. I stepped out onto the damp grass, and jogged toward him, Titan loping ahead, his ears up, gait relaxed.

"Hey." He tossed a ball toward me as I approached.

I caught it and hefted it back. "Hey."

"Had given up on you coming."

"Yet you're here."

"Oh, you thought I came here to see you?" He smirked, and my heart soared. "Not a chance."

"Yeah," I huffed. "Me either."

"So now that we're not here together, want to catch?"

I shrugged, glancing around the field. "I thought I'd go for a run. Knock out some cardio."

"Want some company?"

I gave him an obvious once-over, my eyes clinging to the curve of his biceps, the strength of his stance. "Think you can keep up?"

His grin widened, and Colgate could sell a million tubes off those teeth. "Yeah, I think I'll do just fine."

I tossed the ball toward his bucket and whistled for Titan.

And just like that, we were another step deeper, another bit of my world crumbling off.

I had become a runner. The annoying type who held their breath as they passed others, out of pure competitive spite. One of those who kept Nikes in the back of my SUV, just in case I got a free moment with a treadmill. I'd run over every inch of this complex, down empty hallways and through boardrooms. I'd explored the visitors' locker rooms, our kitchens, and the press boxes. But I'd never gone through the gate where Chase stopped.

"What are you doing?" I jogged in place, lungs starting to warm, our run only just begun.

"Come on." He nodded his head, holding open the gate. *The gate that led off property*. Into the Bronx.

If we took it, we'd pass the Julie Gavin gate. Pictures from the police report flashed through my mind, a flipbook of dark blood, white skin, blonde hair matted, eyes open and unseeing. The killer had underlined the name on the back of the jersey, STERN punctuated with one long line of her blood. "I can't go out there." Titan growled beside me, my indignant tone putting him on alert.

"*Can't?*" His eyes narrowed. "Grant got you on a leash?"

I stopped jogging, my feet unsteady when they stopped. "Don't be ridiculous."

He took a step out, his hand still holding the door, fingers barely gripping it as if he was about to let go. "Then come on."

"It's not safe," I protested.

His face hardened. "I'll kill someone before they touch you. And if I die trying, Killer there will finish them off." He nodded to Titan.

The Bronx, in itself, was probably fine. It certainly felt safe enough, during the day, in our chauffeured rides to and from the stadium. But at one and two in the morning, when I was driving out here, I locked my car doors. Didn't make eye contact at red lights. On foot, on a non-game day … I shifted. Bounced once on my toes to keep my blood flow moving. Watched Chase's eyes drop to the open neck of my pullover. I zipped it up higher, and his eyes rose to mine, his mouth curving a little. "Or are you scared of something else?" He turned, gripping the other gatepost, blocking the exit as he stared me down. "Worried you can't control yourself without eyes on you?" He glanced up briefly, at the security cam in the corner, his meaning clear.

I was too old to be goaded into submission. I should walk away, continue my run in my safe little stadium, the guards watching, my dog following, my virtue protected. Through that gate, there was nothing for me but danger.

I turned away and reached for the phone on the wall. It rang to security and my conscience warred.

"It's Ty," I said, watching Chase, his eyes wary. "I'm leaving for the night."

 **81**

He needed her out of there. Out of Grant's world. Out of the cameras' sight. Every minute together, in that stadium, felt tainted. That should have been their home. They met there—fell in love there. That was *their* place, until it wasn't, until it became hers and Tobey's. And now, he couldn't breathe there. He could crush homers and have every person in it chant his name, but it was still ruined. He could bring them a trophy, and it would still belong to Tobey. *Just like Ty.*

They jogged down, along the fence, away from the lights. She ran quickly, the dog between them, his ears forward, eyes watching. A nasty looking dog. Full German Shepherd, its lack of leash had been intimidating in the stadium. Here, in the open street, it was terrifying. She didn't seem concerned, her occasional commands to the dog obeyed with perfect precision.

They ran past closed restaurants and shops, the streets quiet, cars sparse. She was quiet, and he said nothing, falling a step behind, his eyes on the curve of her ass, the swing of her arms. Like everything else, her run was seamless. Effortless.

"Stop looking at my butt." She tossed the comment over her shoulder, no hitch in her breath, her voice as calm and controlled as if she was standing still. He quickened his steps, lumbering up the hill next to her, his hand reaching out, cupping her elbow, pulling on it.

"Slow down." He sighed. "Walk a minute."

"I forgot." She slowed, looking over with a smile. "You're an old man."

"Yeah. Sure." He pulled his hat lower and made eye contact with a bum, the man looking away as they passed. "I'm ancient, and you're a freak of nature. Happy?"

"Yeah." She smiled, her steps slowing until they hit a speed he could handle without audibly wheezing. Maybe he needed to skip the weights a little. Get in more cardio.

"You do Ironmans in your spare time?" He wanted to grab her arm again. Then her waist. Pin her up against the next building and reclaim that mouth. Before, years ago, he could be around her without touching her. When had he lost that ability? Now, every minute with her was a battle of self-control, a fight to regain all of the years that they missed.

"Ha." She looked down, resting her hands on her hips, and he watched the heave of her chest as she let out a long breath.

He couldn't stop himself; he reached out, his hand settling on her back. "Let's stop, right there." He nodded ahead, at a food truck idling on the side street. "My treat."

 **82**

The beer was cold for the crisp night, but when paired with the hot Cuban sandwich, absolutely heavenly. We sat on a curb, hunched over our food, our shoulders often brushing. "He's a beautiful animal." Chase nodded to Titan.

"Thank you," I mumbled, finishing my mouthful of food. "What ended up happening with Casper?"

He paused for a moment before looking over. "Surprised you remember him."

"Did he move with you?"

He looked back down at his beer. "I wasn't in New York long enough to bring him. I tried in Baltimore, but..." He lifted his shoulders, glancing over at me with a wry smile. "He wasn't happy. And I felt guilty being on the road so much. Some girl once told me it was cruel ... that kind of stuck with me."

"Sounds like a smart girl," I shot back.

"In some ways she was." His smile lost its strength. "In other ways..." He tilted back his beer, watching me.

"I wasn't the only one who made dumb decisions back then, Chase," I said quietly. "You left. And you never came back, you never called." Thoughts I had said so many times in my head, a mantra that I had used, time and time again, to try and stop loving him.

"I was mad. And then, when I calmed down, your number was

disconnected. And then … not even a month later, you were with him." His voice had hardened, raw emotion, anger, still there and I pushed back, just as upset. "You didn't even give me time to sort out anything. To wrap my head around everything. I didn't know how to handle how I felt for you. And I didn't know how to handle it when I was traded. What was I supposed to do?"

"You could have flown here. Called my dad. It wasn't like you didn't have the resources—and I didn't have that. I didn't even have my own money to come and visit you—" My words broke off and I stared at the sandwich, numbly wrapping the paper around it, my appetite gone, four years of emotions welling to the surface. "You could have come." I whispered. *Rescued me.*

"You were engaged. Then married. So fast." He reached over, pulling at my hand, his thumb running over the place where my diamond normally sat. "Why?" he asked.

I swallowed, feeling the familiar push of tears, the thickening of my throat that occurred whenever I thought of the baby. "I was pregnant," I said simply, lifting my eyes to his, steeled for the reaction.

He froze, the only movement in his face the twitch of his eyes. They searched mine, reading everything in the moment before tears blurred my vision. I didn't move, I couldn't speak, couldn't give him any more information. His arm moved, his beer set down, and then he was brushing my hair carefully back, his warm hands cupping my face. "I'm sorry," he whispered.

"It's okay." I blinked, and a tear escaped, his eyes following it down my cheek. I watched him swallow, the part of his lips, a breath of hesitation before he spoke.

"Ty."

It was only one word, but a gruff plea that said everything. I lifted my gaze from his lips to his eyes and saw the hurt in them, the miss, the *need*. Need that I couldn't step away from. Need that I felt in every part of my body. "Take me somewhere, Chase."

He pulled me to my feet and nodded at the hotel, one block down, the sign glowing in the night. "There."

 **83**

I expected him to move fast.
I expected our touches to be frantic.
I thought it would be a fuck, hard and dirty, like an affair was supposed to be.
It was none of those things, yet it was everything.

"Ty." He breathed my name like it was life, shutting the hotel room door and flipping the switch; everything suddenly bathed in warm light. A small room. Wooden desk. Vintage chair. White bedspread. Big pillows. Glass wall. City lights. Chase had bribed the desk clerk to allow Titan's presence and I put him in the bathroom, firmly shutting the door. Chase stepped forward, and I stepped back, my shoulders hitting the door, my eyes closing when his head lowered to mine, the first kiss soft and hesitant, the second deeper, stronger. His fingertips brushed along my side, underneath my layers, and I lifted my hands, our kiss breaking as he rolled my shirt and pullover off. They hit the floor, our mouths met again, and there was the first brush of his bare hands on my skin.

Sweeping over my stomach, upward.
Soft in his cup of my breasts, his gentle lift, squeeze.
He pulled back from my mouth, his eyes falling to his hands, the skim of fingers across delicate skin, around and across my nipples. They stood at attention, and I gasped at the feather-soft contact.

His eyes darted to me at the sound, his fingers repeating the motion, whisper-light over them. "Harder?" he asked.

"No. Just like that."

"Close your eyes. Relax."

I did, leaning against the door, his fingers continuing their tease across my skin. "I've thought about these breasts for four years," he said gruffly. "What they looked like. Felt like." There was the drag of his cheek across the top of them, his hands cupping them against his face, and I gasped, my hands finding the top of his head and gripping his hair. The hot dart of a tongue, flicking across my nipple, a moment of suction, then a kiss, my body leaving the door as I twisted against him. "They are perfect, Ty. Even more perfect than they were before." His hands squeezed, almost too hard, and I inhaled sharply, my eyes opening, the room blurry, then focusing.

His head lifted, my hands fell from his hair, and he pulled me to the bed. "On your back," he choked out, yanking at his clothes, his long-sleeved shirt pulled over his head, his workout pants jerked down, underwear following suit, and I slid to the edge of the bed, my hands reaching for his waist, my eyes on his cock.

I reached out, but he stepped away, frowning, his hand going to it, wrapping around it. "No, Ty."

"I want it," I begged. "I want to touch it."

"Not to be un-gentlemanlike, but I haven't gone to bed in four years without jacking off to the thought of you. And it wasn't you on your knees. I have to touch you, baby. I have to fucking drink you in. And there isn't a thing that you can say to change that fact."

I pulled my eyes from his hand, from his cock, and looked into his face. Saw pain there, his voice almost shaking on his last words, the need in his eyes so strong it screamed.

"On your back," he repeated. "Pants off."

I held his gaze, my sneakers kicked aside, my leggings peeled off. I left on the underwear, a white thong, and he let out a soft sigh, standing alongside the bed, my body stretched out beside him, his hand sliding down, from sternum to tummy, sliding over the white cotton, his eyes closing briefly. "If you only knew, Ty."

I didn't ask. I didn't speak. I didn't think, had he said something else at that moment in time, that I could have handled it. He pulled the panties slowly, carefully, over my hips and off, his fingers lingering on their path, his eyes on his work, face unreadable. When he pulled the thong off my legs, he tossed it aside, looking up to my face.

"Sit up."

I did, propping up my body with my hands, my feet digging into the coverlet, knees raised. He knelt on the bed before me, the mattress sinking under his weight, his hands reaching for me, pulling me, until the backs of my thighs were against his, and we were face to face, my legs wrapping around his waist, my pussy against his cock. His eyes closed briefly, and he winced. "God, you have no idea how much you tempt me."

"It's not temptation if you can have it." I wrapped my arm around his neck, one of his hands tightening on my ass, bringing me closer, the other knotted in my hair, his mouth coming down for a kiss.

"But I don't have you, Ty. And once we do this..." His words fell into a groan, my free hand wrapping around his cock.

"Once we do this ... what?"

"I can't walk away."

I didn't want to have this talk. I wanted to forget life, forget obligations, forget everything but the two of us. I squeezed his hard length, looking down, at the look of us, everything on him hard against my soft, my hair wet with arousal against the ridges and lines of his shaft. I pulled back, away from him, and pushed his cock down, my name hissing from his lips in warning, everything going away the moment it was there, thick and perfect, my legs greedy in their pull closer, his hands tightening on my skin, hips thrusting. And then he pushed in. Deeper, deeper. My hands scrambled against his skin, clawing at it, my world bursting into light as he groaned my name and pushed the final inches home.

I gasped, he stilled, and there was a moment of pure fullness, his lips against mine, one sweet kiss that promised me everything, including heartbreak.

Then his hand tightened on my hair, he pulled from our kiss, lowering his head beside mine, his breath hot on my shoulder, fingertips biting into my ass, and he started to move.

I didn't know what I was thinking, my vision of Chase as a lover. I had thought it would be crude. Quick and dirty, like our meeting in the bathroom. I had thought he would be selfish. Demanding. I had been, in a thousand orgasmic ways, wrong.

I was wrong when he started, like that, our souls face-to-face, impossible to escape.

I was wrong when we moved, on our sides, my back to his front, his whisper on my neck, kisses brushing my shoulder, his hands everywhere, thrusts never stopping, not until the moment that my orgasm came, long and brutal, my body seizing around his cock.

I was wrong when he came, inside of me, my hands gripping the edge of the desk, him standing before me, gasping into our kiss, his hands in my hair, his final push so deep and solid that I bucked against it.

I was wrong when he carried me to the bed, and cleaned me up, his mouth following the washcloth, his tongue gentle, then stronger, knowing everything, leaving nothing, my final orgasm one that broke the record books, his name screamed loud enough that Brooklyn must have heard.

I was wrong when he crawled under the sheets behind me and wrapped his arms around me.

I was wrong when he told me he loved me, and I repeated it back.

"The detectives hadn't even considered an affair. That just wasn't the direction they were looking. Tobey and Ty Grant had always been baseball's golden couple, and the Yankee fans *loved* them. It was because of how iconic they were, of how much so many people believed in them—it was like if *they* didn't succeed as a couple, then there was no hope for the rest of us. And that ideal, that hero worship of their relationship was, quite literally, their kiss of death."

Dan Velacruz, *New York Times*

 **84**

"Stay."

"I can't stay." I sat up, sliding off the bed and eyeing my panties, damp and alone, on the floor. "I have to get back." *Before he wakes up.* I didn't want to turn and see the clock, was terrified of what it might say. It felt like we'd been in this room for decades. First the sex, then the spooning, then the conversation. Words about nothing, each of us trying to stretch out the time, a hopeless feat.

"What are you going to tell him?"

I gathered my clothes and sat at the desk, working on my panties, then my leggings. "I don't know."

He got off the bed, boxer briefs on, and walked over, picking up my shirt and helping me with it, the built-in sports bra a tight fit, his hands taking liberties in their pull of spandex over breasts. I smirked at him despite myself, taking the pullover from his hands and handling it myself.

He didn't smile back. He looked worried. "Maybe I should come with you."

"No." I grabbed my Nikes and sat down in the chair. I didn't know what he thought. That I was going to walk into my house, wake up my husband, and ask for a divorce? I couldn't do that to Tobey. I needed to think, to plan, to figure out—

"This isn't a fling, Ty." His words were hard, and I looked up at him, momentarily pausing my shoe-tying. "You aren't going to go back to him and occasionally fuck me when you are bored."

I finished the knot and stood. "Don't talk to me like that." I glared at him. "Do you think that's what I'm like? Seriously?"

"No." He shook his head with a scowl. "I don't. But I've lost you to him before. And I can't—"

"I understand."

"You *don't* understand. I've been alone for four years, haven't *touched* another woman, and you've been with him every … fucking … night." He gritted out the words and I searched his face, trying to understand the frustration I saw in it.

"You haven't—why not?" I'd seen hundreds of games, thousands of fans. I knew the type of girls, what they wore and how they pounced, especially on the single players, especially on the ones that looked like this man. There had been so many nights where I'd pictured Chase, where I'd cried over what he might be doing and who he might be doing it to. To think that he had been celibate this whole time … it twisted a place deep in my gut. "I didn't ask you to stay faithful," I said helplessly, while inside, a part of me sang.

"You never asked me anything, that was the whole problem, a lack of communication."

It was the merry-go-round of blame that wouldn't stop, each turn more exhausting, both of us equally to blame. I looked away and he let out a loud breath of frustration. "I tried to be with other women, Ty. I just couldn't. Every woman that I touched—it just felt like I was cheating on you. Each time, I couldn't get you out of my head."

It was what he didn't say that I heard the loudest. The fact that I hadn't struggled with the same guilt, the same feelings. For him to not be able to touch another woman—and for me to share Tobey's bed—my feelings must not have been as strong, my morals not as intact, my love incomplete in some way. I didn't have an answer for that, no excuse good enough, my cheeks heating with the shame of it all.

"Do you love him?" There wasn't judgment in his voice, only dread.

"I'm *married* to him," I said helplessly. "We've been ... it's been four years. We created and lost a child together. It's not as simple as..."

"So you love him," he said flatly. "Still."

"I can't just delete feelings because of a trade." *Because of a kiss. Because of a fuck.* I swallowed. "But I can tell you that my love for him..." I stepped closer to him, placing a hand on his chest. "It doesn't touch this. It doesn't even come close. And it never has."

He covered my hand with his, his touch gentle as it pried my palm away, turning it over, his head dipping to kiss the soft skin of my inner wrist. "I know that, Ty. I believe it." His eyes lifted to mine, and there was pure torture in their depths. "And if I didn't love you so strongly, it'd be easier for me to watch you go back to him." His hand tightened on mine. "Promise me you'll leave him."

"For what?" I said, feeling helpless, my world shaky in every piece of its foundation. "What do you want from me?"

His eyes softened, his mouth, when it pressed to me, gentle and soft, a plea of lips against a weak soul. "Everything. I want a life with you. I want to be the father of your children. I want every second we missed and a million more. And I'll give away the world to get it."

A sweet sentiment. But I couldn't leave Tobey, and I couldn't leave the Yankees. Not now. Not when somewhere in this city, a girl's death sentence loomed.

 **85**

I leaned back against his chest, on the balcony of the room, eight floors above the street, his arms around me, his mouth nuzzling at the curve of my neck.

"I have to go," I said softly.

"Don't." His arms tightened for a fraction of a moment, the touch weakening my resolve.

I watched a taxi roll to a stop, a young girl stepping out. I thought of April McIntosh, in that dumpster, and wondered if she was taken there by car or carried. "What do you know about the curse?" I asked, my words so faint I almost repeated them. The curse. Such a stupid phrase, yet so fitting for the dark cloud it put over all of our lives.

He stiffened, his arms dropping and he turned me until we were face to face. "My publicist briefed me on them. When that girl was found in my jersey."

"Julie Gavin."

"Why do you ask?"

It was cold on the balcony, a stiff breeze hitting my bare arms, and I fought the urge to shiver. I leaned against his chest, my cheek on his shirt, and looked down the street, my eyes floating over dark buildings, past hundreds of sleeping bodies and empty offices, the hour too late for life. "I think of them all the time." I said quietly.

"You should have brought me back sooner." There was the hint of a smile in his voice and I frowned.

"We don't exactly know the winning combination," I said, pulling away from him. "We're guessing at everything. What his motivations are, if it's even a man, if he's obsessed with you or the World Series…" Just another part of my life that I didn't know, couldn't control.

"The first girl died the year I left?"

"Yeah." *Rachel, in the alley.*

"And there's been one every year since? Always on the last day of the season? Or the playoffs?"

"Yeah." *April in the dumpster. Julie at the stadium. Tiffany at our home. RachelAprilJulieTiffany.* I shivered, and it had nothing to do with the cold.

"Maybe it will stop this year. If we win."

"And then what—it'll start again if we lose next year?" I pushed away, out of his warmth, and rubbed at my forehead, the stress mounting. It was a possibility that Tobey and I had never discussed, neither wanting to imagine it. This hell might never end. There were just too many people in this city. Too many girls. Too many possible killers. They might never catch this guy. I knew that, in some hopeless part of my heart.

"It's not your problem, Ty. It won't be your problem. You'll be with me."

"Where?" I lifted my arms, gesturing to the city. "This is my home." I turned right, pointing to the stadium in the distance. *Yankee Stadium.* "*That* is my home."

"You chose that home before. Back then." He fixed me with a hard look, his jaw flexing as he crossed his arms over that beautiful chest.

"And it hasn't made you happy."

No, it hadn't. Still, the thought of leaving it, them, him ... it was terrifying. Would I be able to do it?

I rubbed at the empty place where my watch wasn't, my desire to stay trumped by a sudden panic at how long I'd been gone. "I've got to go. Really."

He grabbed my arm, stopping me halfway through the balcony door. "I can't hide this, Ty. The next time I see you, I'm pinning you against a wall and kissing you. I don't care who is nearby; I don't care who sees."

I pulled my arm away and stepped into the room. "Don't threaten me, Chase." I opened the door to the bathroom, Titan ready, body tensed for a command.

"It's not a threat. It's just—I've waited a long time for you, Ty. Don't ask me to wait any longer. Not after tonight."

I reached for the doorknob. "Stay here. I've got Titan with me; I'll be fine on the way back."

"You can't go back alone—" he protested, his hand hard as he held the door shut. I watched the muscles of his forearm flex, and Titan let out a low growl.

I turned my head, looking into his eyes. "I'll be fine."

Our eye contact warred for a moment, and his reluctant push off the door was one that surrendered more than it understood. I opened the door and let Titan out, stepping forward and stealing one last kiss in the moment before I stepped through.

He said nothing. Not *I love you*. Not *goodbye*. He stood in that doorway and watched as I walked down to the elevator, my quick glance back catching his eyes. I could have run to him. Jumped into his arms and let him take me away. Out of this life, away from Tobey and the team and the deaths. He had money, we had love. He could quit the game and we could screw everything and retire to a beach, our days spent with nothing but sunscreen and margaritas, sunrise massages and afternoon orgasms. I'd have babies and he'd coach little league and we'd be happy. I could taste that future as clearly as I could breathe. And I wanted it so hard my chest ached.

Instead, I got on the elevator, Titan licking my shin before settling against my leg, his eyes fixed on the door. I got off the elevator, walked through the lobby, and out onto the street. And there, I ran. I ran as fast as I could, Titan stuck to my side, my heart hard in my chest by the time we hit the stadium gates. I stopped at the security stand, gasping for breath, my hello short and stilted, a genuine smile of relief coming when I saw the guard reach down and hold out my bag. I hadn't thought about it, had left it on the field, my keys and my phone inside.

"You worried us, Mrs. Grant, leaving your bag and your vehicle. You should have let us know you were going for a run. We tried your cell, but—"

"—it was in the bag." I wiped at my face, my hand coming away damp. "I know. Sorry about that."

"Hopefully we didn't disturb Mr. Grant."

I paused. "What?"

"We tried Mr. Grant's cell phone. When we couldn't get yours. Hopefully it wasn't too much of a disturbance."

I wanted to crawl through the window of the security hut and shake the man. Quiz him five ways from Sunday. Did Tobey answer? What did they tell him? Did they pull footage? Mention Chase? I swallowed everything, pulling my phone from my bag. "I'll call him now. Thanks."

"Absolutely, Mrs. Grant. Have a good day."

I nodded, feeling faint, my legs wobbly as I walked through the entrance, taking the side path toward the parking garage, afraid to look at my phone.

I had never been scared of Tobey before. But suddenly, without even seeing my phone, I was terrified.

What had I done?
Why had I done it?
And what would I tell him now?

86

I didn't call Tobey. I didn't want to risk waking him up, on the slim chance that he'd gone back to bed. I loaded Titan into the back, then climbed into my SUV and drove home to face him. Before I pulled out of the garage, I sent him a text. *On my way home. I'm safe. Love you.*

It was four in the morning. Too early in the morning to make a life-changing decision. But too late in the game to lie anymore. I could see myself becoming a different woman, the kind who snuck around, who lied, who cheated. Too easily could I fall into that role. The truth of the matter was, for Chase, I think I was born for that role. I had been his since the moment we met. Everything else, everything with Tobey, had been a lie. A lie I'd told myself since my pregnancy, but started believing in recent years.

The car rolled over bumpy New York streets, and I glanced at the time again, hesitating. Then I reached for my phone, and unlocked it, my dial of digits slow.

It rang only twice, and then he answered.

At the sound of his voice, I started crying.

 **87**

Dad let me cry, not saying anything, his silence comforting across six thousand miles of space. When I finally stopped—hiccupping once, then twice—my final sniffles long and wet, he spoke.

"Tell me what happened, Ty."

"I messed up." I pulled into a closed gas station, putting the Range Rover in park and digging into my center console, finding an abandoned napkin and blowing my nose into it. "And I don't know how to fix it."

"Is it Chase?"

I stopped, surprised by the question. I shouldn't have been. The man knew me better than anyone. "Yeah."

"You slept with him?"

"Yeah."

"Was he Logan's daddy?"

Fresh tears leaked. "No," I whispered. "That was my first ... Tobey was my first. That was the truth."

He let out a hard breath. "I'm sorry, Ty. I wish—" He sighed. "I wish I could have done a better job of protecting you."

I looked out the window, the sky already lighter, my clock ticking. "It wasn't you. I was stupid."

"All teenage girls are stupid, Ty. I shouldn't have let you marry Tobey. Even if it was the decent thing to do."

I said nothing, staring at the skyline, a narrow glimpse of it between two buildings. There was a long stretch of silence before I spoke. "What do I do, Dad?"

"You know what to do, Ty."

"Spikes first?" I guessed, my voice cracking.

"Spikes first."

"You haven't even asked if I love him."
"Oh Ty." He chuckled. "Why do you think I tried so hard to keep you from him? You've been in love with that boy since the moment he set foot in our stadium."

I wiped under my eyes with the napkin, then balled it in my fist. "World Series is in a month."

"I know."

"This will be the fifth year, Dad. The fifth girl."

"You can't think like that, Ty. Whatever psychopath is out there, you can't change fate to please him. And we don't even know, for sure, what he wants. If a World Series ring would even stop this at all."

"I know." I heard the words, but could only think of Tiffany Wharton's face. So pretty. So young—younger than me.

"Dad?" I said, in the moment before he hung up.

"Yeah?"

"I'm sorry for not telling you."

I could hear his smile in his words. "I knew, baby. I *always* knew. I lost that battle from the start."

"Spikes first?" I asked weakly. "You sure?"

"Those men know the danger. You have to go after what you want. You've spent long enough making all of us happy."

"Okay. I love you."

"Love you too."

I hung up the phone, taking a moment to compose myself before pulling out and heading home, my foot stronger on the gas, my hands trembling on the wheel.

I knew what I had to do. And unfortunately, Dad and Chase wouldn't be happy about it.

88

2009 was our last World Series win. Before that, 2002. Since 2009, billions had been spent, all in hopes of one winning season and the series that haunted all of our dreams. A series that would lead to a ring. It was our obsession. We had worked so hard for this. And I'd be damned if I would be the one responsible for us losing, not with it in such clear and attainable sight.

If I told Tobey about Chase, he'd release him. There was no doubt in my mind of that. Regardless of the killer, Tobey wouldn't walk into that stadium and watch my lover in a Yankee uniform. Chase would be gone by morning, and our World Series hopes would be *gone*. Our team wasn't good enough without him. That was the bottom line.

Dad wanted me to go after what I wanted? I wanted our boys to bring home a ring. I wanted the deaths to stop. I wanted to stop lying. I wanted to spend the rest of my life with the man I loved.

I just needed to find a way to accomplish all of that.

I pulled up to our home, my stomach twisted in a hard and painful knot.

 **89**

Tobey was asleep. I stood, shocked, in our bedroom doorway, the rising sun hidden behind our blackout shades. I had practiced a variety of defenses and excuses, fully prepared to walk in the door to a distraught husband. Yet, three or four hours after I normally got home, he was asleep, his hand stretched out on my empty side of the bed, the blankets bunched around his waist, his upper back exposed. I dropped my bag by the door and walked quietly to his bedside table, picking up his cell and unlocking it. His ringer had been off, two missed calls, two voicemails from the stadium, my text unread. I unlocked it and deleted the missed calls, the voicemails, and my text. Then I replaced it, pulling off my clothes and stepping into our bathroom, my shower quick, my sneak into bed done without waking him.

I carefully lifted his hand and slid next to him, his body rolling to his side, eyes remaining closed, his features relaxed in sleep. I studied him for a minute, the first in a long time. When we'd first married, I'd often stared at him in the night, wondering about the man I had walked down the aisle to, so much about him unknown. I had thought, back then, that he was handsome. He'd changed, his boyish good looks faded, his features harder in their lines as he lost any youthful fat. But he was certainly a handsome man. One who turned his fair share of heads. And he loved me, something I seemed to constantly remind myself of. I'd done that for a long time. Overlooked my own depth of love because of our friendship, the strength of our marriage. This would all be easier if he was a jackass. This would all be easier if he had a mistress, or a stable of affairs, or if he was unhappy. I had no excuse for my behavior, nothing to blame it on, except that I'd never really been *in* love with him. My heart, it just hadn't been available to give.

And maybe that was the only reason that mattered. Maybe if I *had* loved him, and he had been a bunch of terrible things, then I would have overlooked all of them, just as he overlooked my lack of love.

When his alarm went off, I closed my eyes and pretended to be asleep.

 **90**

The email was on my phone, waiting there, when I rolled over, light filling the room. Tobey's side of the bed was empty, the house quiet. I didn't see it until after I was dressed, a bagel in hand, stepping out onto the porch to eat. I hadn't expected an email, my hand stalling as I lifted the bagel to my mouth. I sat in one of the rockers, and clicked on the email, one sent to my Boys and Girls Club email, Chase's name in the sender's column.

Ty,
When can I see you again? Call me. 329-222-0114.
I love you.
Chase

I replied to his message, my fingers slow, mind struggling to find the right words.

Chase,
I just need some time. Please give me until the end of the season. But know that I meant everything I said.
Ty

It didn't feel right, typing *I love you* into that email. Not when I was sitting in Tobey's home, wearing his ring. I was still married, despite the things I had done the night before. I sent the email, then stood, resisting the urge to chuck the phone off the side of the porch and to its death.

 **91**

That's three weeks away. I meant what I said last night. If I see you, I will touch you. Kiss you. Take you. And it won't be as gently as it was in that hotel room. That was my worship of you. I have a hundred more ways to make you scream my name and all of them are filthy.
I love you. I want you. Every day for the rest of my life.
Chase

I read the email a second time, memorizing its lines, then deleted it. Sliding my phone into my purse, I smiled a thank you to the waitress, sitting back as she cleared my plate. I watched as Tobey returned, his eyes on me as he strolled toward our table.

"Guess who I saw in the men's room." He sat down, pulling up his chair to the table.

"Who?"

"James Singletary."

I raised my eyebrows in interest, the lines of Chase's email running through my head. "How'd he look?"

"Good. And sober. He said he's with the Mets now."

"I'll ask Nancy about it next time I see her." James had been a pitching coach for us, had helped Dad for a bit, until his drinking had gotten out of control and he'd been fired. I took a sip of my tea, my fingers tightening on the china.

"Everything okay? You seem..." he tilted his head, studying me, "subdued."

Subdued. Maybe that was what depression dipped in false cheer looked like. That was how I felt: depressed. Depressed and deceptive. These three weeks would be hell. I tried my best to smile. "I'm fine."

He raised a hand to catch the waiter's attention. "I've got to meet with Dick. You want to come?" Gone was the man who'd retreated into himself after Tiffany Wharton's death, his stress hitting manic levels. This man was the Tobey of old, one I hadn't seen in years.

Go to the stadium? *If I see you, I will touch you.* "Oh, I can't." I gave my best regretful smile. "I've got a bunch of donations I've got to drop off at the Club."

"Missing your chance to gloat over our record?" He grinned. "This is a prime opportunity to rub our record in Dick's face. Stern's proven to be a game changer for us."

A game changer for us. I suddenly felt sick to my stomach. "Dick chose Stern," I reminded him. "I didn't do anything other than push for Perkins to leave."

"Being modest?" Tobey arched a brow at me. "Who are you, and what have you done with my wife?"

His wife. He thought he knew me. And in some ways, he did. In a thousand other ways, we were still strangers. From the beginning, I'd kept so much from him. Yet he'd still fallen in love with the shell of me. Our waiter saved me, his offer to refill my drink distracting enough to change the course of our conversation.

We stood as one, Tobey's hand soft on my back as we walked out. "Do you want me to come by the house and pick you up for the game?"

"No." I shook my head. "I'll have one of the drivers take me. Meet you in the box?"

"Sure." He leaned down, brushing his lips over mine. "See you around six?"

I nodded, flashing him a smile, and reached for my valet ticket, handing it to the man, the escape to my vehicle quick, my lips still burning from his kiss.

"It was a detective, David Thorpe, who tied the first two girls to Julie Gavin. He created a profile on Julie and then compared it to every unsolved murder, going back five years. Once he'd connected Rachel and April to Julie, and the word 'serial killer' started to be thrown around, the attention on the case exploded. And that's when the pressure on the team, and on Ty and Tobey, really started."

Dan Velacruz, *New York Times*

 **92**

"I don't have a lot of time for this." Tobey glanced at his watch, the gold piece glinting in the dim light of his office.

"It won't take long," the man's voice was gravel, a familiar one heard often in the last few years. Detective Thorpe. The man who came to us about Julie Gavin, then again the afternoon I found Tiffany Wharton. The man who now stood before us, his hands tucked in cheap suit pockets, and tilted his head at me. "This is about you, Mrs. Grant."

"Me?" I met his eyes.

"With the season wrapping up, we'd like you to arrange for extra security. Just in case."

"You think Ty's in danger?" Tobey stepped forward, his hand possessive as it touched the small of my back, his fingers burning through the fabric of my silk shirt.

"With the girls being blonde, and similar to Mrs. Grant, that is reason enough for concern. But each death seems to be getting closer to both of you."

"You're assuming he's going to kill again," Tobey said flatly. "Maybe he won't."

"Extra security wouldn't hurt. Especially on game nights. It looks like you'll be in the playoffs—"

"We will." There was a note of pride in Tobey's voice that I wanted to erase. It didn't belong here, not in this moment.

"But it'd be good for the security to start now. We can provide deputies but figured that you'd have your own security team."

Tobey nodded curtly. "Yes. And we can hire additional resources if necessary."

Any thoughts of sneaking away to see Chase disappeared. I pasted a smile and nodded in agreement. "Thank you for the warning." I didn't want more security. For the same reason that I'd insisted on Titan. My freedom, my independence—even before Chase—was crucial, an ingredient for my sanity.

"It's odd," Margreta said, lifting her wine glass and peering at me over the edge.

"What is?" I took the bait, not particularly interested in the answer. I flipped a page of the magazine, watching as Caleb ran by with a shriek, his hands outstretched for the dog. Behind us, their pool glinted in the late afternoon sun.

"You and Tobey, how much time you spend apart."

I raised my eyebrows at the woman, one whose husband made business trips at every spare opportunity. "We work together," I pointed out. "Every day." Ten hour days, focused on the team, the players, the marketing, the machine. I didn't mind it. I loved it, loved the focus it required. I could get lost in those details, in that goal.

"I know that." She waved her hand, like my time at the Yankees was nothing. "I'm talking about outside of the team. Don't you think a husband and wife should share something other than baseball?"

I wasn't sure exactly what the woman wanted. Tobey to take a dedicated interest in my work with the Boys and Girls Club? Or to start running with me? Or for me to join him on his golf days and poker runs? I swallowed a grimace and turned my head toward the magazine, glancing casually at my watch, my patience with social chitchat waning.

At that time, I couldn't imagine a life like that. One where we did everything together. One where his life started and mine ended, a continuous line without break, without private moments for myself. Those blocks of time away from Tobey ... that was when I could think of Chase.

I thought of him, and how everything had changed since he'd come back. Every moment, whether with others or alone, had become invaded by thoughts of him. It was scary how much I needed him. How much, after so many years apart, the feelings had rushed back. Stronger. More urgent. In 2011, I'd had no fear of loss. I had fallen for him and hadn't thought about anything else. Now, knowing that a life without him could exist ... I was terrified of losing him again. If it happened again, I wouldn't recover. I felt that in every bone of my body. And I feared it, just as strongly.

I watched the detective walk out, Tobey's head bent to him, their voices low and concerned, and mentally counted the days until the Series.

As it turned out, I wasn't the only one counting. And I wasn't the only one watching us all. I thought I was sneaky. I thought our love was invisible.

I was a fool.

 **93**

Chase,
I can't avoid the stadium; I will be at the games with Tobey. I need you to stay away from me. Please.
Ty

The skybox was too hot. I pulled at the front of my shirt and fanned myself with the program. The waitress came by, and I caught her eye.

"Another beer?" she asked.

"Yes. In the bottle, please." I stood and walked to the window, placing my forehead on the glass, cold from the outside air, resisting the urge to yank open my shirt and press my skin against the cool glass. Down on the field, Chase stood, his glove resting against one thigh, his cap low, eyes on the batter, jersey stretched tight over his shoulders. I'd watched him the entire game—every play, every catch, every at-bat. And he hadn't looked up here. Not once.

I should have been happy. All my fears about him pushing the envelope, revealing our relationship with some big obvious gesture, unfounded.

I should have been happy, but I wasn't. Instead, I only wanted him more.

**94**

A meeting with Pepsi finished, my cell phone was out, an email begun, when I stepped off the elevator, into the parking level, my Range Rover waiting, a navy tank of luxury.

I stopped short, the note stuck in the driver's window, tiny and white, like cocaine, deadly in its draw. I unlocked the door, pulling the paper out and palming it, and then stepped into my truck, unnoticed. I unfolded it quickly, spreading it out on my lap.

Same place. Envelope at the desk for you. Now.

The handwriting was tight; the pen used was running out of ink. I wondered when he had written it, how many minutes I had wasted, sitting in that conference room, negotiating sponsorship details and discussing trivial items.

Same place. The hotel we had walked into, a random stop on a Bronx street. I didn't have to go. I could drive by it and get the name. Call the front desk and have them give him a message. Drive back to the house and wait for tonight's game. *I have a hundred more ways to make you scream my name and all of them are filthy.*

I texted Tobey. *Going to run errands. I'll be home in a few hours.* Then I shifted the truck into reverse.

I knew it was wrong. But I was only human.

I didn't notice the car that followed me.

 **95**

Room 908. I didn't check out the view, I didn't examine the furnishings. I opened the door, dropped my jacket and purse on the floor, and saw him.

He stood by the desk, a phone to his ear, and he turned, his eyes skating over me before he spoke into the receiver. "I have to go." He dropped the phone and turned to me, pushing up the sleeves of his sweater and walking toward me, a stalk that turned into a rush, his collision with me one that had his hands in my hair, mouth rough against my own, his body warm and hard. There was the brush of a finger against the bare skin of my cleavage, then he yanked, pulling my blouse over my head, my hands frantically unbuttoning my pants, working them over my hips, my heels kicked off, his eyes dark as he watched. Then he was pulling at his own shirt, red fabric lifting to reveal line after line of perfect abs, his muscles so beautiful, so strong, so capable. I ran my fingers up the side of his stomach, marveling at the definition, his hand shoving my touch lower. "Take it out," he gritted, pushing on my shoulder, his sweater hitting the floor beside me.

"On the bed," I said, starting to stand, his hand assertive, keeping me in place.

"No. Right here, Ty. In front of the mirror. Pull out my cock and wrap those perfect lips around it."

I glanced beside me, noticing, for the first time, the full-length mirrored doors of the closet, the woman in the reflection, half-crouched, her lips swollen, hair everywhere. My breasts half hung out of the top of my bra, my hand gripped his pants, my other on his belt. His body towered over mine, dominance over subservience, our eyes meeting in the mirror. I didn't recognize that reflection, the wild look in my eyes, the urge I had to reach down and touch myself, to relieve the throbbing need there.

I watched his face in the mirror. Watched his hand as it settled on the back of my head. I turned away from the reflection, my knees hitting the carpet, and pulled down his zipper. Reached inside and pulled out his beautiful cock. I stared it at for a full heartbeat, wrapping my fingers around his girth, as it stiffened in my hand, his growl of words pushing me on, his fingers biting into my shoulder as he spoke. "In your mouth. Please. Before I lose it."

I let go, my hands settling on his thighs, their muscles tensing under my touch, a million bucks of talent right there, yet nothing compared to the organ they led to. Just two weeks ago I had it, a taste I still hadn't recovered from. I knew what it could do, knew how it felt, the places it could take me. I leaned forward, my mouth hovering over its base, and exhaled, my hot breath coming out slowly as I moved down his length, it twitching, bobbing against my lips. Chase's hand tightened on me, but I didn't stop, didn't rush, my tongue taking its time as it darted out, tentative, then stronger, my hands staying on his thighs, my mouth exploring the veins of his shaft, the ridge of his head, the thick knot of muscles at his base. When I finally took him in, as deeply in my wet mouth as I could, sucking down the length of him, he cried my name. Whispered a string of unintelligible words as he thrust into my mouth.

I closed my eyes. Cleared my mind. My world dark, the only thing that existed was our connection. My palms, flush against the warm iron of his thighs. His push in and out of my mouth, my tongue against the underside of his cock, the taste of him, the sounds of him…

"Being inside your mouth is better than I fucking imagined, Ty. God, I love how you suck my cock." He bent forward, the angle of his cock changing, and undid my bra, the weight of my breasts suddenly hanging free, my loose bra now one more piece of maddening arousal, the lace of it brushing against my nipples with every thrust of him down my throat.

He suddenly brought me to my feet, pulling from my mouth, his hands on my arms, lifting me up, the bed suddenly underneath me.

Everything the same as before, all of the elements, yet everything was different. He was rougher, wilder, his control questionable, his take of me more of a gorge than a savor. He stripped me of my thong and spread my legs, his fingers slow and careful, running along every part of me, pushing inside, then over my clit, before his tongue took over. Every other sexual experience, my knowledge of the world, dimmed when he put his mouth on me. I clawed at his scalp, I dug my heels into his back, I lost the ability to speak, every piece of me tuned to the swipe of his tongue, the cover of his lips, the heat of his mouth. Inside me, against me, along the most sensitive places. I whispered his name, then screamed it, over and over, my orgasm harder and harder … waves of pleasure building until everything in my body was liquid and everything in my world was lost, then he moved up and pushed himself inside, and everything was found.

"So much happened in those final weeks leading up to the 2015 World Series. With Chase Stern on the team, everything was finally coming together. But with Ty getting involved with him ... everything was also falling apart. Of course the fans didn't know that. The fans, hell, *everyone*, thought that this would be the year. The year that we won. The year that everything in New York returned to normal. And it kind of was. Just not in the way that everyone imagined. Certainly not in the way that I'd imagined."

Dan Velacruz, *New York Times*

 **96**

Chase,
If I leave him now, he will release you, and we will lose the Series. I can't do that.
Ty

It said something about my marriage that Tobey hadn't noticed anything was wrong. That he hadn't noticed that it'd been a month since we'd had sex. Our winning streak had helped, each game, each win, giving another shot of testosterone into his life. With us successful, trudging our way up the hill toward a ring, I didn't think he'd notice if I shaved my head. His focus was one hundred percent on the team. Maybe it'd always been, being one of the things that made our marriage work. Both of us, standing on the Yankee sideline, in our pinstripes, breathing blood, sweat, and tears into the organization, everything focused on their success.

Richards swung, and Tobey and I rose as one, watching as the ball shot, low and deadly, toward third base, skimming past the baseman and bouncing on the grass, our runner shooting off the base and pounding toward home. Tobey's hand grabbed mine, and both of us tensed until the moment his foot hit the plate. We screamed, his arms wrapping tightly around me, his kiss pressed into my hair, his voice gruff as he whispered an *I love you* into my hair.

I loved him too. My best friend. My partner. But whatever embers of love I felt for Tobey was nothing compared to my love for Chase. That was a wildfire, burning hot and mad and out of control, eating everything in sight. It consumed my marriage and left only charred black.

Part of me hated this, hated what I was doing to Tobey, to my marriage. The other part of me just wanted to be free, just wanted to be happy, just wanted to be with the man I loved.

OCTOBER

**97**

American League Championship

Ty,
I hate that you're choosing baseball over us. This feels like a business decision.
Chase

Game 5. We won the championship in spectacular fashion, four games to one. Two homers by Chase brought in a total of four runs, the team clicking, our fielding seamless, the Angels not standing a chance. We popped champagne in the skybox, the air brimming with excitement, Dick pulling me in for a rare hug, shouts and cheers loud in the space. I turned to the field, watching the team jump around each other, bodies colliding, a pile of celebration, more boys than grown men.

I watched the team and tried to find his jersey, number 28 finally spotted. He turned, his eyes finding mine in the skybox, and I smiled. He didn't. His face darkened, and I jumped, caught off guard when Tobey's arms wrapped around my waist, his mouth nuzzling my neck, a kiss against my cheek.

"I love you so much," he murmured, turning me to him, my eyes darting away from Chase, reluctantly pulled by Tobey, his mouth firmly settling on my lips. The kiss saved me from answering, and when we parted, I smiled, glancing back at the field, but couldn't find Chase.

98

Chase
It's less than two weeks. Deal with it. This team has been my world for twelve years. I'm leaving it and everything I know for you.
Ty

I was going crazy from not going to the field, my nightly runs taking Titan and me through the ivy-covered elegance of our neighborhood. The run was boring, but safe, the field too risky, security increased, the chance of Chase there too great.

The other issue, one I didn't want to face, was that he might not be at the field. I would spend two hours running, throwing, sweating … all in an empty stadium, my eyes scanning for a strong build I wouldn't find. It would be a blow that I didn't want to take, my psyche much more comfortable with the thought of him there, waiting. It was a fucked-up thought process, but one that still had me running down a cobblestone street, past private security gates and expensive lanterns, my fingers itching for a glove and ball.

One week, and I would leave my husband. Tonight, he had reached for me, his touch tender as he'd undone my dress, sliding it over my shoulders and down to the floor. I hadn't known what to do, how to act, my kiss reluctant when he'd turned me to him. "I've got to go for a run," I'd whispered. "Can we do this when I get back? Take a shower together then?"

He'd studied me, his fingers running down my arm, closing on my hands and bringing one up to his mouth, a kiss brushed over my knuckles. "Don't take too long," he'd said.

I was now on my sixth mile, my legs pounding up the hill, the night cold against hot muscles, my breath hard. I was far from home, the buildings unfamiliar, and I had a surge of exhilaration at the thought that I might be lost. Then Titan's tail brushed against my legs, his ears up, and I remembered my traveling companion, the animal that could find his way home with his eyes covered.

I couldn't avoid Tobey forever. Maybe stalling was stupid, my quest for a ring just an excuse to put off the inevitable. Maybe I should run home, right then, and tell him I was leaving. I didn't even have to mention Chase. I could just tell him that I wasn't in love with him anymore. That I was unhappy.

The problem was that I still loved Tobey. There was still affection there. History there. We had created and lost a life together.

But I wasn't unhappy. I loved my life, my team. I had spent so much time in pinstripes that it felt like my skin. And leaving Tobey, shaving the Grant off the end of my name ... I would be leaving the Yankees too. *Forever.* Tears pricked the edges of my eyes at just the thought of it.

Stupid to feel such attachment to an organization. But the Yankees weren't just an organization. They were a life force, etched in tradition and history, fortunes, fates and days made on the backs of some of the greatest bats to ever swing in this country. I wasn't just divorcing Tobey. I was cutting out half of my heart and giving the remainder to Chase.

What if he crushed it?

What would I have left?me.

 99

Are you still fucking him?

Tobey was still awake when I climbed the stairs, my turn of our knob quiet, but my heart jumped at the sight of him, sitting by the fire, his shoulders hunched forward, elbows on his knees, eyes on the television. I thought it had been long enough, the hour late, his drinks at dinner heavy, but I was wrong. He clicked off the television and stood, the room suddenly darkened, the flicker of the fire painting his face red, his features half in shadow.

He said nothing, just pulled at my shirt, up and over my head. Then my sports bra. I was taken back to that hotel room, my back against the door, Chase's breath heavy. I opened my eyes and willed it away, meeting Tobey's eyes, his hands quick on their pull at my pants, and he gave me one long kiss before he stepped to the bathroom.

The shower started, a steady patter of drops against tile.
Steam floated off the spray, my hands helping him as he undressed.
The loosening of his tie—pulling the silk slowly through the knot.
The unbuttoning of his shirt—pushing it off, my eyes floating over the tattoo on his shoulder, the initials of our unborn son, the letters curling through an orchid bloom. I swallowed a lump of emotion and pulled at the thick leather of his belt, his hands brushing over my breasts, gentle and soft, as I undid the top of his dress pants and pushed them down.

In the shower, his hands ran over my hair, pulling out the elastic. The froth of bubbles, soap on his palms, slick against my skin. He stood behind me, the sting of water everywhere, our slick bodies constantly touching, brushing. We kissed under the spray, it dripping in my eyes, in our mouths, our touch growing stronger, frantic. I gripped him, and he bit at my lip. He turned me, tilting me forward, his hand brushing over me, fingers sliding in me, and I moaned when he pushed inside, half a cry of pleasure, half one of pain.

I cried in that shower. I held on to the stone wall, his hands settling on my waist, gripping me there, my face turned sideways, cheek pressed against the rough cut of granite, and silently sobbed, every thrust an invasion, not just of my body, but of my heart. He fucked me, and I remembered so much. So many times he was wonderful. So many times he was sweet. So many minute moments that made me love him. I didn't fall, but I grew in love with this man. This man who fucked me in his shower and mistook my cries for pleasure. The one who turned me around, lifting me up, his kiss missing the salt of my tears, the pour of water from overhead erasing all evidence, his cock pushing back in, my legs around his waist, his hands holding me up, our movement slow and beautiful.

Slow and beautiful.
Heart breaking. Of mine as much as his.

And he never knew. He bit out a cry as he finished, thrusting deep inside of me, my nails tightening against his skin, my hands shaking as he lowered my feet to the ground, his final kiss soft and sweet, his thank you almost lost in the sound of the water.

I didn't look at him as I dried off. I didn't speak as I crawled into bed. I waited until the sound of his snores drifted across the room, and then I let myself cry.

I emailed Chase back in the middle of the night, a blanket wrapped around my shoulders, my butt on the bare floor, my back against the foot of the bed, the flames of our fire flickering before me, the phone heavy in my hand as I pressed SEND and dropped it to the floor beside me.

No. not anymore.

 **100**

World Series: Game 1

It was us against the Cubs, the Series starting in New York, and would finish here, in our stadium. My last games in pinstripes.

"Tell me what's going on." My father's voice scraped through the receiver, sounds of the airport behind him. He and Carla were coming home, their flight getting them in with only a couple of hours to spare. They would watch the game from our box, fully clad in team apparel, Dad's number retired and already in the Yankees' Hall of Fame.

"I'm waiting until after the series." I eyed Tobey through the window, by the pool, a phone to his ear, his hands gesturing, face upset. Probably on the phone with his sister. Margreta wasn't coming to the game, a development that had infuriated Tobey and given me a tiny bit of pleasure. The woman liked to chat, and I was the most frequent recipient. I couldn't be polite with her anymore, not today. Not when we were in the World Series, and I was days away from leaving her brother. Not when I had Tobey beside me, and Chase before me, my dad watching the entire thing. It'd be hard enough as it was, without her asking questions, her eyes critical, seeing everything, the woman a damn vulture without a bone.

"This is a big decision, Ty. Are you sure about it?"

"I am." It felt like the first decision I had ever made for myself. Funny that it would be the biggest of my life.

"If he hurts you, I will kill him." My father's threat made me smile, the vigor behind it warming my heart.

"I don't think he'll hurt me. I think he's more worried about me hurting him."

"Good."

I watched Tobey sit down in one of our patio chairs, his legs stretching out. I considered my words carefully before speaking. "I know it was embarrassing, Dad, when I got pregnant."

"You've never been an embarrassment."

"*This* will be embarrassing. Tobey will—" my words broke off. I didn't know what Tobey would do. "He might try to punish you. The tickets, the box ... all of that will be gone."

"You think I care about sitting in an air-conditioned box next to them?" Dad swore, and I heard the shush of Carla next to him. "I care about you. I want you to be happy. It's all I've ever wanted for you. Don't worry about me."

I smiled despite myself. "Thanks."

"See you tonight. Take care of yourself 'til then."

"Always do."

He hung up, and I locked my phone, taking one last look at Tobey before stepping away from the window.

The game was six hours out.

Third inning. Neither team had scored. I stood from my seat and stretched. Walked to the window. Stared down at the dugout. Walked back.

"You don't like baseball?" the idiot of a woman before me tittered, her straw swirling in a drink that looked like piss.

"Of course she likes baseball," another woman chimed in, reaching over the kitchen's island to pluck a carrot from the tray, dragging it through the artichoke dip. "She's Tobey's wife."

The front door was only twenty or third steps behind me. If I took off, I could hit a full sprint in enough time to blast through it, these three-inch heels be damned. "I'm a Yankee fan." I spoke up before these women discussed my whole life right here before me. "Don't have a stake in this game." Only a half-truth. I'd love to be in the other room with the guys, gathered around the giant screen, watching the play and discussing the game. It was the World Series for God's sake. Seven games that the world stopped spinning for. Except that the Orioles had made it. Chase had made it. Which put me here, in this kitchen, staring at these women and trying not to strangle any of them.

"Well, I understand that." One of them grinned, leaning on the counter, her ginormous breasts resting on the granite. "But with Chase Stern playing, I'd watch just for some bedroom inspiration, if you know what I mean." She winked, and I didn't know how anyone could not know what that meant.

"Oh Cayce, stop." An older brunette to my left shushed her.

"Who's Chase Stern?" That question came from the teenage girl, one who looked up from her phone for the first time since the starting pitch. That was how long I'd been in this Godforsaken kitchen. Since the pitch. Now, in the third inning, I was full on finger food and beyond ready to leave.

That question brought a new swell of conversation, all focused on the man who I was hiding from in the kitchen. Only they didn't care about his batting average or wOBA. They cared about things like an Instagram account and a nude spread he had done for Sports Illustrated, *two things I knew nothing about but wanted to see instantly, the pull of my phone almost impossible to resist. The teenager looked him up, and there was a new round of swooning, the iPhone passed from hand to hand, but I stepped back from the action before it was offered to me. I moved to the entrance of the media room, glancing in on the men in hopes of distraction.*

And there he was. In high definition, his jaw tight, eyes looking down the line, his hat pulled low, a day's worth of growth on that face. The camera held him there, held me in place, until the pitch, one low and outside. My hand tightened on the doorframe, willing him to wait, but he didn't. He swung, one hand leaving the bat, the crack loud and crisp, his eyes on the ball until it was gone, the crowd surging to their feet, his eyes moving to the camera and giving it one, cocky wink. I turned from the TV, but was too late to miss it.

I walked through the kitchen and out the front door, the cool fall night a shock to my senses. My butt hit their front steps, and I wrapped my arms around my knees, his face, that wink, stuck in my mind. And there, on a stranger's empty front porch, for a long breath of time, I mourned a life lost.

A life I had now found. It was there, in my grasp, that man down there one who had waited for me. Four years he had waited. I suddenly wanted to run out of the box, like I had fled that party, taking the halls, elevator, and ramp down to the field. I wanted to burst into that dugout and wrap my arms around his neck. Jump into his arms and kiss his lips, inhaling the scent of sweat and clay and leather.

I didn't. I stared down, watching him from above as he leaned against the dugout fence, one foot resting on the ledge, his eyes on the game, on the action. Then I turned back to the room, and found my seat next to Tobey.

 **101**

World Series: Game 2

I didn't know what happened when lives split. Couldn't imagine sitting in this bedroom and packing up my things. I didn't have much, not that was just mine and not ours. Some memorabilia from my ball girl days that Tobey had framed and mounted. A few things in the baby's room … the shrine that still sat, two rooms away, neither of us able to bear the task of returning it to a study. After I left, I was sure he would. I was sure he'd take my library and turn it into a cigar room. Would probably have the gardeners tear out my orchids and replace them with something else. Something without memories. I would do all of that, if I were him. I would burn this place to the ground without a moment's guilt.

I had less than a week left in this house. Not enough, yet hundreds of hours too long. I walked through the library, my hand drifting over the spines, thousands of hardcovers—some read, some not. I spent most evenings in this room, Tobey off with the guys, me with my plots and heroines. Fell into other worlds, Chase seen in every hero, his build in every description, his touch in every sexual scene. He had rescued me from burning buildings, solved murders, and seduced me a hundred ways. I smiled, thinking of all of the times I had pictured actual sex with Chase and expected it would fall short, my expectations that of the bestselling erotica variety.

But he hadn't fallen short. He had been a hundred thousand times better. As a teenager, he had corrupted me. As a woman, he had ruined me.

I heard steps behind me and turned, Tobey in the doorway, smiling at

345

me. "One win down."

"Yeah." I smiled as widely as I could manage. We had barely eked out a win the night before, the Cubs leading up until the last inning.

He glanced at his watch. "You ready? We should leave soon."

I nodded. "I'll meet you downstairs."

He glanced around the room. "Need more bookshelves? I can have that wall blown out, if you don't mind sawdust and construction for a few months."

A few months. The guilt was climbing up my chest, clawing into my heart with long nails. "I'm fine," I said faintly.

"You feeling okay?" He looked at me closely. "You've been quiet."

"Just nerves," I said quickly. "We're so close."

"I know." He smiled. "I'm ready to bring that trophy home. Already had them prepare a spot in the cabinet for it."

"Great!" The response came out too loud, too forced, and he studied me for a moment before nodding.

"I'll be downstairs. Let's try to leave in the next ten minutes, okay?"

"Yeah." I turned away from him and straightened a bookend. When I heard him leave, I jogged upstairs, wanting to check my email before we left.

 **102**

World Series: Game 3

This is driving me crazy. Every time I see you with him, I feel a piece of me break.

Tension was in the air, the bodies that passed our seats subdued, everyone on edge, short greetings tossed our way. Game 2 had been bad, a loss by four runs, the team's cohesion off, everyone batting shit, errors right and left. I had stayed at the skybox's glass, tension building with each inning, the drinks Tobey kept passing me not helping, nothing helping. I almost went down there. Just wanted to see his face, to hear his voice. I needed it, each of these days without him were torture.

Now, Tobey and I sat in the first seats of the jet, each new body in the open door causing my heart to skip, my eyes frantic in their game of avoidance and need. I tried not to look, but I failed. Then, there was the moment of glance and stick—his head ducking through the opening, a hat on his head, his eyes finding mine, the edge of his mouth barely lifting, his chin nodding, his eyes going from me to Tobey, and his mouth flattened. "Mr. Grant," he drawled. "Mrs. Grant." He nodded and moved past, down the aisle. It took every muscle in my neck to keep my head trained forward, to not turn my head and watch his exit. I wondered if he turned around. If he glanced up at us when he sat. I hated sitting next to Tobey. Being on this jet with both of them. I tried to get Tobey to fly out separately, but he refused.

If he wasn't here, I'd have your seat leaned back and my face between your thighs.

I saw the email twenty minutes after we took off, the jostle of turbulence covering up my small reactionary gasp, the uncomfortable cross of my legs. I tilted the phone away from Tobey, rereading the email, committing it to memory before I pushed the delete button.

There. *Gone.* I shifted in my seat, needing some relief from the sudden ache between my legs. Tobey leaned over, kissing my neck, and the familiar stab of guilt returned. It'd been haunting me, getting stronger by the day, gaining momentum with every touch of my husband's hand, every whisper in my ear. I wished I could hate him. I wished I didn't feel pity for him. He was too good for pity. He was too good for any of this.

Three more games.
Five more days.
Then, the lies and the deaths would all be over.

 **103**

World Series: Game 4

We had won Game 3. A short-lived victory since we were now down by four runs. Chase swung, the ball ripping from his bat, going high, high, high … gone. I watched fans in the upper decks scramble for the ball, bodies jumping off seats, a claw of arms and elbows until one lone figure cheered, his arm stretched high in the air, the ball clenched in his fist. It didn't matter. No one was on base. One run in, three more needed just to tie up the game. And in the sixth inning, our prospects looked bleak.

I tipped back my beer and sank into the chair. Took another pull. I'd been using alcohol to avoid sex with Tobey. Guzzling drinks and then stumbling into our room at night. Funny, since alcohol was what put us in bed together the first night. That chug of his beer, then the next round of shots, the fuzz they brought when they hit my virgin system. The recklessness it had pushed him to. I doubt Harvard boy would have fucked little Rollins without a condom, had his head been on straight.

Another inning, another run brought in by the Cubs. Tobey growled under his breath next to me, the entire box quiet as we watched. We should have changed pitchers earlier. Should have put Franks before Chase in the lineup. Should have, should have, should have. I should have ended things with Tobey a long time ago. I could have done it before the attachment, before the love. Then maybe this wouldn't feel so seedy. I was a woman unaccustomed to guilt, and it drowned me—pulling me deeper, cutting off my air supply.

I stood at the final pitch, tossing my empty beer bottle into the trash, the loss painful as I stared at the final scoreboard. Two more losses and we'd lose the World Series. Two more losses and ... what? Would another girl die?

I stumbled for the door, and Tobey caught my arm, holding me steady, his hand a shackle I reluctantly leaned on for support.

It was too much pressure, all of it. Baseball shouldn't be life or death. Baseball shouldn't determine fates.

 **104**

World Series: Game 5

Our last day in Chicago. I stepped from the elevator, into the huge lobby, one that towered upward, its grandeur constructed over a century ago. I paused, my eyes sweeping the room, looking for Tobey. He'd come down fifteen minutes earlier, anxious for our lunch with Dick and John. Not seeing him, I headed for the restaurant, walking quickly, tension knotting my veins, any public experience always running the risk of—

"Ty." Chase. Freshly shaven, a nick on his jaw, his hair wet. He wore sweatpants and a long-sleeve T-shirt, the smell of soap drifting off his skin, a duffel bag hanging from one shoulder. He joined me, our steps carrying us closer to the restaurant, and I glanced around.

"I'm meeting a group for lunch," I said quickly.

"Right here," he ordered, herding me left, down a short hall and through a doorway. I stopped just inside, a long desk holding three computers and a printer—the business center.

"Chase," I argued quietly, reaching for the handle, his hand covering mine for a moment, one dip in heartbeat, before he reached higher and locked the latch, my eyes following his movement as he reached for the blinds, twisting slowly, our window to the outside world reduced, then shut off. There was a dull thud when he dropped his duffel.

"Don't fight me on this, Ty." He stopped before me and rested his forehead on mine, inhaling deeply, his voice gruff, hands sliding up my arms and into my hair. "Five minutes. Please."

"What is this?" I asked faintly, my eyes closing as his fingers traced across the scoop of my sweater and down, over my breasts, his mouth soft as he pressed just under my ear, then on my collarbone, then up to my mouth.

"This is a dying man's taste," he whispered, brushing his lips over mine. Softly. Harder. "This is me reminding you of what we have."

"I don't need reminding," I mumbled, stumbling back as he stepped forward, pushing me until my butt hit the desk, and he broke from my mouth, his hands at the back of my pants. Unzipping. Pulling.

"Turn around," he choked out, pulling up my sweater, the scrape of his nails against my skin when he yanked at my bra.

I did. I turned around.
I turned around, and he bent me over, my name a hiss between his lips when he pushed—bare and thick and hard—inside of me. My panties stretched around my thighs, my pants not even at my knees, my sweater and bra pushed just high enough that my breasts hung out for him to grip, to squeeze, to tease as he began to fuck me.

And that was what it was. Hard fucks that knocked across the desk, my fingers grasping for some hold, one of his hands hard on my back, pushing me forward, until my bare breasts were flat on the cool surface, my cheek turned sideways, hair falling in my face. I gasped, hiccupping for breath, the steady motion one of absolute need and lust, my right butt cheek gripped hard by his hand, pulling me on and off him in rhythm with his thrusts, the hum of the idle printer broken by the loud sounds of our bodies connecting.

"Tell me that you love me," he begged, his fucks increasing in speed, the staccato building my own climax, both of us racing to the top. I squeezed with my inner muscles, and he almost came out of his shoes, a swear crossing his lips, one hand reaching down and gripping my waist.

"I love you," I gasped. "I love you so much it hurts."

He didn't slow when he came, he kept at it, fucking and fucking and fucking, my own orgasm coming, his cry of my name only pushing me higher and higher and higher until I reached heaven and fell back down, his arms catching me, crushing me against his chest, both of us collapsing into a kiss that didn't want to end, never wanted to stop.

Certain loves can't be fought. The harder you tried, the harder you would be knocked back, over and over again, until it beat you into submission, until your heart caved and body surrendered. Love like that didn't know the rules of society; it didn't care about life mistakes. It only knew what must be, and what would happen—no matter what.

I kissed him and didn't care about the Series anymore. I kissed him and only wanted to run away. I kissed him and tasted our future.

 **105**

World Series: Game 6

We were back home, our stadium full, fans roaring, energy everywhere, and we needed it. With our win in Game 5, we just needed one more win, and we were *done*, the championship in hand. I needed my Yankee career to end on this note. I needed to give this to Tobey to ease the stab of my betrayal. I needed this for the girls' families, and for every single blonde in NYC.

But one more win didn't seem to be in the cards. Not when we were in the ninth inning and down by two. Cook hit a ball, low and far, dirt leaving his heels as he sprinted to first, making it just in time, a sigh of relief passing through the box as the ump called him safe. Chase was two batters down. One out already on the board. If either runner made it to base, we had a chance.

I ate sunflower seeds at a rapid pace, my lips dry and chapped, a cup in hand, my spitting of shells quite unladylike but noticed by none. Dad sat to my left, Carla beside him, Tobey pacing as soon as the game began, stadium lights bright, the windows open, no one bitching about the chill. I had dressed up for the occasion, upgrading to heels, a blazer pulled over a navy silk cami.

"When are you telling him?" Dad spoke low, leaning into me, his eyes on the game.

"Tomorrow. Maybe tonight … if," I spit into the cup, "you know."

"That'll kill the buzz of a win."

"I know." He was right. No way I could ruin the biggest moment of our marriage, of our life so far, with the news of me leaving. I'd have to at least wait until the next morning. Really should wait a few days after. Especially if, God forbid, we lost. But I couldn't wait. Not when every minute with him felt like infidelity, and Chase's patience was already stretched thin.

I watched Cinns try to bunt, his short legs not fast enough, and I cursed, rising in my seat, just high enough to watch him get tagged out, the scoreboard changing, boos erupting from fans as our outs increased to two.

"You can't win them all, Ty. You know that, right?" Chase spoke quietly, the words barely heard as he bent over the water cooler, filling his cup. I slouched on the bench next to it, the end of my ponytail in my mouth, nerves fried as the freaking Marlins handed us our asses.

I snorted, spitting out my ponytail. "You see that on a motivational poster? That's bullshit. We can win them all. We're—"

"The Yankees," he finished with a smile, tipping back his cup. "Yeah, I heard you were a little fanatical."

"It's called loyalty," I retorted, my eyes back on the field.

"I like it." He tossed his cup into the trash. "It's cute."

I didn't look up, instead stared at the field, but knew the moment he looked away, the moment he walked away, saying something to the first base coach, our conversation over.

Ball three. I watched in interest, gnawing through another seed, as the pitcher spoke with his coach. I glanced at Dad. "Think they'll walk him?"

"They'd be stupid to." He watched the conversation on the mound. "Not with Chase up next. He needs to throw him out."

"Only one strike on the board." Unnecessary words, spoken only to fill the conversation, to distract.

"Curveball," he muttered, reaching over and grabbing a handful of my seeds. "That's what I'd do."

It was a curveball, Dad's prophesy coming true, but it was too wide, too high, and Franks watched it go by, the energy in the stadium amping up as he took the free base, two runners on, our star—*my* star—now stepped up to the plate.

I rose in my seat, my cup left behind. Chase carried the bat by its end and flipped it, his head turning in my direction, his chin lifting until our eyes met. Just a second, a moment of connection, then he looked away, his cleats digging into place, the pants tight on his thighs, his ass. His forearms clenched as he wrapped his fingers around the bat's handle, and then it swung slowly back, everything in him tensing as he waited, his eyes on the pitcher. I held my breath, watching him, the first pitch wild, his body never moving, the catcher behind him lunging for the ball. I caught my breath, eyes darting to first and second, where we had runners. Both taking leads, the second runner's a little too generous for my taste. I looked back to Chase, his lead foot moving slightly in the dirt, then he stilled. Everything in our stadium stilled with him, fans on their feet, breaths held, hearts in throats.

An inside pitch, but he swung, his face tight, a blur of beautiful movement, the connection loud and crisp, the ball soaring, high and fast, disappearing into the lights of the stadium, then *gone*, to the moon. *A moonshot.* I was yanked sideways, Tobey's arms around me, his body jumping up and down, our box filled with cheers, my body shook from others' arms, my gaze staying on Chase, who slowly tossed his bat to the side, his face turning up to our box, his arms spread out from his body as he looked up to us.

"Yes!" Tobey shouted, pounding the glass. "Yes, you son-of-a-bitch! Run!"

Chase wasn't looking at him. He held my gaze, then spun slowly, raising a fist to the crowd, and then jogged toward first, slapping hands with Rich at first base, my eyes on him the entire lap, his gaze reconnecting with me in the moment before he crossed home, the entire team there to greet him. Around him, around me, the stadium exploded.

Three runs. One enough to take the lead. One enough to end the series.

It was over. We had won the World Series. On a moonshot of all things. A moonshot off the most beautiful bat, from the most beautiful man I had ever seen. Somewhere behind me, champagne sprayed. And before us, the sky exploded in fireworks. I watched the brilliant display, lighting thousands of faces, the faces of Yankee nation, all of my boys in a pile of exuberance on the field, and felt a piece of me, the last tie of my childhood, break away. I choked back tears, smiling bigger than I ever had, and pressed my hands to the glass, devouring the scene, my last from this life.

It was a beautiful final moment.
It was a beautiful goodbye.

106

I left in the middle of the celebration, our security distracted, like everyone else, by the win. I yanked off my heels and sprinted down the private stairwell, passing through secret halls until I was underground, on field level, by the equipment bays, the muffled sounds of the stadium everywhere, celebrations in full force. I grabbed the ball boy when he ran by, stuffing a hundred-dollar-bill in his hand and told him to get Chase. He recognized me, the teenager old enough to understand the problems with the owner's wife wanting a private meeting with a player. But he took the money, disappearing onto the field, and a few moments later, Chase was there, my hands pulling off his hat, his shirt damp with sweat, his clay-streaked baseball pants pushing against my hips, our mouths frantic as we kissed. With boxes of balls at my back, his hands cupped my face, my hands raked through his hair, and we kissed as if it was our breath, necessary for the beating of our hearts, the flow of blood through our veins.

"I love you," he said, pulling at the holder of my ponytail.

"I love you too," I gasped, kissing his neck, the taste of it salty champagne, my hands gripping at his uniform.

"Come home with me tonight. We won. You promised."

"Tomorrow morning," I swore. "Just give me until tomorrow."

"I can't wait that long." He kissed me again, his fingers tangling in my hair.

"Yes, you can." I stepped back, his hands falling, my chest heaving.

"I'll tell him tomorrow."

"I love you," he repeated, his eyes stuck on me.

"Always." I smiled, pulling my hair back, tucking in my shirt. "I'll call you when I'm on my way."

I ran back to him for one last kiss, then turned and slipped through the door, leaving him in the dark room, the taste of him still on my lips, my promise hanging in the air. I ran up the service stairwell, toward the sky level, back to Tobey. One flight before the top, I stopped, pulling on my heels, smoothing down my hair, my heart still pounding. Taking a deep breath, I slowly climbed the final stairs, back to Tobey.

107

Even though the deaths had stalked my mind, invaded my thoughts, and dominated my nightmares for over two years, I'd never felt in danger. I'd felt pressure, I'd felt blame, I'd felt guilt—but never fear.

That changed when I rounded the final bend in the stairs and came face to face with evil. The man stood at the top of the landing, and I knew. I knew it instantly, as clearly as I knew my love for Chase. As clearly as I recognized my mistake. *As clearly as I now knew a win would not satisfy.*

I hesitated, his name taking a second, my mind sluggish in the face of danger. Finally, it came, a squeak off my lips.

"It wasn't about me trying to be God. I was just in a unique position to see into a part of the Grants' lives that no one else could. And that position came with a degree of responsibility. Tobey and Ty were one of those meant-to-be couples. And that was really that. They just couldn't seem to move out of their own way to make that happen."

Dan Velacruz, *New York Times*

 **108**

"Dan?"

Of anyone I'd ever pictured, Dan Velacruz was the last person I'd ever thought capable of murder. I'd known him for over a decade, his face appearing whenever anything newsworthy happened, his pieces guaranteed to paint us in a positive light.

Nothing, in that moment, in that empty stairwell, seemed positive. I stared at him and tried to figure out the pieces I was missing from this puzzle. He pulled his hand out of his cheap suit pocket, and I watched, time stuttering to a stop, as he opened the blade.

I stepped backward, and felt the edge of the stair, my descent stopped as I balanced at the top of the flight. "Please." The word was tissue paper against fire, a whisper of smoke that he couldn't have heard. He stepped toward me, and my hand tightened on the railing.

I could run. I could kick off these damn heels and sprint, barefoot, down the flight. But kicking off Louboutin slingbacks wasn't an easy task, and it would certainly eat up precious seconds, seconds where his fingers would close on me and that knife could gut me. Just like Rachel's side. Just like April's neck. An image of Tiffany flashed before me, her eyes blank, her mouth open, her caked and dried tongue sticking out slightly through the opening in her lips. My tongue would not dry. I'd be found before then, unless he planned on sneaking me out of Yankee Damn Stadium after a World Series win. The win reminded me of the curse, a curse that should be beaten, our fans safe. I found my voice, the edge of my left heel hanging off the edge of the step. "We won," I said weakly. "Shouldn't everything be fine? I mean…"

"You thought the killings would stop," he stated, seeing my thought process, a look, almost pity, crossing his face.

"Yes." He shouldn't be here, in this stairwell. It was a private one, for staff only, used for emergencies when the staff elevators were too busy, the stale air in here proof of their non-use.

"I didn't kill them because of the World Series, Ty. That..." he waved his hand into empty space, the knife in it flashing, "that was an assumption the papers made, an assumption the police adopted, all of it embraced by the fans. Only Yankee fans would make this all about baseball."

"It wasn't a stretch," I pointed out, my stupid mouth unable to contain itself. "The Yankees' necklace, the girl in the jersey right outside our gates—"

"Oh, Ty," he interrupted, his voice quiet and sad, stepping forward. Closer. Closer. The knife in arm's reach. If he punched out, right now, it could hit so many vulnerable places. My stomach, cutting across the faint stretch marks that showed in harsh light. My heart, so full and happy, just minutes earlier. My lungs, empty caverns that had suddenly forgotten how to function. I watched it, his hands stilling as he stopped, and I lifted my gaze slowly, carefully, to his face. A face filled with so much pity that I almost forgot he was the enemy. "You are so much smarter than this. *Think*."

I tried to think. I tried to understand. I tried to see an escape to this madness. But my mind failed me on all three fronts. Instead, I began to panic, painful bits of the past pushing forward.

"The baby." I looked out on the water, not turning when Tobey stepped closer, shuddering when his hand gently touched the top of mine. I pulled it away, and he didn't come closer. "It's gone."

He didn't respond. I needed a response from him. I needed to know how he felt, if he was as shaken as I was. I needed him to push through my resistance and pull me against his chest. I needed to sob and scream and break down, and I needed him to be the strong one, to pick up my pieces and put me back together. But he didn't. He only stood there, next to me, both of us staring out into the dark, and said nothing.

"Rachel Frepp," Dan said. "What do you know about her?"

Nothing. She'd gone to a few games. She worked as a valet. Was just like all of them, blonde and gorgeous. I shook my head, my hysteria rising. "I won't tell anyone," I whispered. "You can just go, right now. The police will never know. I promise." In that moment, I meant it. I would let him go, would risk another woman's life just to remove myself from danger. I stared him down and let him see the sincerity in my eyes. I was so close to finally leaving Tobey, to leaving this life, to being happy. I couldn't die now, not when I was in reach of everything I'd ever wanted.

His expression soured, and I saw the minute his patience stopped.

"You misunderstand what I'm doing here, Ty. I'm here for you."

"The issue was, when someone is blessed with things, like Tobey, you have to appreciate those things. *Preserve* those things. Whether Tobey Grant knew it or not, I was *helping* him. I was putting him on the right path, one that saved his marriage, one that saved his team. And I was in the perfect position to do that. Because I could see. I could see the mistakes before he made them. Take Rachel Frepp for example. If it wasn't for me, he'd have never married Ty. He didn't care about the baby, he was in love with Rachel. I knew it the first time I asked him about the engagement—could see that something was off, that he was a panicked man. It hadn't taken much digging to find out who he'd been dating. Hell, who he was *still* dating, even with a pregnant Ty Rollins packing up her stuff and moving into his family's mansion. She had to be eliminated. It was the only option."

Dan Velacruz, *New York Times*

 **109**

"Me?" The warnings of Detective Thorpe echoed in my mind, every slip of me past security, every time I argued for freedom—stupid decisions from a stupid girl. I had thought myself invincible. I had thought that just because I was happy, that I deserved life.

"Everything had finally come together. After Tiffany, Tobey had stopped. Had been faithful. And then you. *You. You* had to mess everything up."

It was too many words, too much at one time, my brain slow in its filter. "Tobey had stopped?" I asked faintly. "Stopped what?" But I knew. April McIntosh's Yankees' pendant. Just like the one Tobey gave me, so many years ago, just after our wedding. Tiffany Wharton. A girl more beautiful than I could ever hope to be. Her bright smile growing each time Tobey stopped by HR. A department he had never needed to visit, until she was hired. The dark periods after each girl was found, each death affecting him much worse than me. I'd chalked it up to sensitivity, a quality I was grateful for in a husband.

"Do you know that when Rachel died, he didn't even notice?" Dan reached out, the knife in hand, and ran the tip of it slowly across my neckline. "She disappeared, and he never even called the police. He didn't realize she had *died* until the police started to tie the deaths together. He was going to leave you Ty, and he DIDN'T EVEN NOTICE her death." His voice had changed, growing sharper and meaner, the hand holding the knife beginning to tremble, the line across my skin becoming jagged. I lifted my hands off the railing, and his eyes sharpened. "Put your hands behind you, Ty. Link your hands back there."

April McIntosh had fought. I'd seen the photos myself, the defensive wounds on her palms. She'd also been the most disfigured, the one who'd taken the longest to die. I obeyed his directions, carefully moving my hands, behind my back, the backs of my hands bumping, at the moment before they linked, at the hard object in my back pocket. *My phone.*

I kept eye contact with him, pushing out my chest slightly as the fingers of one hand quietly slid into my back pocket, pulling at the edge of the phone, and sliding it carefully out.

"I'm sorry," I said, hoping to distract him, hoping to cover my movements as I pressed my thumb against the home button of my phone. "I didn't know—about Tobey. I didn't know he was—"

"Of course you didn't," he crowed, his eyes on my face, a smirk playing at one corner of his mouth. "You were so focused on the team that you didn't notice anything. That's why you needed me. I was the one who watched. I was the one who saw *everything*. And your husband?" He dropped back his head with a laugh. "He did a terrible job of covering his tracks." I moved my fingers blindly across the screen of my phone and prayed that I was opening up the phone app. Dan brought his chin back down, his laughter abruptly ending. "Almost as poorly as you. And that, Ty, just isn't acceptable."

"You're crazy," I choked out, tapping blindly at the front of my phone, praying for help, praying for a call, praying that someone would answer and understand everything. He must have seen me leave through this staircase. Followed me, then waited for me to come back.

"I'm not crazy," he said simply, his free hand reaching out and sliding my shirt carefully over one shoulder, his fingers gentle as they ran over the exposed skin, as a painter would do with a fresh canvas. "I'm not crazy," he repeated. "I'm dedicated to this team. To this family." His touch hardened, and I stiffened as I felt those fingers slide up and wrap around my neck. He smiled then, a lift of two cheeks that didn't match the cold look in his eyes. "Loyalty, dear Ty, is the key to success. I tried to keep Tobey loyal. For *you*. And then you went and—"

I swiftly brought up my knee, hitting the soft area between his legs, and twisted, his grip on my neck loosening as he wheezed. I shoved one hand forward at his chest. But when my foot stepped back, toward escape, there was nothing there but stairs, my ankle turning as one heel hit an edge, my arms pin-wheeling, my phone flying, and then I was falling. A shoulder slammed against one hard stair, and I tucked my head, my hands coming up to shield myself, the impact on the concrete landing the worst, most excruciating pain I had ever experienced.

When I opened my eyes, he was there, his eyes furious, his knife out. I inhaled and tasted blood, something in my mouth loose, my head pounding. He put one dress shoe on my chest, leaning hard, putting his weight on it as he reached forward with the knife. "You shouldn't have done that, Ty. Not after everything I've done for you." Around us, the stadium shook, a cheer going up, the trophy ceremony underway. He lifted his head and listened, a smile crossing his face. "*I* did that, Ty. I brought back Chase Stern, *I* got this team focused, and *I* won this Series for New York."

"I'm sorry." The apology gasped out of me, my lungs struggling for breath, his weight on my sternum a vice that barely allowed movement. Maybe he wouldn't hurt me. Maybe he just wanted an audience, recognition.

"Me too, Ty." I wished he would stop saying my name, his mouth caressing the short syllable. He leaned forward and brought the knife down, just under my ear. "I thought you were different. I thought you were such a good wife. I thought that, with Tobey behaving, you two could finally be happy. Now, it looks like you never will be."

And I saw in his eyes, that this was the end.

 **110**

"Run away with me," Chase whispered, his leg wrapped around me, my body tucked into his chest, my cheek against the smooth muscle of his chest. The hotel room was dark, the sounds of the Bronx subdued.

"I can't," I said quietly. "You know I can't."

"He doesn't love you like I do. He can't."

"It's been four years, Chase. I was here that whole time." And he hadn't come. I had waited, in Tobey's parents' home, listening to every ring of the bell, every call on the phone. I had waited for Chase, and he had never come for me.

"I didn't know about the baby, Ty. I thought—I thought you had just left me. Chose him."

"I would never have chosen him." I looked up at him, surprised to see his eyes wet with emotion.

"Then don't choose him now."

There was so much blood. All over the front of my shirt, the wet smear of it worsened by his hands, gripping at me, claws of contact, the knife swinging at me, wild, red, wet motions that were suddenly farther away, space between us as he was pulled away. *Horace.* I recognized his face, one of our security guards. *Mitch.* Another familiar face. There were more, the stairwell getting crowded, a glimpse of Dan's face, eyes frenzied, through a space between black uniform and a pinstriped shirt. I held onto those eyes for the split second that was allowed. Then someone moved in front of me, said something to me, hands gentle as they raised my feet.

"Ty?" Dad's voice, through the blood, through the pain. "TY!" he shouted at me, and I reached out for him, unsure of where he was, everything going dark.

111

Chase sat in the locker room, his hands on his head, trying to clear his head, to say a prayer of thanks, the weight of the last season, of the last decade, suddenly gone. They had won. He had her. Champagne sprayed, cold mist showering, and he was pulled to his feet, pushed into the center of the room, hands everywhere, on his back, his head, his arms. Smiles all around, love in the air. For the first time, since high school, he really felt the love, the bind, the feel of family. Funny how quickly hearts warmed when championships were won. Or maybe he was just now open to it, everything rosy when he had her in his future. He was gripped tightly and he smiled, a smile that hurt in its stretch. A chant started, and he tilted his chin back and yelled, a belt of joy that joined in on the chorus.

She was right. This team *was* a family. One she was leaving for him. The depth of the sacrifice warmed his heart, his devotion to her aching in its ferocity. All the more reason to start their own family. Together, with their love, they could have it all. Together, they would build it all.

For a moment where everything had finally come together, something felt off.

112

I had pictured the end of Tobey and I so many times. Early on in our marriage, I had contemplated running away. Everyone would wake, on Tuesday morning, and I'd be gone. There were times in our relationship where I didn't think he'd even notice. Then later, our friendship weaving tighter and tighter with strands of love, it became harder. I didn't know how difficult it was to leave a husband. But my business partner, my friend ... over the years, it had become impossible. Until Chase.

I knew the minute our eyes met beside that plane, that I would leave Tobey. In that moment, it was no longer a choice, but a necessity. Regardless of whatever happened with Chase. Staying with Tobey when I loved another man so fiercely—it wasn't fair to him.

In the months since that decision, I'd pictured the end of our marriage a handful of different ways. I'd rehearsed what to say. I'd pictured his reaction. I'd dreaded it all.

I never thought the end would come in a police station.

We sat next to each other in a small room, Detective Thorpe across the table, the case files spread out between us. The images I'd seen before, paper clipped to thick reports, thousands of words that captured none of the girls' lives but every detail of their deaths. I took a deep breath, my chest burning, the stitches along my collar itching, a pile of gauze preventing my scratch. Twenty-nine stitches. Overkill for a surface wound, my blackout most likely caused by shock. Being cleared by the doc had taken two hours in the Yankees' infirmary, my insistence at avoiding the hospital met with a fair amount of opposition. But, I couldn't drag this out. I couldn't lose focus. All I wanted, in my first minutes of rescued life, was to end the one I was living.

"We've gotten a full confession from Dan Velacruz," Detective Thorpe said, his voice hard, no pride in the tones. "He says that you had relationships with each of the women."

I shouldn't be there. The detective had wanted to question Tobey privately, but he'd insisted I be present. Now, his hand tight on mine, I only wanted to run. I didn't want to hear the details of Tobey's affairs. I didn't care. Maybe another wife would. Maybe another wife would feel hurt and betrayed. But that all seemed a little hypocritical when all I wanted to do was burst from this seat, sprint through the station, and out into the night. I wanted to find Chase, jump into his arms and escape. I didn't want to see the guilt in Tobey's eyes, hear the pain in his voice.

"Relationships is a fairly strong word, for some of the women." Tobey swallowed, his hand tightening on mine. "For the first girls, yes. Rachel … I was in love with her. And April and I had a thing … for a while. Mostly sexual." He turned to me, and I pulled my hand away, his eyes dropping to it before he returned to my face. "Ty, I stopped. Julie was nothing and after Tiffany, I swear to God, I stopped *everything*. I never even slept with Tiffany. I took her to lunch twice—nothing else. That man was crazy. I saw that after Tiffany."

"Do you realize, had you shared this information with me earlier, years ago, how we could have saved their lives? Maybe caught the son-of-a-bitch?" Thorpe interrupted us, the hard edge of his voice caused Tobey's face to stiffen.

Thorpe was right. What kind of asshole sat on that information? What kind of asshole sat next to me, in countless strategy sessions about the team, and allowed us to all think that the killings had to do with the Series? I half listened to Tobey's sputter of defense, something weak and spineless. I wondered, absently, if he had broken a law. I wondered if they'd ever asked him if he'd known all of the victims. I didn't think they ever asked me. Then again, when they had sat in our home, when we had pored over the case files, they would have probably assumed we would have mentioned it. Who wouldn't have offered that from the start? *Tobey.*

My phone call, in that stairwell with Dan, went to my dad. His phone hadn't rung, the call sent straight to voicemail, his eyes catching the indicator when it flashed on his screen. The voicemail was almost a minute long, Dan's and my conversation clear, the acoustics of the concrete stairwell helpful in their search. That message played on repeat between countless parties. That voicemail saved my life. It also aired our secrets to every listener.

"I should have told you." I didn't know if Tobey was talking to me or the detective, but he was right. He should have told me that he wasn't happy. He should have told me, when I was pregnant with Logan, that he was in love with Rachel. He should have told Detective Thorpe that the killing wasn't about the World Fucking Series, or Chase Stern, at all. He should have told him that the girls all had one very clear connection to each other: him. I thought of Tiffany Wharton's face, the blood staining her cream sweater, the unnatural bend of her elbows. Two meals with my husband had cost her her life. Damn him for not controlling himself. Damn him for keeping his affairs a secret … for what? To preserve our empty fucking shell of a marriage?

"I don't mean to interrupt the questioning," I said carefully, meeting Detective Thorpe's eyes respectfully before turning to my husband. "But I have something I need to say to Tobey."

Just six months ago, I thought I knew everything about this man. The glint in his stare when a spark of anger burned. The way he loved his steak, started on the grill and finished in the oven. The sound that hissed through his teeth when I took him in my mouth. Obviously, I was wrong. There were many signs I missed, or ignored. Secrets that he held close to his heart, lives he lived away from my side. But I still recognized the look in his eyes when he looked into my face. One long moment of connection, one that lasted for an eternity. One where our relationship died in that tormented pause. "I'm leaving."

The sigh tumbled out of him, loud and heavy, his shoulders sagging, as he lowered his head, that thick head of hair, wild and unkempt in the midnight hour, to my shoulder. And there, my husband, his hands fisting against my jeans, for the first time since I'd known him, silently cried.

I felt the shudder, the tremble of his shoulders, his grip on me more desperate, one long, wet inhale against my neck, his mouth close to the start of my bandage. The weight of him almost hurt, his hands heavy and hard against my thighs, his knees bumping against my own, and he hiccupped once, before turning his head, his cheek against my shoulder, and spoke.

"Please don't," he whispered.

Despite myself, I bent into him, wrapping my arms around him, hugging him as best I could, and closed my eyes, a few of my own tears leaking out. "I have to," I said quietly.

I had always thought it would be hard, and I was right.

 **113**

"Are you sure?" Tobey sat against the table, his hands in the pockets of his suit pants, us finally alone in the room. Detective Thorpe had excused himself, giving us a moment of privacy after telling me that I was free to go.

I met his eyes, the sadness in them pulling at every seam of my heart. "I am. You weren't the only one unhappy. There's..." I swallowed. "Someone else."

He stopped breathing, his face tightening, an edge coming to his sorrow. "How long?"

Such a hard question to answer. It felt like I'd loved Chase since the day I was born. "A few months," I managed.

"Chase Stern?" he asked, looking up at me.

I wondered how he knew. I wondered how transparent I'd been. I nodded tightly, but it was unneeded. He had seen the truth in my face as soon as he'd said the name.

"Shit, Ty."

"It started way back," I said. "When I was a ball girl. But then—"

"...you got pregnant," he said flatly.

"Yeah."

I said nothing, and neither did he, a long moment of silence, the air vent in the room humming to life, cool air hitting my face, and I shivered. He noticed the movement and wrapped a hand around my shoulders, pulling me carefully into his chest, a kiss pressed against my head. "Love you, Ty."

Part of me hated him. For his weakness. For keeping the key to all of this from the police. He'd cheated. He'd put our lives in jeopardy. But we had also shared so many years, so many memories, such a large chunk of our lives. "I love you, too."

"I'll miss you. So will the team."

I nodded, without speaking, more tears threatening. *The team.* My relationship with them had changed so much in the last four years, my life from them more removed when up in the skybox, a new distance present when my last name changed to Grant. I wasn't really losing the team. That loss had started four years ago, the last day I dressed out.

"I'll have to trade Chase." He looked away, stepping back. "I can't … I'm sorry. I know what the team means to you."

"I know." I nodded, wiping at my eyes before the tears fell.

"I want you to be happy. You know that, right?" He rolled his lips tightly, the tremble of them almost hidden by the movement, his own eyes wet as he looked at me. I didn't care what secrets he'd hid. There was good in him. There was love between us. It just wasn't true. It just wasn't enough.

I nodded and stepped away from him before I reached out. "I'm gonna go."

"When are you leaving?"

"I'll go home now and pack a bag."

"Wow." He winced. "Not how I pictured celebrating the win." I started to speak, and he stopped me. "No. I'm fine. Go. Take Titan with you." He reached forward and pulled me into another hug, this one hard and tight before he roughly stepped away, nodding to the door. "Check in with the doc. I'll have him call you in the morning."

Goodbye seemed too trivial of a word, so I only nodded, turning on my heel and walking out the door, Detective Thorpe pushing off the opposite wall, his eyes meeting mine.

"Do you have anything else for me?" I asked.

"Not that can't be done tomorrow via phone. Take care of yourself, Mrs. Grant." He held out his hand, and I took it, shaking it firmly.

"It's Ty." God, that last name haunted me. I would reclaim Rollins as soon as I could.

I think he understood, his kind smile the sort that spoke volumes. "Be safe, Ty. I'll have a deputy escort you home."

"That won't be necessary." I said the words without thinking, no ride set up, no one waiting outside. But the thought of a uniform, the thought of someone guarding me … it was stifling at a time when I only wanted freedom. And it was unimportant when the threat to my life was now behind bars. I smiled a goodbye and moved past him, down a long hall, then to an elevator, people everywhere despite the late hour. My hands trembled around the strap of my purse, my throat dry when I swallowed. I wanted to run, to kick off my shoes and sprint out the double doors. My steps quickened, a click clack along the concrete floor, the glass doors closer, closer, closer. Then I was through, the night air cool and clear, a shot of adrenaline zipping through me. I was free. I was alive.

Back home, my dad and Carla waited, expecting for me to ride home with Tobey. I had no idea where Chase was, my phone breaking in its tumble down the stairs, the touch screen useless, calls unanswerable. My frustration and elation warred, my desperation to see Chase competing with the need to hug my father, to tell him everything, to grab my bag and Titan, and get in my car and GO—out of the Grant world, out of the Yankee bubble.

My bags were already packed and tucked into the back of my closet. Monday, I would have our house manager pack my items and send them to the auction house. I had no need for the furs and gowns, the matching luggage sets and jewelry. They would bring a high price at auction, the proceeds sent to the Boys and Girls Club.

I looked down the street, the wind whipping between the tall buildings, the night alive with the smells of the city, trash competing with a food truck, cigarette smoke drifting over from a nearby group. There were no taxis in site, and I waited, wrapping my arms around myself and taking a deep breath. I was alive. It was a blessing easy to forget, in the rush of everyday life. How precious that simple gift was.

A navy sedan skidded to a stop beside me, and its door opening, Chase stepping out. He stood for just a second, looking at me as if testing his sight, and then everything inside of me broke open as he rushed forward.

"Oh Ty." He clutched my face, his eyes searching over me, noticing the bandage, the bruises. "Fucking game traffic. I didn't hear the news until I got home. Then I went to your house, and th—"

I shushed him, grabbing at the front of his T-shirt and lifting to my toes, pressing my lips to his. "Take me there?" I asked.

"I'll take you anywhere." He kissed my forehead so gently I wanted to cry. "I love you."

"I love you too."

In his arms, in the back of the car, shuddering over potholes as it carried me to the house, I cried. I cried out every emotion left inside of me. And somewhere between the Bronx station and the security gates of my home, I found peace.

It was over.

All of it.

 **114**

Six Months Later

"Let's talk about your happiness." My therapist's favorite topic. I often wondered, hitting this stage of the appointment, if Tracy recycled the question with everyone in her life, every damn member of her family forced to prove, on an everyday basis, that their smiles and laughter were real.

"I'm happy." I looked away from a wrinkle in her cleavage and to her eyes, sharp holes of black behind bright red glasses. "Everything is great." It was. It was better than great. It was a painful happiness, the kind so precious that it scares, each moment filled with an edge of panic that it will all be lost. A person should not be this happy, our love should not be this strong—it just didn't seem fair, seem possible, to be so blessed.

"How is the public handling your engagement?"

I shrugged. "I'm not sure. I haven't paid attention." Probably not well. Yankee Nation hadn't been pleased when their first lady had abandoned her post. They'd ignored the carefully worded press release that Tobey and I had given. The one that emphasized our continuing friendship, and the joint decision we had made to end our four-year marriage. The paparazzi had caught my climb onto the private jet, Chase behind me. They'd seen our kisses on the beach in Bali. Overnight, I'd been branded a cheater. I hadn't cared, not when it had been the truth. I had cheated. There wasn't really any getting around that. Besides, Tobey had been in the trenches right next to me, Dan's mouth as loud in prison as it'd been outside of it. Everyone knew about his affairs, the media all but having a field day between the two of us. It was comical, though I seemed to be the only one seeing the humor in all of it.

"When is the wedding?"

I glanced down at my hand, at the simple band there. We'd skipped a diamond, Chase wanting something that could be worn under a glove. I preferred it, every giant rock reminding me of my first one, the stone that had seemed more like a shackle than a symbol of love. "In six months." I wasn't in a rush, though Chase seemed to be counting down the seconds, frantic to change my name and haul me off to his cave where he could properly claim me as his own.

"Anything else happen since our last session?"

"I visited Dan again."

Her brows raised. "Why?"

I didn't know. But she didn't like answers like that. She liked to dissect, the process exhausting yet helpful. Every session, I told myself I wouldn't come back. And every session, when I checked out and the perky receptionist asked if I wanted to book another appointment, I did. It was a cycle I wasn't yet ready to stop. Like peeling chapped lips.

I slid my palms under my thighs, knuckles against jeans, and tried to work through her question. "I like seeing him. It makes me feel in control."

"What did you talk about?"

"Love."

"You know what I don't understand?" I folded over the gum wrapper, my nail sliding across the edge, each bend in the foil drawing Dan's eyes to it.

"What?" There was glass between us. Dirty glass, fogged at the top, a few greasy handprints scattered over its surface. He peered at me and waited.

"You wanted Tobey and I to be together—that's why you did all of it, right?" He said nothing, and I pressed forward. "But then you were going to kill me. Which would have meant that we wouldn't be together. It would have defeated the entire purpose."

I don't know how I never saw his crazy before. Maybe I just hadn't known where to look. Didn't know that the slow tilt of his head meant that he was turning over a lie in his head before he spoke it. Or that he smiled when I said something that angered him, and he frowned when he was thinking. Now, he smiled, but it was a sad one. An almost genuine one.

"I read an article about you and Stern. A nice piece actually. Vanity Fair, I believe."

I nodded. The only interview I had done, one published just last week. An interview where I had bared my soul, my first time speaking aloud the thoughts, the dreams, the feelings that I'd hidden for so long. The piece had been my confession, and the only time I would speak publicly on any of it. After that, should the fans hate me, so be it. But at least they would know the how. The when. The why.

"The last line of it. Powerful stuff." He saw my confusion and leaned forward, so close that his breath fogged the glass. "Our love … I knew I would never find another like it. I had to protect it. I had to respect it. Even if it hurt Tobey. Even if it hurt the fans. Even if it meant leaving everything that I knew. I had to choose him. And I'd make the same decision now, even if he didn't love me back. Because next to it, anything else was a lie. And anything else wasn't fair to either of us."

"I meant it. I love Chase. And I never felt—"

"I know you didn't." He cut me off, his head shaking but staying in place, close to the glass, his fingers biting into the table. I glanced at those fingers, the same ones that had held the knife to my skin, the same ones that had wrapped around my throat and squeezed.

"Then …" I flicked my eyes back, suddenly understanding.

"I thought he was happy with you." He said softly, and there was madness in those eyes. Love does that to a person. I understood that, on a much milder scale. "I'd wanted him to be happy. And I thought you were worthy of him."

"Until I wasn't."

He smiled, a slow one that showed a piece of food stuffed near an incisor. I couldn't believe that this was the man, the one who terrorized our lives, our team, our city. This man who settled back into his plastic chair, scratching at a place on his neck.

"I don't understand." Tracy tilted her head, her pen tapping at the edge of her notepad, toes curling into the brown cork of her sandals.

"Despite the ten-year age difference, despite Dan's ex-wife, we never saw it. We had simply appreciated his undying loyalty to the Yankees. But it wasn't about them." I paused, weighing the words in my mind before using them. "He loved *Tobey*. That's why he did it all."

So simple. And so heartbreakingly stupid.

I glanced at the clock, then at her face, three minutes left in this examination of my sanity. "I don't think I'll see him again. I think I'm done."

It's odd that I chose that day to make that decision. Even as I said it, I wasn't sure it was final. I had some perverse need to stare at him, locked in that prison, on the other side of that glass. But, I never had another opportunity to. That night, Dan Velacruz hung himself in his cell.

 **115**

Four Years Later

I'm a Texas Ranger now. I wear red and navy, drive a pickup truck, and run with Titan through horse pastures across our ranch. We have two goats and four horses to keep him company, all but one named after baseball players. Moonshot is the exception. Chase spent a month tracking him down, following racetrack records and stud channels until he found him, retired from a sad career and studded out. He flew him to Dallas with some romantic notion that I'd care. I did. I almost fell out of the truck when we pulled up to the ranch, and I saw him trot across the field.

Right now, at nine o'clock on a Friday night, I'm in Globe Life Park in Arlington—Section 34, Row A, Seats 1-5—and that's our home, the seats right next to the dugout, close enough that I can hang over the side and pretend, for a brief moment, I'm in it. Close enough that my husband can look over and catch me when I try to sneak our daughter a sip of my soda. Close enough that when I scream at the ump, he can hear my voice. Close enough that when my man rips a homerun, he can lean over the rail and get a kiss. He gets lots of kisses. And his team is keeping up, their record putting them in the standings for the American League Championship. Never mind that the Yankees are the other front-runner. We aren't focusing on that right now.

We are focused on juggling life with a toddler. One hundred sixty-two games are a lot different with a two-year-old in hand. Dad and Carla sold the Alpine home and moved to Dallas. They have a ranch a half-mile away from ours, and keep Laura during most of the home games. The away games are still a work-in-progress. I now understand why Mom had stopped traveling with the team when I was born. My love for baseball is nothing compared to my child. *Everything* changed the moment she was born.

I avoid New York entirely. Haven't set foot in Yankee Stadium since that last game. I don't think I ever will. Partially out of respect for Tobey, and partially out of respect for my heart. I think it would be too hard for me. I'd rather my last memory of that field be that championship moment. I will always, secretly, be a Yankee, no matter whose colors I'm wearing.

My divorce with Tobey was quiet and quick, no child to fight over, no assets contested. I got Titan and my car. He offered more, a bulk settlement with alimony, but I refused. We had taken four years out of each other's lives. Anything else was ridiculous.

He's dating a supermodel now, one of those Victoria's Secret Angels who wears million-dollar bras and blows kisses into cameras. She looks good in pinstripes, and in every photo I've seen of them, he looks happy.

Chase steps up to bat, and I stand, my daughter peeking up at me, her pink Converses sparkling as they jut out from her seat, not long enough to hang over the side. "Daddy up?" she asks.

"Yep." I lean forward, watching, her attention returning to the coloring book before her, a big chubby marker awkwardly gripped in her hand, purple colored over half of the page.

"Come on…" I breathe, wrapping my hands around the railing and watch him, the strong line of his back, the cock of his head, the slow roll of his bat before he settles into place.

"Mom."

I ignore the command, my eyes darting from the pitcher to Chase.

"Mom," she insists.

"Wait." Pitch. Swing. High and left. *Foul.* I sigh and glance back at her. "Yes?"

"Need new marker." Laura holds out the grape-scented stick. We named her after my mom, all other ideas abandoned once Chase made that suggestion.

"Daddy is at bat, don't you want to see?" I bend down and pick her up, holding her against my chest until her soles rest on the railing.

"New marker." She waves it in the air, her eyes away from the game, still stuck on her coloring book.

"She's two," Dad calls, from his seat next to us. "You think you cared anything about baseball at two?"

"I was young and dumb," I remark, watching as the pitcher throws to first, trying to catch Cortez as he dives back to the bag.

"Give her time, she'll come around," Carla coos to Laura and lifts her away, my hand-off quick, eyes back on the field, and there is a moment of hushed silence before the pitcher curls, Chase tenses, and then...

Action.

Contact.

High and up...

Moonshot.

Thank you for reading Moonshot, by Alessandra Torre. If you would like to be notified when Alessandra's next book releases, please visit www.nextnovel.com.

Other novels by Alessandra

Suspense:
The Girl in 6E
Do Not Disturb
If You Dare
Tight

Contemporary Romance:
Hollywood Dirt
Love Chloe

Erotic Romance:
Black Lies
Mrs. Dumont
Sex Love Repeat
Blindfolded Innocence (Innocence #1)
Masked Innocence (Innocence #2)
End of the Innocence (Innocence #3

Note from the Author

Each book has a different journey and I feel differently at each completion. With Tight, I was exhausted, having gone through four complete rewrites, with completely different story lines and endings. With If You Dare, I felt a sad elation–similar to the last day of high school when you are happy, yet miss that part of your life already. With Moonshot, I wasn't quite ready to let go. I finished this book and didn't want to leave its world. I didn't want to step out of Ty's head and back into my life. I loved so many parts of this book and wanted, for just a few more hours, to savor it.

I have never been an athlete. I am terribly uncoordinated. I was more interested in horses than tennis. I played the piano instead of soccer. During PE, I prayed fervently that the ball would never head in my direction. I knew nothing about sports and couldn't tell you if a first down was a football or basketball term.

Then, I met Pudge Rodriguez. Well ... I didn't exactly *meet* him. I stood, way up in the nosebleed section of Ranger Stadium, a foam finger firmly on my ten-year-old finger, and watched him play. Me and fifty thousand other fans.

I don't know why I liked Pudge. Probably because his nickname was Pudge and it stuck out to me. All I know is, I left that stadium and knew *something* about sports. I had a team. I had a t-shirt! And later that summer, in a small sports store in Dallas, I bought his baseball card. Baseball, unlike football, was easy for me to understand. I didn't feel like an idiot, or cheer at the wrong time. It was my first step into the world of sports, but it wouldn't be my last.

Twelve years later, I married an athlete. My husband is the type of man who grew up with a ball in his hand. He had football *and* baseball scholarships offers. He lived in some world I was a stranger in, one where ESPN played constantly, life changed drastically depending on the sports season, and vacations were planned around the closest sporting events.

I am still uncoordinated. Throw me a ball and I'll duck for cover. But I can oil a glove. Rattle off a fair amount of sports statistics. I've screamed at hockey umps, stomped my feet on a hundred baseball stands and revolve much of my life around SEC football. My life has changed due to sports. It's become better. And I can't help but sometimes wish that I grew up like Ty did.

Some of my husband's fondest memories, out of everything, are from his days as a Minnesota Twins bat boy. He spent thee years on their dugout bench. He traveled to some games. He stayed at some of their homes, babysat their kids. He was my resource for much of this book's content. He approached cute girls for the players. He ran across the street in search of batteries for their Walkmans. He mudded balls, did laundry and got stuffed in lockers. I've heard his stories for a decade. I'm glad this book gave me a chance to use some of them.

It's been thirty-some years since he was a bat boy. I'm sure some things have changed. If I described an improbably scenario, please don't roast me. Please take the spirit of the book as it was intended. I hope you enjoyed it. If so, please check out my other books. If you'd like to be notified of my writing progress and new releases, please visit www.nextnovel.com.

About The Author

Alessandra Torre is an award-winning New York Times bestselling author of thirteen novels. Her books focus on romance and suspense, all with a strong dose of sexuality. Torre has been featured in Elle and Elle UK, Dirty Sexy Funny with Jenny McCarthy, as well as guest blogged for the Huffington Post and RT Book Reviews. She was also the Bedroom Blogger for Cosmopolitan.com.

Learn more about Alessandra on her website at
www.alessandratorre.com.